Bascom Hill Publishing Group

Bascom Hill Publishing Group
212 3rd Avenue North, Suite 570
Minneapolis, MN 55401
1.888.645.5248
www.bascomhillpublishing.com
Order online: www.amendment-28.com

ISBN 13 DIGIT - 9780979846748
ISBN 10 DIGIT - 0979846749
LCCN - 2007939984

BASCOM HILL
PUBLISHING GROUP

Book sales for North America and international:
Itasca Books, 3501 Highway 100 South, Suite220
Minneapolis, MN 55416
Phone: 952.345.4488 (toll free 1.800.901.3480)
Fax: 952.920.0541; email to orders@itascabooks.com

Cover Design by Wes Moore
Interior Design by Jennifer Wheeler

Printed in the United States of America

THE 28TH AMENDMENT

NEAL RECHTMAN

Inspired by

Gore Vidal

Author's Note

The 28th Amendment is a story about an actor who portrays a fictional US President on television, does his job a little too well, and gets drawn into real-world politics.

In my book the TV show is called *The Oval Office*, but anyone who watched the now-retired NBC series *The West Wing* will quickly see the similarity. Think *Martin Sheen (Almost) Goes to Washington*.

Even those who are not familiar with The *West Wing* will recognize the very real potential for conflict between entertainment and politics in our media-defined age. My book explores the logical extremes of this conflict, even as-real life examples abound: Fred Thompson made it into the 2008 Republican Presidential primary not because he was an unremarkable former Senator from Tennessee, but because he gained national recognition as an avuncular district attorney on the television series *Law & Order*.

My story includes numerous references to the card game bridge. You certainly don't have to know how to play bridge to enjoy this book, but you may enjoy it more if you know how bridge is played. I have therefore also added an Appendix that provides a basic outline of the game for the non-player.

If you've gotten this far, there is a statistically high probability that you'll turn to the next page, so now would be the right time to advise you that this is a work of fiction: any similarity to real people or events is unintended and purely *coincidental.*

All of the *coincidences* described in the book, however, are based on real events that I have personally experienced.

Neal Rechtman
Ossining, NY
July 2008

1	November 20, 2019 Beverly Hills

In the few minutes that had passed since his lawyer called, Victor Glade managed to work himself into a state of high anxiety. He knew that his long-time friend, and for the past three years his Executive Producer and General Counsel, wouldn't be stopping by just to *schmooze*. Jeremy Lerner was ruthlessly efficient with his own time, and equally protective of Victor's, *ergo* any in-person meeting on short notice like this could only mean trouble.

Glade was half-seated on a stool in the middle of his dressing room after a morning of retakes that pretty much concluded *The Oval Office*'s production for the week. A makeup assistant whose name he could never remember wrestled his tie off and unfastened the top four buttons of his starched, white dress shirt. She then disappeared behind him, threw a wide vinyl cape over his shoulders, and began her cotton swabbing of his cheeks and eyebrows and ears. *What had Jeremy been working on that might blow up? The distribution deal with Paramount?* A red-vested wardrobe assistant, also nameless, knelt beside him and began removing his presidential cufflinks. *They're already making out like bandits, what more could they possibly want?*

Three front-to-back strokes of a comb took the spray starch out of his masterfully dyed hair, a mottled charcoal black with silver highlights, and then off came the cape. Now Glade stood up, and in one seamless motion pulled his undershirt and long-sleeve shirt over his head and handed them to Robin red-vest, who in return was holding out for him the navy blue golf shirt that he had worn to work that morning. When he retrieved it, remaining in her outstretched hand, like magic, was a deodorant stick, which he frowned at and then grabbed. *It could also be just another lawsuit, but it would have to be a pretty big one to bring it to me in the middle of the day like this.*

He stretched the shirt over his head, popped his arms through, and nipped it down over his belt. Then two steps sideways and a squint into the illuminated mirror ten feet away: *well there's nothing I can do about it, is there?* The "it" being his age, which was sixty-five; his hair, which was far thinner in person than it appeared on the pate of President Alvin Bosco, his *Oval Office* alter ego; and his physique, which used to be athletic and was now as boxy as his Brooks Brothers shirts. He sighed, ran his hand once through his hair—*at least there was still something there*—and then darted out of the dressing room. His bodyguard, a ruddy, six-foot Scotsman and former Royal Navy Seal named Grainger Wells, was waiting for him in the hallway and accompanied him in the elevator up to his eleventh floor office.

During the ten seconds of vertical silence Victor's synapses suddenly fired out the answer: Jeremy's unscheduled visit must be about Bill Clinton's call. The ex-President had telephoned earlier that morning, but Victor had been in a final rehearsal of a scene involving five other actors, was completely in character, and had the call forwarded to Jeremy. He hadn't thought about it again until just now.

Grainger left him off at his corner office, where his private secretary, Caroline, a posture-perfect, bespectacled ex-librarian of forty-nine, was waiting for him at the door with her steno pad tucked officially under one arm. (A native of Gibraltar, she had at some point served in the British army and acquired various military habits.) She followed him to his desk, a rectangular slab of glass mounted on two sawed-off olive tree trunks that appeared to grow naturally out of the polished hardwood floor. Behind the desk, a curtain-wall window framed a panoramic view of the UCLA campus.

He plopped down in his leather swivel chair, immediately untied his Oxfords and chucked them off. "Wardrobe's going to come for these," he said, bending down to massage his feet through thin-ribbed socks. "When they do, tell them I need to be refit or something—these are killing me." He looked up at Caroline, who stood alongside the desk nodding with her usual good cheer.

"Good morning again, sir," she said. "I understand Jeremy is on his way over. He should be here any moment. The call from Clinton, perhaps."

"That's what I figure." He finished his foot massage and sat up.

Caroline glanced at her watch. "Well, if you can keep it under fifteen minutes, the rest of your day will stay on track. It's almost 11:15 now; at 11:30 you're due to meet with Evelyn Vaughn, from the 28th Amendment. That includes lunch and however long you want to spend with her afterwards. Then you're signing correspondence and making some decisions about your calendar, and then . . . *then* you are free to go!" It was Thanksgiving Day eve, and everything was winding down early. "'The world is your oyster,' if that's an appropriate use of your American aphorism."

There was a knock on the doorpost and Jeremy stuck his head in. "Anyone home?"

"Greetings, greetings, come in please." Victor stood up and waved Jeremy in, and then nodded a silent thanks to Caroline. She dispensed a low-handed wave to Jeremy as they crossed paths, and exited into her adjoining office.

As always, even on the day before Thanksgiving, even in LA in seventy-five-degree weather, Jeremy was wearing a suit and tie. He was divorced; he didn't know how to match sport clothes, so he stuck with what he knew. At sixty-six he was a year older than Victor, and his hair even thinner, but it drove Victor crazy that Jeremy kept his thirty-two-inch waist and his tapered shirts without limiting his food intake or exercising at all. Jeremy attributed it all to his fast metabolism, which Victor agreed must be true. He walked rapidly, talked rapidly, and was constantly on the alert, always observing, evaluating, processing. When he was really busy even his body language seemed spring-loaded.

Now Victor was sure Jeremy's grin was a little too contrived to be genuinely celebratory. He was masking something. A shoe was about to drop, but it wouldn't be anything *really* terrible, otherwise there would be no grin at all. "Should I be seated for any reason?" Victor asked, standing beside his desk, still in his socks. "Are you the bearer of any dramatic news?"

Jeremy immediately saw his friend's distress. "Sit, stand, levitate, do as you please. Nothing I have to say is going to make you faint." He came over and extended his fist to Victor across the desk for their traditional bump-grind.

Victor shot him a disbelieving stare and Jeremy laughed. "What do you want me to say? Actually, the reason I've come by is because of something that's going on with *me* that I think you should know about. It's not all about *you*, you know."

This was said in good humor, and Victor took it that way, but it had its zing. "Got it. By all means, lay it on me. Are you okay? Your kids are okay?"

"Everyone was intact and thriving the last I checked." Jeremy pulled from the breast pocket of his suit jacket a stapled packet of sheets that he unfolded and passed across the glass tabletop.

"These are your hourlies from when, this morning?" Victor tried focusing on the small print, and began to paw at the papers scattered on his desk to find his reading glasses.

"Indeed they are. You don't need to read them now—I'll explain everything. I brought them because they outline a sequence of events."

"I see here the call from Clinton. I'll certainly want to hear about that."

"All will be revealed, but in proper order, please."

"Okay, I'm all yours."

"So, you know about my coincidence condition, right? My attraction to extremely unlikely coincidences?"

"Of course, no need to explain." Beginning in his early adult years, Jeremy came to recognize that he encountered astonishing, often outrageously implausible coincidences far more frequently than most people, and everyone who knew him knew it was true. As a hobby he documented these "coincidence events," as he called them, in a private blog that he shared with his close friends and family.

"Well, this entire morning has been one continuous coincidence. This will definitely end up as an entry in my blog. I could actually just paste in a copy of my hourlies."

"How so? What happened?"

"Starting with the 8:30am Security Memo"— Jeremy gestured to the papers Victor was scanning—"everything that I touched for the rest of the morning, every phone call, every e-mail, everything I have handled today up until this very minute has all been about you running for President."

Victor kept an impassive expression. If this was what it was all about, he could relax. "I thought you said this was something about you, that it wasn't all about me."

"This *is* about me. It's about my morning. I didn't engineer these calls and e-mails; they all came to me from different, independent sources, in the space of a few hours. There could not possibly have been any collusion or coordination. I know you don't want to run for President, and I didn't come here to change your mind. But when I encounter a coincidence like this I sit up and take notice. And, to get to the heart of the matter, at least one of the calls I took has public repercussions that you'll need to address."

"Uh-oh, here it comes! I knew I was in trouble! *Now* you've got my attention." Victor finally found his reading glasses and slipped them on. He focused on the first page. "Okay, I see the security review here. What does this have to do with me running for President?"

"Nothing, on the face of it, but it starts the whole ball rolling. Stay with me here. This was a technical report I ordered to re-evaluate the Threat Index we have assigned to our friend Morley James in the *real* White House," Jeremy said, referring to President Burton Grove's theocratic Chief of Staff. "As you know, we've identified him as someone who might try to sabotage or close down *The Oval Office*. The hypothesis being evaluated was that James's motivation to act against us might be increased because of recent events in the Middle East."

Victor understood this issue right away. In the past few months the Grove Administration had suffered numerous major setbacks in the Middle East, the most visible being the assassination of Saudi Arabia's Prime Minister. This was the third PM in a row to be killed; he had only been in the position for five months, and before he took the job it had been vacant for over a year. And in Egypt, the elections so ardently encouraged and supported by the Administration ended up giving fundamentalist clerics outright control of Parliament, and the stage was now set for a showdown with the military, *a là* Algeria.

During this same period, *The Oval Office* had been reeling out a subplot about a Middle East peace initiative that President Alvin Bosco (portrayed by Victor) hatches one evening over dinner with a brainy, Democratic ex-President named Wendell Chapman—to any sentient observer a Bill Clinton stand-in.

After plying him with wine, President Bosco recruits Chapman to serve as America's *ex-officio* emissary to the Islamic clerical world. Chapman agrees to the assignment, but insists that nothing be announced until he's had an opportunity to prepare for it. He then begins intensive training in Arabic language, and devotes most of his other waking hours to studying Islamic history and culture. Various highlights of his education, conveniently dispensed by State Department experts acting as private tutors, are scripted into numerous episodes of *The Oval Office* over several weeks, in effect delivering a survey course on Islam to their viewers. Finally, after weeks of preparation, Chapman begins making private overtures to Islamic leaders of all sects, flying off to dozens of countries to meet with them in person—and ultimately persuades most to attend an Islamic Unity Conference where terrorism and suicide bombing are to be publicly renounced. In the same week that the Unity Conference was portrayed on *The Oval Office*, the marked Saudi Prime Minister was incinerated by a spectacularly powerful roadside bomb that killed twenty-three other people.

Because of the timing, it was inevitable that the PC crowd— pundits and columnists, in Jeremy's lingo—would end up comparing *The Oval Office*'s fictional happy ending to the somewhat grim reality faced by the Grove Administration. When comment was solicited from *The Oval Office*, reporters were referred to their stock legal disclaimer, which was included as both static text and simultaneous voice-over, at the beginning of every episode: "The characters and events portrayed in *The Oval Office* are the exclusive product of our writers' imaginations. Any resemblance to real people or actual events is unintended and coincidental." When Deputy Press Secretary Gale Rose was asked if the White House had any comment, she replied with a statement that had obviously been prepared in advance: "We believe *The Oval Office* is blurring the lines between entertainment and the serious business of diplomacy and national security."

Jeremy—who, before coming to work for Victor in 2016, had been Chief Counsel to the Senate Foreign Relations Committee for twenty-five years—had highly refined senses when it came to interpreting official statements of this type. To him, it was a bludgeoning, an alarming escalation not only of rhetoric but of actual threat—hence his request for the security review.

"It's irrelevant," Jeremy said to Victor, "what the conclusion of the report was. They did end up increasing the Threat Index, but it doesn't matter. The point I want to get to is that after reading the report, I sat back and remarked to myself how absurd this whole situation is. Here you are, a fictional President with real leadership ability and practical policies, and we're stuck with a *real* President whose world view is a fiction and whose policies are a disaster. So this starts me thinking about you running for President."

"Jeremy, I'm not going to run for President. We've been through this. Why are we even talking about this?"

"No, no, no! That's not it. Stick with this. All I'm saying is that after I read the report, I was *thinking* about you running for President, but at that point I had no intention of visiting you this morning. I was just filing it away, planning to lay it on you at some carefully selected moment."

"So what happened?"

"So now, look back at the hourlies. I was on the report until 8:48am, when the call from Bill Clinton comes in, a call for you that you sent to me."

"I get it," Victor said, nodding, "he was calling to talk to me about running."

"*Voilà!* He was in finest form, I might add, positively oozing charm and persuasion. He insisted that I arrange a meeting with you. By the end of the call, he had framed that as my assignment; it was my job to get you to lunch or dinner with him sometime soon, within the next week, and the fate of all of humanity rested on it."

"Let me guess again: he suggests that I have a moral obligation to run for President."

"We didn't get that far, but you're going to find there are a lot people—me included—who feel that way."

"Oh spare me."

"I will spare you. For now. I'm here to tell you about my morning, right? Just be here for me, okay?"

"I'm here for you, Jeremy." Victor could not suppress his grin.

"So, next on the list"—Jeremy pointed toward the paper in Victor's hand—"is an e-mail from Gordon Kramer," who was *The Oval Office*'s private pollster and a closely guarded secret. "The e-mail has a link to the still-unreleased results of a McKesson poll he got hold of. I didn't ask him for this poll; he never mentioned it to me before. He just sent it to me with a note that he thought I might find it of interest. The poll showed you at the top of a list of six potential candidates for next year."

"Who were the other — actually, you know what? Skip that, don't answer that. I don't want to know about polls. Who's next on your list?"

"Hold it, I'm not finished yet with Kramer. At this point I started to suspect that one of my coincidence events might be starting up, so I called Kramer to find out why it was that he sent me this e-mail, and in any event I wanted to make sure there was no perception, anywhere, that we were commissioning this kind of poll. He assured me that we were not, but pointed out that virtually everyone else was. The e-mail, he claims, was completely his idea—an FYI thing. He thought I might like to know about it, especially since he knows we don't do this poll. At the end, he asked me if it was possible that you might run, and wanted me to tell you that according to him, you could win. I of course quickly denied that you had any interest."

"Got it. Okay, who's next . . . Walter Trask called? The software guy who bought Gulf Pemblico? Why does *he* want me to run for President?"

"Based on my one conversation with him, I can't say I know *why* he wants you to run, but he wants you to run badly enough to launch a Draft Glade campaign, and to drop a pretty piece of change

17

into it for starters."

"You're not serious."

Jeremy raised an eyebrow, but said nothing.

"How did you handle it? You of course told him I was not a candidate and would not be a candidate."

"His call was not to consult with you. It was, as he said, a courtesy to let you know what he is doing. He is announcing it for tomorrow's papers—a brilliant stroke, actually. Thanksgiving is the perfect day to pull a stunt like this. There's no other news, it'll be all over the headlines, and everybody's gathered together at big family events where this kind of news travels fast."

Victor leaned back in his chair, expressing no outward sign of respiration, much less any verbal reaction. Jeremy made no effort to fill the silence.

"Is there anyone else involved with it?" Victor asked. "This guy by himself is a lightweight."

"I'm not aware of him being connected to anything or anyone bigger, but it doesn't matter. He's putting in twenty million dollars to start it up, which . . ."

"Jesus, twenty million dollars?" Victor's voice diminished to a croak.

" . . . which would suggest he plans to buy some heavyweight talent, and *a lot* of media. You underestimate your draw as a candidate, or as a non-candidate, I should say."

"I don't underestimate or overestimate, because I'm *not* a candidate, and I'm *not going to be* a candidate." Victor paused, and Jeremy again let it ride.

"Why do I have to do anything about it?" Victor pleaded. "I could ignore it completely. My schedule is packed—I don't have time for anything else."

"Victor, Victor! *Vey iz mir!*" Jeremy moaned, rocking his head between his hands. "Leave aside for now the fact that *the press is gonna fuckin' lay siege to this place.* Don't you see, the bigger danger is the Administration? This Trask thing is just going to fuel their paranoia about you as a political opponent. Talk about Threat Reviews!"

Victor sat back in his chair, perfectly aghast.

"Also," Jeremy continued, "you should consider the possibility that *really* doing nothing—not responding *at all*—may have the opposite of your intended effect. The silence might be construed as vacillation by you."

"Okay, I got it, I got it," Victor snapped. "Jesus, *son-of-a-bitch*." Pause. "Who's next on your list? This is about *you*, remember?"

"Absolutely. Look at the log, you'll see. The next call I took was from Carla Sanders."

"Of the DNC."

"The same."

"Well you know what I think of her. If I *were* running, I wouldn't *want* her endorsement."

"Notice she didn't even try to reach you—she called me directly."

"She's known you for two decades!"

"We're both native Alabamans; it's a bond. Anyhow, her take on it is slightly different. She wants you to run, but recognizes that you really don't want to. If you don't, she believes you must be persuaded—pressured is the word she used—to endorse someone else. A Democrat of course."

"Okay, okay, who's next? How many people called you this morning about me running for President?"

"Including the e-mails, a total of eight so far." Jeremy looked at his watch. "By now there could be more. I left my office about fifteen minutes ago."

"Okay, just tell me who the eight are. I get the picture." Victor scanned the hourlies, trying to pick out the names.

"Well, there's me first, with my security report. Then, coming in order after that are: Bill Clinton, Gordon Kramer, Walter Trask, Carla Sanders, Admiral Corbett, and then Tom Friedman, who got advance notice from Trask and was calling to offer his support and to invite you to appear on his Sunday morning program. And then about fifteen minutes ago, Irving Liman." Liman was the ninety-one-year-old *majordomo* of Democratic campaign consultants, whose sage advice Jeremy and Victor had relied on for years.

Victor raised his eyebrows for Liman, but didn't take the

bait. "So tell me," he said, "what these coincidences mean when you encounter them. Are they an omen of anything? Is there a superstition or something I should know about?"

"No, nothing like that. This kind of stuff just happens to me all the time. It's the most bizarre thing."

"No kidding." Victor cast him a sincere look, and paused, thinking. Jeremy kept his eyes on Victor, but said nothing.

"So." Victor's tone changed the subject. "What you said earlier about public repercussions—you're referring to the Trask thing, this draft effort."

Jeremy nodded.

"What are your thoughts about this, and about this guy?"

"My personal thoughts are that I want to send him a donation and a letter of encouragement. Wearing my *Oval Office* hat, my thoughts are the following. A, you're not going to be able to stop him. He's going to go forward regardless of your reaction. B, if he's going to be out there doing his thing, we need to figure out what your most effective response would be. We will bring in the finest spinners to do our work for us. I know some great people for situations like this."

"I appreciate your sacrifice of personal feelings on my behalf. But I'm not running for President, so with that in mind, how do you think I should respond?"

"Your objective is . . . ?"

"To spend as little time on it as possible."

"Then let's just issue a stock denial through the press office. It needn't take a minute of your time."

"Jeremy, don't be coy. I'm serious about this; now will you advise me or not?"

"Of course, of course. Okay." Jeremy paused and put on his most appreciative smile, masking an internal conflict that was, he knew, inevitable.

"I've only had a little while to consider this, but here's where I'm at. As I said, I think the worst consequence of this is that, regardless of your statements, Trask's effort will raise your profile as a potential presidential candidate. That in turn will make the Administration see you and *The Oval Office* as even more of a threat. *Ergo,* my sense is that we should respond to Trask, immediately and publicly, with the strongest possible message that you are not a candidate and that they are wasting their time and money. If we emphasize the wasted money part, and we keep that up as the theme of our response, that might curtail their donations and maybe cause them to re-evaluate their position."

"We also could run ads," posited Victor, "cautioning people not to throw their money away."

"You're not serious!" This was a twist Jeremy had not foreseen.

"Why not? I would think that would be very effective."

"You would actually spend money on advertising to stay *out* of political office?"

"Sort of gives 'negative campaigning' a whole new meaning, doesn't it?" Victor was very pleased with himself.

Jeremy's heart sank. He didn't want to do anything that might preclude a last-minute run, and negative ads like this would do just that. "I don't know that we'll need to go that far, and we certainly don't have to do that now. Right now we just need to be as outspoken as possible about your position. Are we in agreement on this?"

"Absolutely." Victor loved having Jeremy in charge—he knew how to get things done. He was so *efficient*. "What do you recommend?"

Jeremy now came to the actual, ultimate, final moment of truth. He knew what outcome he wanted, he just wasn't sure what to say in order to get it. He could only go with his gut. "You are looking to spend as little time on this as possible, right? My recommendation is that I man the front lines. I'll do the interview with Friedman on Sunday, and maybe take another as well, just to cover more territory. I'm familiar with the format, I know a lot of the people, it will be fun for me. What *you* should do, behind the scenes, is call Trask and speak to him yourself, but not in a threatening or negative way. Maybe loosen him up a little. Do your charm thing, throw in a little humor, and then gently lay it on the line. You've convinced me that you're never going to run, and I desperately don't want to believe you. Maybe you can convince him too."

"That's all?"

"What do you mean?"

"That's all we're going to do? Two interviews and a phone call?

I get the feeling there's a lot at stake here."

"There is, but that's all we *can* do for the next four days."

Victor plucked a bag of M&M's from a box on his desk, tore it open, dispensed several of the colored candies onto a note pad on his desk, and began tinkering with them. After some inscrutable twirling and rearranging, he shifted his gaze to Jeremy, who again made no effort to disrupt the quiet.

"How effective will you be denying my candidacy if you really want to see me running?" Victor suddenly asked.

"If your question is 'can you trust me?' the answer is an unequivocal yes. If your question is 'am I the best person for the job,' the answer is an equivocal no. You would probably do it better, but I'm certainly the second-best person for the job. I think you'll be very satisfied with the result."

Victor resumed his rearrangement of the M&M's. Through the silence Jeremy noticed the chime of the elevator and, he thought, the subsequent faint hiss of the elevator doors opening and closing. How was that possible? He constructed a mental plan of the 9th Floor: the elevator had to be at least eighty feet away, and the sound would have to travel through three closed rooms—at least a half-dozen walls. The chime sound he could see getting through, but maybe the hissing was a phantom sound, something he heard because it was expected? Like the famous phantom limb syndrome? Subconsciously he filed the question for future research.

Victor interrupted his acoustic ruminations. "What do you think of *me* doing the interviews?"

Jeremy remained outwardly calm, but his adrenalin kicked in. This would be the best possible outcome! If Victor did the interviews himself, it wouldn't matter what he said about running. It would establish a public perception of Victor Glade as himself, the real Victor Glade, as opposed to President Alvin Bosco, his *Oval Office* persona. Jeremy saw this as an absolute prerequisite to any scenario of late entry into the race. He had not recommended it directly to Victor because he was sure Victor would have resisted; it was something that could only work if he came to it himself.

"On any issue that is important to you," Jeremy replied carefully, "you will always be your own best advocate. I didn't recommend it because you said you wanted to spend as little time on this as possible, and I would certainly do an adequate job of it."

Victor's reaction was a further relapse into silence, his thinking now fueled by the serial consumption of M&M's in some indiscernible color-coded sequence. He then said, suddenly, "Let's do it this way." His voice took on a decisive timbre that Jeremy well recognized. "I'll take the interview with Friedman. I'm going to be in Philadelphia anyway for the Thanksgiving holiday—it's easy enough to stop in DC on my way back, do the deed in person. Much more effective, I find, than those remote links—whatever they call them."

Jeremy veered into a mental jig, but caught himself and recaptured his focus. Now was not the time to blow it. "It's up to you," he said. "If you want to put in the time, you'll at least be left with the feeling that you did all that you could do at a crucial moment."

"I'm taking time now because I can see that if this gets out of hand it could take a lot more time later. However," Victor continued, "since you obviously are willing, I would ask that you also do an interview. Call your friend Fred Sherman at CNN and see if he can get you on one of their shows—*Dateline*, or whatever it is."

"I think it's likely, after Trask's announcement hits the Web, we'll have a number of invitations to choose from."

"One more thing," Victor added. I'd also like us to come up with a formal statement, press-release style, not more than a page, that declares my position and makes it official. I want you to do a first draft because I want it to have a legalistic sound and I want to leave absolutely no room for interpretation. We also need it to make sure that you and I are saying exactly the same thing."

Jeremy nodded. "I'll get a draft to you first thing Friday morning, which is the next day I'm picking things up. Speaking of press releases, you'll see in my hourlies, towards the end, a link to the press release that Trask has prepared. It hasn't been made public yet, but it will be by tomorrow. You should read it so you at least know how they're making their case."

"Great, I can't wait." Victor rolled his eyes.

"Is there anything else?" Jeremy asked, getting up out of his chair and stretching himself in a backwards arch. Victor also pushed his chair back and stood up.

"Actually there is. Remember I'm meeting with Evelyn Vaughn today? The woman who runs the 28th Amendment organization?"

Jeremy nodded. "You're going to talk about writing the 28th Amendment into the show, if I understand correctly?"

"Well, we only want to do it if it's going to help her cause, which is why your take on things might be valuable for both of us, I think. Can I get you to join us for a little while?"

"Absolutely, I'd love to meet her." Jeremy looked at his watch. "I have a conference call with Paramount in a few minutes, and I need to be in my office for that. As far as I know it should be quick. My next thing I can push back. But I absolutely need to be out by 12:15 for a luncheon outside. Why don't you . . . if you don't mind, the way to maximize my time with you would be to bring her to my office."

"Excellent plan. I see its inherent *efficiency*." He extended his fist over his desk and Jeremy tapped it with his own.

After Jeremy left, Victor dropped down into his chair again, picked up the hourlies, remounted his reading glasses, and found the Web link to Trask's press release. He tapped the URL into the open tablet on his desk and it came up instantly:

For Release 11/20/2019 at 20:00 hours.

COMMITTEE FORMED TO DRAFT VICTOR GLADE FOR 2020 PRESIDENTIAL RACE

Technology entrepreneur Walter Trask and other interested parties have announced the formation of a Political Action Committee (PAC) called "2020 Vision." The Committee is dedicated to bringing the writer/actor Victor Glade into the 2020 Presidential Race as a Draft Candidate, and is soliciting funds from the general public in furtherance of this effort.

Simultaneous to its formation, Trask has made an initial $20 million contribution to 2020 Vision. "I have taken this step," Trask says, "because I am convinced that Victor Glade is the only widely recognized public figure who has the ability and credibility to lead this country back to greatness, as *a role model and guiding light for other nations."*

"The first objective of this Committee is to learn how broad and deep the public's support for a Glade candidacy is, Trask stated. If we can demonstrate overwhelming support, we hope that will inspire him to seriously consider running."

"Glade's experience makes him by far the most qualified candidate," says Trask. *He cites Glade's two terms in Congress, in 1986 and 1988, representing the 1ˢᵗ District of Massachusetts, as proof of his political savvy and electability. "It is important to remember," says Trask, "that Victor Glade is not just an actor, he is central to every episode of* The Oval Office. *He's the lead writer and approves every script that is produced. All you need to do to see his vision of a better America is to watch the show. I think it's perfectly natural that Americans would want their government to function the way Glade portrays it, and I anticipate an overwhelming response to our draft effort."*

Further information can be found, and donations can be made, at www.2020Vision.com

*   *   *   *   *

"It's truly an honor to meet you in person, " Evelyn Vaughn introduced herself to Victor, offering her hand and a warm smile. "I'm very excited . . . I've been a fan for years."

"The honor is mine, I assure you." Victor bent forward to accommodate Evelyn's short stature, raised her hand to his lips, and gave it a continental kiss. "What I do is easy, it's all pretend. What you're doing is *real*, a much neater trick, and much harder."

"Thank you, that's very kind of you." Evelyn practically swooned. Like millions of other women, she found him strikingly handsome in the traditional all-American mold: tall, straight-featured, clean-shaven, with intense blue eyes and a default smile that radiated confidence. It quickly occurred to her that it might be embarrassing for a fifty-six-year-old former US Attorney and law professor to act like a rock star groupie, and then just as quickly she decided she didn't care. Who was watching? They were standing in the carpeted 9th floor elevator lobby of *The Oval Office's* complex on Olympic Avenue.

"What you've accomplished so far is nothing short of remarkable," Victor continued, guiding her into a wider, busier hallway. "But I also see how much further there is to go, and that's what got me wondering if we couldn't find some way to help you." When he had invited Evelyn to LA to discuss his idea for writing a sub-plot into *The Oval Office* that would help publicize the 28th Amendment—if not by name, at least by some clear allusion—Evelyn had responded enthusiastically, not only because she loved the idea, but also because of the fundraising potential. Almost a billionaire, Victor Glade was by far the biggest fish she had ever gotten this close to.

"Well, your help so far has been nothing short of remarkable," Evelyn replied. "You're probably not even aware, but the air taxi you arranged for me last night in Detroit may well have saved my life. If your pilot hadn't found me, I was otherwise planning to be on the United flight that was shot down!" Since Al-Qaeda's first missile attack on a domestic airliner on September 11, 2016, more than twenty other attacks had been staged. Most were unsuccessful, but on two prior occasions, and now this third time, the results had been devastating. The previous evening in Detroit, a total of five shoulder-launched missiles were thought to have been fired as the plane took off, and it crashed a mile beyond the runway in a busy commercial area, killing all 183 people on board and an unknown number of people on the ground.

"Whoaaaa!" Victor's eyebrows shot up. The front pages of the morning papers had all carried the same gruesome aerial photo of the burning plane. "You were booked on that flight? Holy Toledo, how close a call can you have!"

"I was watching CNN this morning in my hotel room," Evelyn said. "When I realized it was the flight I would have been on, I went into shock. I could actually hear my heart pounding."

"And you're saying you weren't on it because of an air taxi that I arranged for you?"

"Maybe not you, personally. The pilot said he had been asked by *The Oval Office* to track me down and offer me a lift."

"Agghhhh." Victor was earnest in his disappointment. "This pains me so. I must quickly decline any credit for having saved your life. I wasn't the one who ordered the air taxi, but as you can see," he gestured broadly in front of them as they walked down the cubicle-lined corridor, "this place is huge, and we should find out who did the deed so you can thank them—or him, or her—whoever it is. Maybe I'll be lucky and it will be someone I personally hired; then at least I can share in some reflected glory."

They reached the end of the hallway and Victor signaled to the right. "Fortunately, we're about to meet my Executive Producer, whose name is Jeremy Lerner. He'd be the one to know about your CAT flight, or find out if he doesn't. I've invited him to join in our discussions—initially at least—because he was a Capitol Hill insider for many years. He's got a political perspective that we'll both find valuable. And another right, here." He directed her into an enormous corner office. On their left was a sunken living room, complete with sectional sofas, armchairs, floor lamps, a full-size conference table, and two huge video panels mounted on the far wall. On the right, a full twenty feet away, Jeremy was standing behind a spotless white tempera desk. Arrayed in front of it was a small forest of guest chairs of different types and sizes. He pointed to his ear set with his index finger, and then held up three fingers to mark his ETA. It was sunny outside, but the curtain windows had turned dark to compensate, and the whole office was suffused with a filtered, yellow-gray light.

"Let's hold here for a second until he's off. Unless you'd prefer to sit down?" Victor gestured toward the sunken seating.

Evelyn quickly declined. "No thanks, I could get lost down there." Although in no danger of being considered petite (she had enough of a frame to make her presence known), Evelyn topped out at 5' 1", and by habit tended to avoid places that made her look even shorter. She rested her briefcase between her legs, ran her fingers through her short-clipped hair—originally a deep brunette, now dominated by gray—and then shook her head. The hair settled into a kind of aerodynamic helmet, with a single inch-wide streak of white running from her forehead back; as artificial as it looked, it was completely natural. She struggled to let go of the plastered grin. *Time to get back to work.*

"Your colleague's name again is Jeremy? My short-term memory is horrendous."

"Jeremy Lerner is correct. I have known him for over thirty years. We first met in law school, actually—he was a year behind me. When I decided to run for Congress in 1985, he joined the campaign, and when we won he worked on my staff in Washington."

"What did he do when you left politics?"

"When I left for Greece in 1990 he took a position as Counsel to the Senate Foreign Relations Committee, which he stayed with for over twenty years. While he was there he learned three or four languages—I can't remember how many—just so he could do the best possible job for the Senators. Then I hired him back to work at *The Oval Office*. The man's an organizational genius—he's the key to a lot of what goes on here."

Evelyn cast her appraising eye at the genius, who instantly— from a distance of twenty paces—connected with her gaze, so she had to move on without a detailed impression. What had registered was a trim, business-suited, sixty-something Jewish man, on the tall side, with thinning salt and pepper hair. She would have assumed him to be a lawyer if she passed him on the street. As she edged her field of view back toward him, she could see he was engrossed in his phone call but was also watching a bank of displays that was built into his desktop, and he occasionally tapped at a keyboard. And then he caught her eye again, but this time he was smiling warmly, as though they already knew each other. From the drabness of his tie she concluded he was not married or in a relationship.

"After the first couple of years," Victor continued, "I was ready to pack it in. By the time Jeremy got here, *The Oval Office*'s audience had grown to three times the size of the original *West Wing* from twenty years ago, but for me it was starting to wear thin. It was Jeremy who came up with the segments concept. Now we've got a total of four shows in regular production; it's this incredible challenge, and I'm absolutely fascinated by it."

Evelyn knew from the briefing memos she had read during the previous week, as well as from her own experience watching *The Oval Office*, that these "segments" were separately titled spin-off programs that incorporated characters and plot lines from *The Oval Office,* giving viewers three additional windows into the same fictional Bosco Administration. The first, *The Press Room,* which began airing in 2016, portrayed *Oval Office* events through the eyes of Press Secretary Andrea Pfeiffer.

In the following year, two additional segments were launched, *Dunmorgan* and *Goose! Dunmorgan* followed the same public events as *The Oval Office,* but from the perspective of a powerful Republican Senator. This had the intended effect of appealing to an entirely new audience of conservatives, while continuing to draw a significant percentage of regular *Oval Office* viewers. *Goose!* was about an eccentric career diplomat, of that nickname, who heads the China desk at the State Department and advises the Bosco Administration's befuddled Secretary of State. According to Evelyn's many friends who watched the show, it was by far the funniest, and most irreverent, of the four.

"To maintain our 'reality edge,' as I like to call it," Victor said, "each segment produces a new one-hour episode almost every week. For the four shows, we have sixty-one actors under contract, 135 writers, hundreds of production personnel—almost two thousand people altogether. The first six floors of this building are used just by our IT and security departments."

Jeremy tapped a button on his desk, pulled the phone set from his ear, and walked over to them. "My apologies for keeping you waiting, Ms. Vaughn. I'm Jeremy Lerner"—he extended his hand—"Victor's old friend and lawyer, as I'm sure he has told you." He being 6'0", and she about 5'0", standing two feet apart, Jeremy subconsciously calculated their handshake was being executed at a 22.5 degree angle. "Please join me." He led them over to his desk.

"Evelyn, please pick a chair you think you'll enjoy," Victor continued, "and good morning to you again, sir." Jeremy and Victor and exchanged nods. Victor pulled over a medium-height stool where he sat half-perched, propping himself up with one straight leg to the ground. Evelyn finally settled on an adjustable height armchair.

"Jeremy, I assume you heard about the terrorist attack in Detroit last night?" Victor started out.

"Indeed," he said. "Makes 'Homeland Security' seem like an

oxymoron."

"So it turns out that Evelyn here was at Detroit Metro last night, and was actually booked on the flight that was hit—but at the airport she was offered a CAT flight courtesy of *The Oval Office*. Is that something you arranged?"

"Hmm . . ." Jeremy paused, thinking. "I wish I could say it was; it would have been a thoughtful thing to do. Now I feel guilty for *not* thinking of it, and I'm a little bit hard-pressed to think who would have."

"Maybe the travel office?" Victor suggested.

"I doubt it," Jeremy replied. "They wouldn't know anything about your schedule," he explained, turning to Evelyn, "for security reasons."

Evelyn started to feel queasy. "How very strange," she said. "This pilot knew I was at the Detroit airport—he had me paged. His name was Loughran, Bernard Loughran. He knew that I was headed to LA for a meeting with you."

"I'll put one of my EA's on it," Jeremy said, pushing a button on his desk. The door opened and a freshly scrubbed young man, in khakis and a starched, button-down blue shirt, strode in quickly. Jeremy explained the AirShares mystery and asked the assistant to investigate. "Let me know what you've found when I get back from lunch. Also, would anyone care for a drink? Evelyn, we have respectable coffee, tea, juice, water . . . ?" There were no takers, and the assistant nodded and left.

"In the meantime, Evelyn," Victor picked up, "I'm glad you made it here safely, and I thank you for taking the time and trouble to visit me in LA. Traveling for me is such a production that I tend to avoid it whenever possible."

"You mean with the security?"

Victor nodded. "Alvin Bosco is a fictional president, but I'm better protected than the *real* President." He shot Jeremy a look like it was his fault.

"Well, I'm glad to know it," Evelyn said. "There are millions of people, me among them, who depend on you for their political sanity. I'm a big fan of your show; I have watched it for years."

"Thank you. As I'm sure you can tell, we work very hard at it. And one of the things that makes it so interesting is that we can take current, real-world events and issues, like the 28th Amendment, fictionalize them a little bit to stay out of trouble, and write them into our scripts. With the size of our audience, we could generate a lot of buzz about the 28th Amendment, or if not specifically about your organization, about the general concept of publicly funded elections. But we only want to do this if you think it will be helpful to the cause."

"It depends on how you fictionalize it."

"On that and a whole lot more. That's why I asked Jeremy to join us here for a while. He's not only the driving force behind all of our expanded programming, he is also a former Washington insider whose political sense is far better tuned than my own."

Jeremy picked up. "Evelyn, what can you tell us about the support the 28th Amendment has drawn so far. What are your demographics?"

"Well, I assume you know the objectives. Amendments to the US Constitution, once passed by a two-thirds majority of Congress, then must be ratified by a simple majority of three-fourths of the state legislatures. If you work with an assumption that ninety percent of all Democrats are on board, in the Senate we need twenty-two Republicans and in the House we need about eighty-eight. We already have ten Republican Senators and twenty-one Congressmen."

"That in itself is amazing," Jeremy said. "Why do you think that is?"

"I know why it is, because they tell me. Campaigning has for years been a full-time endeavor. Running for office is so money-driven that you have no choice but to raise money all the time—throughout your entire term. There are many from both parties, more than you might otherwise imagine, who actually want to do their jobs: legislate, set policy, manage the taxpayers' money, advocate for their district, and they have had it with the constant fundraising. Those that have the safest seats, as you can imagine, are the ones who have come out in support."

"So I take it," Jeremy said, "since you've gotten some Republicans on board, that you think it's just a matter of time."

"That is what I hope, for the Congressional part of the equation. I think it could be passed by the next year, depending upon how certain key elections go next fall."

"I suppose you have those contests identified?" Victor asked.

"Certainly. I couldn't name them all for you off-hand, but there are about a half-dozen."

"I didn't want to go into the specifics now," Victor said, "I just wanted to make sure the homework has been done. It's background music, in any event, to the main event I have in mind, which is to add a long-term subplot to *The Oval Office*, running over several weeks or maybe months, about a constitutional amendment—not exactly your amendment, but something close enough so that the association will be made."

"Victor, before we get into the content, I just have one more question for Evelyn about the political side. If we stipulate for now that Congress will approve the 28th Amendment sometime in the next two years, what is the broadest outline of its prospects in the state legislatures?"

Evelyn gave them her analysis. With minor exceptions, it was pretty much a red state, blue state battleground. A different parse of the same data yielded a similar result; states whose economies were dominated by agriculture would be the hardest to win. Rural legislators, she explained, tended to have a disproportionately large influence in agricultural states, relative to their populations. Farm and agribusiness lobbies would work very hard at the state level to stop ratification of an amendment that would eliminate their influence over a hundred billion dollars worth of crop subsidies every year.

"What can you tell us about your funding?" Jeremy continued. "Where do you stand now, who are your contributors, and how is most of the money coming in?"

"Most of the small money comes in over the Web. I personally spend a lot of my time going after large donors and foundation support."

"And how do *you* like the rubber chicken circuit?" Victor asked. "You must be learning what it's like to run for Congress!"

"I see it as part of the job, which is probably how Congressmen see it," she replied. "But it's certainly not my favorite part of the job. Do you know anyone who actually likes it?"

"Bill Clinton," Jeremy replied instantly. "And he still does a fair amount of it. For him it's pure protein."

"So your bigger money comes from . . . what are its demographics?" Victor asked.

"No one wants to guess? You fellows are at least as expert as anyone I'm dealing with."

Victor rose to the bait. "I would guess the majority of your big money comes from Hollywood and small business; the majority of your small money from academia and middle class, mostly urban, Democrats."

"How did you know?" Evelyn played along. "That's about it, in a nutshell."

"I'm impressed," Jeremy said to Victor. Evelyn couldn't tell if he was being serious or not.

A double chirp came out of Jeremy's desk, and he paused to read something from a screen embedded in it. Evelyn and Victor sat quietly as he processed the new information. Victor looked at his watch.

"Evelyn, I apologize," Jeremy said, summoning his most sincere voice, "Victor is needed for a brief phone call, and I need to go over it with him first. May I propose a break for a few minutes? I'm hoping not more than five."

"Oh, by all means," she replied. "Actually, this gives me a chance to check in with my office."

"Why don't you set up shop downstairs," Jeremy suggested, pointing to a desk in the far corner of the sunken living room, a good fifteen yards away. "There's a cubicle there for some privacy, and a land line if you need it."

Evelyn took her briefcase with her and opened up her tablet at the small desk, but nothing in her in-box needed immediate attention. She thought of checking in by phone, but instead fell into a surreptitious trance, watching Victor Glade talk to his Executive Producer from a corner of her eye.

To keep from staring, she opened the file about Glade that she had been reviewing all week and scrolled through it again. Forbes had him listed as the 721st wealthiest person in the US, with a net worth of $880 million. Far more interesting than the size of his stash, however—in Evelyn's mind at least—was how he had acquired it. He graduated from Harvard Law in 1980, worked for five years in a large Boston firm, and then ran for Congress in the 1st District of Massachusetts. He won in 1986 and 1988, and could easily have been re-elected to a third term, but quit politics, moved to Greece and became a writer. His first novel, *Demosthenes*, a political thriller from the 4th Century BC, landed on the *New York Times* Best Seller list for almost two years. Two subsequent novels had their own, more modest success.

In 1999 he returned to the US to take over a faltering production of the film version of *Demosthenes*, cast himself in a supporting role, and turned it into an international box office success grossing $750 million over twenty years. As a sideline, apparently, he invested in real estate and the stock market, cashing out of the latter weeks before the dot.com crash in 2000.

In 2001 he married Melissa Brant, also a lawyer, and began raising two daughters, Andrea and Rachel. In 2004 he certified his celebrity status by describing in an interview with *Esquire* magazine the bi-sexual lifestyle he adopted during the years in Greece when he was writing *Demosthenes*. He then began investing in film projects and taking acting lessons, and took on an assortment of minor acting roles in the movies he produced. In 2011, he tried acquiring the rights to future episodes of *The West Wing* from Warner Brothers; when they could not come to an agreement, he created *The Oval Office*, wrote the first four one-hour scripts, cast himself as President, and began production in 2014 without any outside investment.

By 2019, *The Oval Office* and its related segments typically attracted ninety million viewers worldwide every week. In the process, Victor became one of the most widely recognized personalities on the planet, and even though he regularly disavowed any interest in politics, recent polls showed that almost fifty percent of eligible voters would seriously consider voting for him if he ran. In head-to-head match-ups, he was basically in a dead heat with the incumbent Republican, Burton Grove, polling far better than any other Democratic front-runner.

Evelyn now watched as both Glade and Lerner, who were

standing alongside the window behind Jeremy's desk, twisted phone sets into their ears and began their call. She wondered why she hadn't gotten any advance information about this Lerner fellow, who obviously was a major influence on Glade. Not that she thought he represented an obstacle in any way. He seemed genuine and smart, and possessed at least a modicum of wit, which after many years of observation Evelyn had learned was the most reliable barometer of her compatibility with a man. If he had a sense of humor, she could relate to him; if he took himself too seriously, that spelled trouble.

She opened a new e-mail to her assistant, intending to ask for background information on Jeremy Lerner, when she saw him pull the phone from his ear and look across the room. When their eyes met he flashed a broad smile and headed toward her. Evelyn quickly killed the e-mail, closed her tablet, and stood up to greet him.

"I'm sorry I won't be able to join you and Victor for lunch," he said as he arrived. "I have an engagement out of the office, but I'm sure we'll be speaking again. I know Victor is very keen on your organization, and I think we can definitely help bring your message to our audience. Are you still on board? With the concept, I mean?"

"I'm hard pressed to see how it could harm us, although I would want to know more about how we would be portrayed."

"Well, that's Part Two. Victor does the creative work, and I think he plans to share some of his script ideas with you over lunch."

"Could I ask you a question off the record?" Evelyn lowered her voice a notch. "I know the official answer, but maybe there's an unofficial one also."

"Sure," Jeremy said. "What's on your mind?"

"Do you think there's any chance Victor might run for President next year? He might be our best bet for beating Grove."

"That's funny," Jeremy replied, lifting one eyebrow. "You're not the first person today to ask me that question."

*   *   *   *   *

By the time she was sitting with Victor in the Executive Dining Room on the 7th floor, Evelyn had grown accustomed to the peripheral glances and outright stares that he attracted wherever he went—in hallways, elevators, now at lunch. Before the appetizers had been cleared away, Victor had praised Evelyn for her leadership, described the 28th Amendment as a cause very near and dear to his heart, and committed forty million dollars to the effort. Evelyn's jaw simply lost motor control; she had not even had a chance to ask. She sat in a daze, her lucid moments interspersed with fantasy flashes of heavyweight talent running huge media campaigns in battleground states.

When she came to, the practicality of it started to sink in. "You of course know," she reminded Victor, "that the 28th Amendment is a Non-Connected PAC, and there are limits to what we can take in. How will we get around that?"

"That's what lawyers are for!" Victor proclaimed merrily. Giving away large chunks of money always left him in a fine mood. "There must be half-a-dozen ways to bring this money into play. Jeremy will handle that aspect of it for me, but you are probably just as familiar with the ins and outs of this stuff as he is. How will you approach it, do you think?"

"I have some ideas—a separate PAC is one way, for sure, but this is not the first time this kind situation has ever come up, so we'll figure out the best way to do it. I assure you I'm grateful for your support no matter how it arrives."

Waiters cleared away their first course, and water glasses were topped off.

"So, Evelyn, tell me something about yourself. I've not had an opportunity to read the *Times Magazine* article, and I glanced through this portfolio I was given before our meeting, but I don't think I remember a thing from it, except that you were a law professor at UC Hastings."

"I still am, technically; I'm on a leave. But about myself, let's see . . . I'll give you the quick rundown. I'm fifty-six, I was born outside of Philadelphia in a really interesting place, actually . . . my parents were tenants of Mother Divine. Do you remember Father Divine?"

"He was a charismatic preacher of some kind? A black man?" Victor replied.

"Very good!" Evelyn was amazed.

"Hey, I'm sixty-five! I'm a fount of ancient knowledge!"

"My parents had rented a carriage house on Mother Divine's estate, and that's where I grew up as a young child."

"Your parents were . . .?"

"My dad was a lawyer, a labor lawyer representing railroad unions. My mother was pretty much stay-at-home, the norm for the day, but she was incredibly well read. While other mothers were doing laundry or cleaning house, my mother was reading everything from Nabokov to Jung."

Their meals arrived. When the waiters had finished, Evelyn picked up again while she investigated her plate. "Then, let's see, I was undergrad at Penn, went to Georgetown Law graduating in '83, clerked for two years, and then worked in the US Attorney's office for seventeen years."

"Where was that?" Victor asked.

"Ninth Circuit; I ended up as the US Attorney in the Northern District of California."

"That must have been some experience."

"That it was. It's a really good spot to view the widest possible spectrum of human behavior."

"But it's also not hard to see how at some point you might get tired of that spot. So from there you went into teaching?" Victor picked up his sandwich and took a bite.

"Well, it coincided with my marriage and children. It's hard to be a US Attorney and raise a family."

Victor nodded for a moment as he chewed. "I could only imagine. Why don't you take a moment and have some lunch."

Evelyn obliged and they both worked on their meals for a short time.

"And that's where you first came across the 28th Amendment—when you were teaching?" Victor resumed. "Do I have that part of it right?"

Evelyn nodded as she swallowed. "I first saw the 28th Amendment—the actual language—in 2011, in the form of a paper submitted by a 3L in my ConLaw class. At the time, I gave the paper some considerable attention in class, and, of course, a good grade.

The student who wrote it then graduates and goes away, but with his permission I continue to use his paper—without attribution—as part of my ConLaw curriculum. So after a few years, there are a lot of UC Hastings grads who've heard of this, and one of them who had access to some money sponsored some newspaper ads and a Website, and the organization was born. Two years after it was started, the founders, mostly my former students, came to me and asked me to head it up. The University gave me a leave . . . how could I say no?"

"Well they couldn't have picked a better person to lead the charge. You are just a little terrier! I saw a clip of your appearance on *Timeline* from a few weeks ago and was howling. You left the poor guy in shreds. Sliced and diced; it was uncomfortable to watch. I can see how you must have been very effective in court."

"My litigation mentor at Georgetown was a very short man— Landrieu was his name. Joshua Landrieu. Anyhow, one of his favorite expressions was: 'You never want to get on the wrong side of a short litigator.'"

"Indeed, I will remember that." Victor paused to give Evelyn some more eating time.

"Would you like some wine?" he asked as he signaled to the waiter. "Or other beverage?"

"Not for me," she said, pointing to her water.

"I'll have a sweetened iced tea," Victor told the waiter.

"Ooh, okay, I'll have one of those too," said Evelyn, suddenly inspired. The waiter left.

"Who was the original author of the Amendment?" Victor resumed. "The student, what is his name?"

"Believe it or not, he—or she—the person has asked not to be identified, and I haven't."

"That's what I had read! I'm amazed at that . . . that's really surprising."

"All of his classmates from 2011, the people who were in the class where it was first presented, all know who it is. So my guess is that it will eventually come out, but so far I think everyone has been respecting his request." She resumed eating, and Victor joined her. The iced tea arrived and they both drank.

"You mentioned you have children," Victor said. "They are grown now, or still at home?"

"I have a son and a daughter, thirteen and fifteen. Nominally they live with me, but now I'm traveling all the time, so they pretty much live at their father's house. It's only a few blocks away, and we've been divorced for five years already, so they're pretty much adjusted to it. I like to think so, anyway. I miss them a lot, but I'm also getting a lot of satisfaction from what I'm doing."

"Mmm . . . I'm in a similar spot with my daughters. They're fifteen and seventeen, and I almost never see them; I work six days a week, often until eight or nine at night. A couple of years ago, when they were younger and we were just doing the original *Oval Office*, I spent more time with them. Now, though, we're producing four shows a week—I'm working twelve hour days and loving it."

. "What more can you tell me, if I may ask, about your colleague Jeremy? This was all his invention, this segment thing? It really is fantastic the way you have a whole alternate reality going here, week in and week out."

"All his concept and execution, and it's the execution part that is his real talent. Imagine what it takes to produce four new one-hour programs every week that share common characters and adhere to the same fictional time line. The logistics are phenomenal. This is really complicated stuff."

Evelyn thought about this. "Very creative for a guy who's been trained as a lawyer. We try to wring all that stuff out of you when you're in law school, but thankfully our time-honored system of legal education failed in his case."

"He's a great lawyer, but that's only a small part of his job here. He's much more of an Executive Producer or COO."

"What's his background?" Evelyn asked.

"Somewhat offbeat, actually," Victor answered. "Jeremy was born and grew up in the Deep South, in rural Alabama. He got his undergraduate degree in math from Brandeis, then finished 5th in his class at Harvard Law, which is where I first met him. Like me he went into private practice after law school, and then he joined me when I decided to run for Congress. Then, I think I told you, he worked for the Senate as counsel to the Foreign Relations Committee."

"He grew up Jewish in rural Alabama? That qualifies as offbeat . . . how did that come to be?"

"Ask him, he'll tell you. It's a whole long *megillah*."

"I'm sure it is." Evelyn laughed and laid her knife and fork over her plate, pushing it away. "I saw the pictures on his desk . . . those are his children?"

Victor nodded. "He has two really fine sons, both much older now than in the pictures. One works in the State Department—a very interesting job, actually—and the other is a filmmaker."

Evelyn paused for a few moments, considering. "No spouse picture though, I noticed. Is he interested in meeting single women, do you know?"

Victor was only momentarily flustered. "You are inquiring on behalf of yourself, or a friend . . .?"

"Myself. I'm fifty-six, I'm busy, and I've lost any inhibitions I once had about the mating ritual. I just tell it like it is."

Victor was delighted. "In that same spirit, which I share, I am happy to advise you. Jeremy has been divorced for many years now. He does not, to my knowledge, seek out dates with women, but he's probably as eligible a bachelor as you'll ever find." Victor leaned forward to give her an additional tip, *sotto voce*: "*I happen to know he makes a nice living.*" Then, resuming his regular voice, "If you can figure out a way to penetrate his schedule, you might have a shot at it."

"Surely he doesn't work all day and all night," Evelyn probed.

"That is true, but when he's not working, he's usually playing."

"Playing? Playing what?"

"Bridge," Victor replied. "The card game."

"Ahhhhh." Evelyn nodded. "Of course he's quite accomplished at that as well."

"Quite. Do you know the game at all?"

"I was taught as a teenager, but I don't think I ever got the hang of it. All I remember is it seemed very complicated."

"It is and it isn't. If you just want to have fun, it's easy. If you play competitively and want to win, it's complicated. Jeremy plays to win."

*   *   *   *   *

Jeremy was ambivalent at best—paranoid at worst—about meeting his cousin Tzvi Zalmanovitch for lunch. Tzvi was a retired Israeli Air Force general whom he had seen only a handful of times since they first met in Jerusalem in 1973. It was not that he didn't enjoy his cousin's company; he was actually fascinated by him. The problem was that whenever they got together, their meeting always seemed to coincide with some high-profile violent event related to the Middle East conflict.

Before starting his junior year at the Hebrew University, Jeremy had made it part of his mission in Israel to locate and establish contact with several long-lost relatives, descendants of a great aunt on his mother's side. Using as guides a partially legible letter and envelope of undetermined date, the current Jerusalem phone book, and a street map, he came to a barn-like cottage in the shadow of a Wissotzky Tea warehouse on the northern edge of Giv'at Sha'ul, overlooking the Tel Aviv highway. When he knocked and identified himself, he was ushered into a room where a celebration was already underway—a birthday party for Tzvi—who, as it turns out, like Jeremy, was born on June 30, 1953. When Jeremy told his newfound relatives that it was his twentieth birthday as well, the room erupted in cheers. Toasts were made, and another round of "Happy Birthday" was sung.

Tzvi, Jeremy soon learned, was the great-grandson of his maternal grandmother's notorious younger half-sister Ruchel (who, astonishingly, turned out to be quite alive; ancient and wheelchair-bound, but unquestionably alert.) He was of average height, blond complexion, and angular features, with a beaming, broad smile. In another setting Jeremy might have taken him to be a German or a Swede; as it was, the small leather yarmulke and Israel Defense Forces uniform blew his Aryan cover. When the party broke up, Jeremy and Tzvi walked together to the bus stops on S'derot Herzl, about twenty minutes away, in animated conversation, with Tzvi insisting that he speak only English and that Jeremy speak only Hebrew.

On their walk Jeremy learned that Tzvi had recently been accepted into the Air Force's pilot training program, and that the birthday party had also been in celebration of that. They mapped out the genealogy that connected them, and agreed that they should investigate what time of day they were born, to see how close the coincidence was.

Jeremy also expressed surprise that Ruchel was still alive, and calculated mentally how this news would be received by his family back home, where her notoriety stemmed from a five thousand dollar loan she had received from Jeremy's grandmother Beryl in the early 1920's. As rendered to Jeremy by his mother, the story was this: Ruchel and her husband, Meyer, had arrived in Palestine from Poland in 1919 and managed to open a small dairy on the outskirts of Jerusalem. Several years later, a fire broke out in the barns, killing all of the cows and devastating their livelihood. Ruchel wrote to her half-sister in Detroit repeatedly, painting a vivid picture of near-starvation, and pleading for assistance. In desperation, Beryl borrowed money from every person she knew, added to it her family's own modest savings, and sent it to Ruchel within weeks of first learning about the disaster. Ruchel wrote back immediately, thanking her sister profusely, and added that she had given half of the money to a Rebbe, in thanks to God for the miracle. Jeremy's grandmother responded in fury, demanding the immediate return of all of the money, and asserting that there would be no further contact until the loan was repaid. There was no record of any subsequent correspondence between the two, and Jeremy's mother assumed that the loan had never been settled.

By now feeling comfortable with Tzvi, Jeremy asked if he had ever heard such a story, or knew of any circumstances surrounding a fire in a dairy, or a loan shared with a *Rebbe*. Tzvi howled with laughter, and kept sputtering uncontrollably. He finally composed himself and replied through a toothy, plastered grin: he had heard of the fire—Ruchel's current home, where they had just been, was a remnant of one of the original dairy buildings—but knew nothing of a loan from anyone in the States. He promised to make some discreet inquiries, adding that if it was true, he surely knew who the *Rebbe* had been. They reached the eastern crest of the hill and began the descent into S'derot Herzl's orange aura, cast down from tall sodium streetlights that lined the boulevard, spaced neatly between towering palms. They hugged and parted ways, and Jeremy accepted Tzvi's invitation to spend Yom Kippur with him at his parents' home in nearby Kiryat Moshe.

Several weeks later, on the morning of Yom Kippur, Jeremy

was seated with Tzvi on a sidewall bench in a small, neighborhood synagogue, listening to the minor-key drone of the High Holiday prayers, when a tall soldier in fatigues, obviously out of breath, appeared from nowhere and pulled Tzvi into the aisle, gesturing and whispering frantically. "*Apikoras!*" someone shouted. "Apostate! Cover your head!" Anonymous arms reached up to try and plant a yarmulke on the soldier's head, but at that moment the wail of an air raid siren rose, and everyone stopped exactly where they were. There was total silence for two or three seconds, and then the small room erupted in a mad scramble. Jeremy raced outside behind Tzvi, who turned suddenly and said in Hebrew, "Syria and Egypt have attacked! We don't know yet about Jordan. I'm leaving for my unit; you must go back to my parents' home and tell them that! Please go now!" Jeremy stood still, stunned. "Do you understand?" Tzvi shouted in English as he ran toward the street. Jeremy nodded and watched as dozens of men, prayer shawls flapping, ran in both directions on Rehov Raines. Tzvi vaulted into a jeep with the soldier who had come for him, several others piled in, and they sped off. By the time Jeremy reached Tzvi's parents' house, a ten minute walk, the streets were deserted; everyone was either on their way to the war, or at home listening to it on the radio. The siren kept wailing, high and low.

Jeremy remained in Israel for another ten months, until August of 1974. He visited Tzvi's parents regularly, hoping to meet up with him, and when Tante Ruchel died, he spent the entire day with the family, at the funeral and afterwards sitting shiva, keeping an eye peeled for Tzvi. Wartime leaves were short and infrequent, however, and the hoped-for encounter did not materialize.

After Jeremy returned to the US, they maintained a modest correspondence over a period of years, but did not speak again until June of 1981, when Jeremy was visiting Israel with his wife, Samantha, on a delayed honeymoon (they had been married in April). Jeremy was reluctant to call on relatives on his honeymoon—where was the romance in that?—but Samantha was keen to learn more about her new family, so he telephoned Tzvi upon their arrival. Amid an outpouring of gracious and insistent offers and invitations, including the use of a car (which they found hard to turn down), Jeremy and Samantha agreed to spend three days with Tzvi, also now married and with two daughters, at their home on an Israeli air base near Beersheba.

Much to their puzzlement, the address Tzvi gave them turned out to be one side of a two-family home, with a lawn and driveway, on a quiet residential street that might have been mistaken for a suburb of Los Angeles. Their taxi had passed an information kiosk a few blocks before with a sign welcoming visitors to Tel Rad, but there was otherwise no sign of an air base. The driver assured them that this was the correct address, and seconds after they pulled up to the curb, Tzvi bounded out the front door to greet them.

Tzvi's wife, Ditza, and Samantha soon discovered that they were both teachers, and otherwise shared the common ground of being married into the same extended family—plenty of grist for both of their mills. Jeremy and Tzvi were able to pick up threads of their conversations about Israeli and international politics from years earlier, and bring them up to date with subsequent events. Their first evening there, both Jeremy and Samantha asked about Tzvi's work and experience in the air force, but he openly discouraged them from asking questions, saying there was very little he could share with them. When they asked where the actual air base was, Tzvi and Ditza smiled at each other and he explained that it was all around them, but carefully camouflaged. "We go to great lengths to disguise it," he said, volunteering nothing further.

"Well, you do a great job of it." Jeremy was nonplussed. "You would absolutely never know."

"You'll hear the planes early in the morning," Ditza advised. "It can be very loud. Don't be alarmed."

As promised, at 5am Jeremy and Samantha were wakened by a distant roar of jet engines, but instead of the sound dissipating, it quickly grew louder, and in moments the entire house was shaking on its foundations, the roar of a jet engine seemingly directly beneath their bed. After idling at this deafening pitch for some time, an additional shrieking whine rose that in turn made the windows in the house begin to ping. A final, grand finale roar was unleashed, and the plane, wherever it was, took off with enormous acceleration, the shattering sound and vibration rapidly fading away. His heart pounding, Jeremy threw on some shorts and ran into the kitchen, where Ditza was sitting on a stool next to the kitchen counter, eating yogurt from a plastic container and reading the newspaper. "Good morning," she said, looking up as Jeremy, barefoot, quickly padded to the glass doors opening to the back yard. Peering out, he saw nothing but a cloudy dawn breaking over a playground. "Where are the planes?" Jeremy pleaded. Ditza smiled and shrugged, pointing all around, and at the end glanced down at the floor. "They're everywhere. Would you like some coffee?"

Over the course of their visit, Jeremy came to see Tzvi as, increasingly, both complex and anachronistic. On one hand, he had the super-rational intelligence of an engineer (his degree from the Technion was in aeronautical engineering), but he was also deeply religious in both observance and faith. In Tzvi's world, all non-spiritual problems could be rationally solved through logical analysis and the application of the laws of mathematics and physics, while all spiritual dilemmas (birth/death, free will/fate, divinity/chaos) were inherently ineffable, unknowable, and impervious to human resolution. The best one could do to master the spiritual realm was to study God's words, the *Torah*, and to study the words of those who have mastered the art of *Torah* study, the *Talmud*.

Jeremy's primary exposure to Jewish religious ritual had been his Bar Mitzvah. In his adult life he made the minimum commitments needed to get his own sons past that milestone, but he had no inherent sense of spiritual dilemma, and no room in his legalistic mind for a divine presence of any kind. Certainly there was no empiric evidence to support Tzvi's core belief that the words in the *Torah* were dictated to Moses by the one and only Yahweh, God of the Hebrews, in a one-on-one meeting some three thousand years ago, but this didn't seem to trouble Tzvi. He had somehow compartmentalized his thinking, Jeremy concluded, in a way that allowed him to suspend all logic and critical judgment in this one realm only.

While fascinated with this paradox, it in no way diminished Jeremy's respect for Tzvi, who was, after all, a twenty-eight-year-old captain in the Israeli Air Force. On his current rotation, he left for work at 2am, returned home around noon, and slept through the afternoon. At 6pm he went to a quick evening prayer service at a nearby chapel, and afterwards joined a handful of other officers for an hour, sometimes two, of *Daf Yomi*—the Daily Page, a synchronized reading of the *Talmud*, at the rate of one page a day, that is followed by tens of thousands of amateur Talmudists on six continents. Tzvi was home by 8pm, when Ditza and their two young daughters would join him for a late evening meal followed by a ten minute *Birkat HaMazon*—a full rendition of the ritual grace after meals. Afterwards there was an hour or two of family time, much of which was devoted to keeping Tzvi apprised of the exploits of various relatives, a seemingly endless cast of characters. Late at night he would pick up books again for a couple of hours before work—sometimes *Torah* commentaries, sometimes weapons training manuals.

"Depending upon his mood, do you think?" Jeremy had wondered out loud to Samantha as they lay entwined in bed at 6:00am, in between the rocket launchings beneath their mattress. "Do you think he asks himself, 'Hmm, what should I read about tonight . . . Bombs or *Psalms?*'"

Both Tzvi and Ditza were completely attuned to world events, to stock markets, to local news, to politics (both American and Israeli), and were otherwise intense conversationalists on almost any topic. They were fascinated with the United States and asked innumerable questions about the cost of living and what salaries represented in purchasing power for Americans—how many hours you have to work to buy a car, an airplane ticket, a turkey. Before the two daughters came along, Ditza had been a world history teacher in a *gymnasia*, a secular high school, in the seaside resort town of Herzliya, as secular a community as you'll find anywhere in Israel. But as a homemaker, she had assumed the traditional role of *ba'alaboosta*, the family manager, working long hours and saving every *shekel* so that her husband could devote as much time as possible to *Torah* study—presumably while he wasn't out practicing dogfights.

The day before Jeremy and Samantha's departure, Tzvi received a visit from a base messenger after lunch, and apologized to everyone; he had to take an earlier shift. Tzvi made his goodbyes, saying he expected to be late the next day and he didn't want them to wait. The two cousins embraced, and jokingly congratulated each other on having spent two days in close proximity without starting a war.

The following morning they stayed through breakfast to see if

Tzvi would re-appear. When he did not, Ditza telephoned for a car service to take them to their next destination, which was the port city of Ashkelon. Just as they pulled away from the curb, the music station the driver was listening to was interrupted by a news bulletin. Jeremy didn't quite follow the rapid Hebrew, so he caught the driver's attention in the rear view mirror and asked him what the news was. The driver's eyes were wide. "Our Air Force," he said, "has bombed Iraq's nuclear reactor. The place is called Osirak. They flew one thousand kilometers over Jordan and Saudia Arabia in the middle of the afternoon, destroyed it in one pass, and returned the same way without being detected."

"This just happened?" Jeremy asked.

"No, they are announcing only now. The attack took place yesterday, in the early evening."

Several months later, in October of 1981, Tzvi called Jeremy at his office one morning from a pay phone in Union Station. Jeremy invited him right over, and they were soon hugging each other, exchanging family updates and otherwise trying to pick up where they left off. Only minutes later, an assistant buzzed the intercom and urged Jeremy to turn on the television in his office, where all networks had pre-empted their programming to report the assassination of Anwar Sadat at a military parade on an airbase outside of Cairo. Others crowded into his office, and they all watched as the grainy sequence of events was played and replayed on the television—the snappy, unscheduled turn of the honor guard, Sadat rising to accept their salute, the sudden crack of live rifle fire, and finally his terrified colleagues trying to shield him by tipping chairs over his body.

After the office had cleared, their mood was much subdued. Inquiring about his visit, Jeremy was at first amused by Tzvi's explanation that he was a member of an Israeli dance troupe performing at an international folk dance festival in Missouri. Jeremy's rapid mental translation: he was taking flight training at McDonnell-Douglas in St. Louis, or was picking up a Phantom F-4 and ferrying it back to Israel. His amusement dissipated quickly, however, when he realized that Tzvi was not amused. "This is a vacation for me!" Tzvi insisted, looking pained. "I love folk dancing!"

Jeremy steered the conversation elsewhere, and Tzvi left after another half-hour to rejoin his "dance troupe." Jeremy complained that he had not been given an opportunity to reciprocate his Israeli cousin's hospitality, but Tzvi politely begged off and did not get in touch on his return through Washington, as he had said he would try to do.

More than a decade of incidental correspondence ensued—mostly holiday cards initiated by Samantha and Ditza—until the Fall of 1995, when Tzvi wrote that he would be in Washington DC for several days "on business" and suggested that he visit them for a dinner one evening while he was in town. While still holding the letter in his hand, Jeremy reached Ditza by telephone, insisted that Tzvi stay with his family while in Washington, and assured her they would be insulted if he didn't.

Tzvi arrived at the Lerner's Cathedral Avenue townhouse by taxi on Halloween evening and was escorted up the steps by trick-or-treaters. He quickly cued himself into the scene, and when Samantha answered the door he was standing ramrod straight in a formal air force salute, flanked by pint-sized Star Wars characters wielding light sabers and pillowcases. The greetings were effusive, and after settling in Tzvi joined Jeremy and Samantha in their living room, sipping wine and asking about the origins and significance of the various costumes as they appeared at the front door. When Samantha asked him if his family had seen the movie Star Wars, Tzvi had replied, somewhat morbidly, Jeremy thought, "Who knows how much time we have? We choose not to spend time on these fantasies."

Eleven-year-old Jonathan, hair slicked back and nattily handsome in a vested suit and tie, soon returned home and proudly opened his candy-laden briefcase for adult inspection. When Tzvi asked him about his costume, he explained that he was a dressed as a lawyer and handed Tzvi his business card:

Jonathan Lerner, Esq.
Senior Partner, Tax Evasion Practice
Greed, Babbitt & Morgan
1919 Cathedral Avenue NW
Washington DC 20016
Influence Peddlers since 1984
"There's Nothing Your Money Can't Buy"

This struck Tzvi as uproariously funny, and the laughter continued throughout the evening along with the wine and a haphazard mutual accounting of family and events over the previous decade.

They soon learned that Tzvi was no longer an active pilot, but had decided to remain in the Air Force as a career officer. He was now a Brigadier General, and his reference to being in DC on business was just that. He had four days of meetings with American counterparts at the Pentagon about a "joint technology initiative," and planned to spend the Sabbath in Washington and then leave for Brussels late Saturday night on his way back to Israel. Jeremy described his work as Counsel to the Senate Foreign Relations Committee, and this caused their conversation to veer quickly to the Middle East and Israeli politics.

At the time, Jeremy had had high hopes for the Oslo Accords. He had been consulted several times by the American negotiator Dennis Ross regarding language in the final Accords during the weeks leading up to the Clinton-brokered handshake between Yitzhak Rabin and Yasir Arafat. Jeremy felt peace was in the offing—indeed, that it had arrived—and was pleased with the role the United States had played. Tzvi distrusted Arafat, and saw the Oslo Accords as a policy leading to an inevitable Jewish civil war. There were tens of thousands of Israelis, he argued, who believed that the land of Israel, including Judea and Samaria, had been given to the Jews by God, and they would take to arms, against others Jews and against the Jewish State, to retain the right to live wherever they wanted within God's promised homeland. When Jeremy asked point blank if he was one of those Israelis, Tzvi split his response; he believed Jews had been given the land, and had every right to live there if they chose, but he would not take up arms against the State. "I'm a chain-of-command man," he had said, his eyes darting to the stripes on his shoulders. "But there are many more who aren't."

Over the next several days Tzvi left early, worked late, and was a ghost of a guest. Friday afternoon, however, he was back at their home by three in the afternoon. By dinnertime he had napped, showered, and shaved, and was in fine humor. Samantha had proposed to Tzvi in advance that their Sabbath dinner be prepared and served by a kosher caterer—she had in mind the same caterer that the White House used, if that was acceptable to him. "That's some *heksher*," Tzvi had said, laughing, and warmly thanked her. "I would love such a meal."

At Jeremy's request, Tzvi took charge of the various blessings both before and after the meal, which he rendered respectfully but with a minimum of tune and a maximum of dispatch. After dinner their heated discussion about Israel's future resumed. Totally in character, Tzvi laid out his positions with all of the rationality and precision of a scientist, and was very persuasive, but Jeremy saw it as faith-based logic that was intrinsically irrational. "I read in the paper yesterday," Jeremy had said, "Rabin was quoted as saying that the Bible is not a legal deed for real estate, it's an historical document. If you take away your premise that the Jews have a God-given right to live wherever they want in Biblical Palestine, regardless of modern political considerations, your entire argument collapses." Tzvi's immediate response was, "If you take away the premise that the Jews have a God-given right to the land, all of Zionism collapses. Rabin is a serious man, I know him personally, and I have total respect for him as a soldier, but if he said something like what you say, he is moving into dangerous territory. Without God's promise, there's no basis for the State of Israel."

Saturday morning Tzvi and Jeremy walked two miles in the brisk autumn air to a small Chabad synagogue that Jeremy had located near Rock Creek Park. Jeremy felt no personal connection to the ritual, but some of the tunes were familiar and it gave him a chance to exercise his spoken Hebrew. It was after they had returned home and were drinking coffee together in the kitchen that they simultaneously overheard the televised special news bulletin from another room: Yitzhak Rabin had been assassinated.

As horrified as they both were, Tzvi was completely immobilized. He sprawled in a low armchair in the den, silent, watching the television through one squinting eye—as if more light would cause greater pain. Jeremy had the benefit of distraction; almost immediately the phone had started to ring, and he stood in the back of the den talking quietly to Committee members and staffers as he watched. Dennis Ross called. Jeremy called Senator Pell, the Committee's outgoing Chair. Senator Helms's Chief of Staff called.

Both Tzvi and Jeremy immediately saw themselves in an eerie replay of their experience fourteen years earlier, in 1981, when Sadat was assassinated. The sense of déjà vu was magnified by dozens of television replays of the event, this time Rabin's entire security detail walking backwards, craning up at balconies and scouring the crowds, totally oblivious to the danger from within. Jeremy asked Tzvi, in Hebrew, if he thought Rabin's murder was God's will, as claimed by the assassin. Tzvi made eye contact for a second and then turned away. "I don't know," he finally said, and then kept repeating "I don't know" quietly to himself in Hebrew.

The very last time they had been together in person was on September 11, 2001. Tzvi and Ditza had come to the States for their first-ever vacation without children (for their "second moon-honey," Tzvi had written in his e-mail, failing to transpose the Hebrew expression) and also to celebrate Tzvi's retirement from the Air Force. He had gotten a job in the private sector in an airline security consulting company with contracts in the United States, and had several work-related appointments in the Washington area. They planned to spend four days in Washington, but declined Jeremy's offer of accommodations in favor of a downtown hotel suite provided by his new employer. Jeremy, for his part, did not protest too loudly; his Committee was in session and he was already working ten-hour days. He did arrange on Tuesday, however, to give them an early morning private tour of the Senate chambers. Tzvi and Jeremy were alone together in Jeremy's office, Ditza having left for the bathroom, when the first report was received of the attacks on the World Trade Center in New York. They turned on the television in his office, and CNN was already showing slow motion replays of the second plane hitting the World Trade Center. They immediately exchanged incredulous looks. "Is this us?" Tzvi asked, both amazed and mortified. "It's happening again. Are we doing this?"

"I'm sure this has far more to do with me than with you." Jeremy started to explain to Tzvi about his coincidence condition, but then CNN reported that the Pentagon had been hit. The announcer's voice cracked with panic. Jeremy sat stunned, silent. Tzvi stared intently at the television, as if trying to read a coded message in the text scrolling across the bottom of the screen. Suddenly he shouted, "Where is Ditza?! Take me to where she is! We must leave the building at once! Quickly!" Jeremy hesitated for a moment, in shock, but now

Tzvi barked like an officer giving orders. "Take me to the bathrooms now! This building is a target! We must leave! Bring your phone with you!" Jeremy finally understood and leapt from his chair. As they ran down the narrow corridor outside his office, Tzvi called out, "Use your phone! Call to empty the building! Everyone must leave!"

"What about a fire alarm? Why not just pull the alarm?"

"Yes! Do it!"

Jeremy spotted a red box on the wall opposite the bathrooms, opened it, and pulled the handle. The alarm yelped, a whooping, submarine-dive siren that produced a fugue as it echoed down the marble colonnade.

"Good!" Tzvi shouted. Ditza was now on his arm, and they were out of the building in less than a minute. From the top of the Capitol steps, the sidewalks on Constitution and Louisiana looked like human rivers, all flowing northward away from the Mall. Smoke from the Pentagon strike poured into the Western horizon. They parted ways quickly, with promises to be in touch; Tzvi and Ditza heading to their hotel, Jeremy to his wife's office in Georgetown. That evening Tzvi called Jeremy at home to let him know they were okay, and immediately declined Jeremy's invitation to have them leave the hotel to stay at their house. "I'm very curious to hear about your attraction to extreme coincidences, but perhaps by e-mail would be safer."

In subsequent years they did in fact exchange occasional e-mails, but until Tzvi telephoned Jeremy at home the previous Sunday to invite him to lunch, they had not heard each other's voices in almost two decades. Caught completely off guard, Jeremy had blurted out, "Are you sure you want to do this? You know our history; it would be so easy to meet on the Web."

"Don't be so superstitious!" Tzvi was jovial. "I'm only going to be in LA this one day and would love to see you. I will bring you up-to-date on family matters, and I'm a big fan of *The Oval Office*—Ditza downloads it every week."

Jeremy quickly agreed to meet. Tzvi's self-invitation was completely artificial; family news had not been a focus of their few exchanges since Jeremy's divorce in 1998, and he was hard pressed to believe that someone who never went to the movies and spent most of his free time studying the *Talmud* would somehow, even after 20 years, evolve into an *Oval Office* groupie. When he learned that Tzvi wanted to meet at Il Monello, an expensive and very private trattoria in Beverly Hills, he was sure he was right: there was some other agenda that Tzvi either could not or would not reveal.

*   *   *   *   *

Tzvi strode toward the table, grinning broadly. Jeremy swept past his outstretched arm and gave him a full chest hug. He seemed shorter than when they last saw each other, and smaller in frame. Jeremy realized during their embrace that Tzvi probably had the same impression of him—he had also lost two inches in the past fifteen years.

They parted and stepped back. "*Nu, mah nishmah?*" Jeremy started out in Hebrew, only to realize that Tzvi was mumbling a prayer which he soon recognized as the *Sheh'heh-cheyanu,* thanking God for having been granted life up until this moment.

"*Ameyn,*" Jeremy added with emphasis, and they sat down at the small table beaming at each other. Aside from being smaller, Tzvi looked much the same. He was wearing the traditional Sabra uniform of khaki trousers and an open-collared white shirt, but also, oddly, to Jeremy's eye, a finely tailored linen summer jacket. His blond hair, always thin, was thinner yet, but still sufficient to keep a small knitted yarmulke clipped to his head. His face was more lined, but the grin and the gleam were still there.

Aproned minions converged from all directions with mineral water, bread, olive oil, menus. "Thanks for meeting during the day—I know how busy it must be for you. I would have asked you for dinner but I'm flying out this evening."

"I was surprised, actually, that you wanted to meet in person. You're not concerned that we might trigger a war or an assassination?"

"God forbid. I gave it careful thought, though. In fact, a more thorough analysis than you might ever imagine."

"What do you mean?" Jeremy was puzzled.

"Is complicated," Tzvi replied. "I'll tell you, but I must tell you something else first."

A waiter interrupted to take drink orders and to describe the restaurant's specials. Squinting over his reading glasses, Jeremy gave his order, Tzvi gave his, and the waiter retreated.

"Nu?" Jeremy coaxed his cousin to continue.

Tzvi laughed. "You're going to find this hard to believe at first, but please be patient and I will explain." He paused again and shifted his weight forward slightly. His voice softened. "You know that after I left the air force I got a job in the airline security business? Well, this job is actually a cover for other work that I do for one of Israel's intelligence services. And completely by coincidence—or perhaps not, since you are apparently the King of Coincidence—you have turned up in the middle of one of our most sensitive operations."

Jeremy practically snorted a laugh. "You can't be serious. You're joking."

"Have you ever known me to make jokes? Do you think I'd travel all the way here to *eck velt* to make a joke? Of course I'm serious." Tzvi smiled, but didn't laugh and didn't change his expression.

"I thought you were here on other business."

"My dear cousin, I am here on other business, but that business has crossed paths with you . . . *again* . . . in the biggest way."

Jeremy was slack-jawed. "What is your business that involves me?"

"Well, to start with, you'd probably like to know how Evelyn Vaughn came to be on a CAT flight last night, and not on the commercial flight that was attacked by a terrorist."

"What could you possibly have to do with that?"

"It was our organization that picked her up and flew her to Burbank last night. The pilot was Bernard Loughran."

"How could you know anything about this? How do you know Evelyn Vaughn?"

"I will answer that question and many others that you will surely have, but for now the most important thing to know is that Evelyn Vaughn is a target—someone is trying to kill her and she should be told this as soon as possible, but not by telephone."

"Why not by telephone?"

"Because your telephones may be bugged. Your e-mail servers

are bugged, and you should assume your offices are as well. The 28th Amendment headquarters in San Francisco is also under surveillance."

Jeremy was now truly jolted, but working in the Senate for over twenty years he had encountered a lot of bombshells, and he maintained his composure.

"Tzvi, where are you getting this information? How do you even know Evelyn Vaughn is visiting us?"

"We know about Vaughn only because a terrorist we are tracking suddenly changed his target to her flight. Her flight information was obtained from an e-mail she sent to your office—we later intercepted it ourselves as it came in to the terrorist."

Jeremy paused for some time, trying to process it all. "Let me understand," he resumed. "I'm not going to call Vaughn, I'm going to go back to my office and tell her in person that someone is trying to kill her, and I know this because my cousin, who is an Israeli spy, told me so?"

"You are not to attribute anything to me. This also we must discuss right away,"—and his voice trailed off as a server came with appetizers. After he left, Tzvi continued in the same lowered tone, with added urgency.

"I have taken a huge risk to bring you this information. I'll explain to you anything you need to know to convince you that my information is correct, but you must promise that none of what I tell you will be attributed to me."

"And if I don't agree?"

"Well, you have the two pieces of information I already gave you, and we would go our separate ways. No matter what you do, I will deny any knowledge of this conversation. I'm your cousin visiting you from Israel and we have talked about family and other personal matters."

Jeremy was practically dizzy. "Tell me again. What are the two pieces of information you are giving me?"

"The first is that there is a contract out on your friend Evelyn Vaughn. The second is that your e-mail, at least, is being intercepted. My guess is that your phones are wired also."

"And what is the arrangement you are proposing? If I agree not to tell anyone how I got this information, you will tell me how *you* got it?"

Tzvi contemplated this for several moments, and then repeated it to himself. "I never thought of it that way, but that's basically it."

Jeremy paused to process what he had taken in as quickly as he could. He knew he was being manipulated, but could almost always detect an outright lie and this didn't have that feel. Yet this was an entirely different Tzvi than the Tzvi he knew, or thought he knew. In a momentary flash he was reminded of his visit in 1981 to Tzvi's house on the air base; it had seemed like an ordinary suburban home until a jet engine lit up under his bed.

"Tzvi, when we met for the first time at Tante Ruchel's house, you walked with me back to S'derot Herzl and I told you a family story that you thought was very funny. Do you remember the story?"

"You mean about the loan from America that Tante Ruchel gave to the *Rebbe*? How could I forget? This is one of the best family stories of all time! What is reminding you of this story, why are you asking?"

"I just wanted to make sure you're the same Tzvi I've known in the past."

"Ahhh." Tzvi nodded slowly.

Jeremy kept his gaze focused on Tzvi. "You said you are taking a big risk by coming to me with this. What exactly is your big risk?"

"The risk I'm taking is that I will be exposed. Before today there were, *God willing*, seventeen people who know about my second job. Now there are eighteen. Each time this number increases, the potential threat to me and my operations increases exponentially. If you tell someone about me, that person could then talk to other people, and so on."

"And please explain to me again, why have you come to me with this information?"

"We are fighting terrorism and trying to prevent terrorist acts. I don't know why terrorists are trying to kill Ms. Vaughn, but they are, and the longer she stays alive, the better chance we have of catching our 'big fish,' as you Americans say."

"Another question. You claim our offices are bugged—I would question your source. Our phones, our offices, our computers, our cars—everything is swept at least once a month. We would know if there was a bug."

"You would know if the company you used to do your sweeping was not compromised. But your sweep work is done by Corel Associates, which cooperates privately with your Department of Homeland Security."

Jeremy now shed all pretense of calmness. "What do you mean they 'cooperate'?" His voice almost squeaked.

"Corel has on several . . . many occasions set up surveillance of their own customers when requested—unofficially, of course—by your DHS. They then naturally cover up their surveillance during their sweeps. Corel is not the only company that does this, but they are the biggest by far."

Jeremy found his expectations were adjusting quickly. It was no longer even surprising that Tzvi knew things like who their security contractors were—that was small potatoes compared to the surveillance. Their offices and e-mail were bugged? Private security firms were doubling for the government? "Does this mean," Jeremy asked, "that DHS is trying to kill Vaughn?"

"Not necessarily. I'm saying only this: the people who are trying to kill Vaughn got their information from a bug that was planted by your sweep, probably at the request of DHS. There may be other leaks along this path, or the information may have been lifted out of DHS—their organization is not as tight as they would like to think it is."

Jeremy had to remind himself that he was no longer Chief Counsel to the Senate Foreign Relations Committee; he was a business executive with a fiduciary obligation to his employer. Although he knew he was being used, the information he had gotten so far, if it proved to be true, was invaluable.

They paused while their food was delivered. Tzvi reached up and tapped his head to make sure his yarmulke was still clipped to his hair, whispered to himself a Hebrew prayer, and eagerly embarked on his salad. Jeremy absently pulled apart a roll and dabbed it at the olive butter. His mind raced. Tzvi was right. If someone was eavesdropping on *The Oval Office*, it was essential, it was absolutely crucial to learn who it was, and the only way to do that would be to trace it backwards.

Which meant keeping quiet about it. *Of course Tzvi was right. He had this all worked out in advance.*

Still chewing, Tzvi looked up and met Jeremy's gaze but made no attempt to disengage or to fill the temporary silence. Jeremy resumed. "Tzvi, as you know, I encounter a lot of incredible things, but this one is going to win a prize. My cousin is an Israeli spy?"

Tzvi finished chewing and swallowed some water. "No prizes, please. First of all, don't think of me as a spy. I'm not a spy, at least not in the sense of someone working undercover in the field, because no cover is being used. You are my cousin, I have known you for many years, we are catching up on family news. The only reason I'm in the field like this is because I can have this conversation without having to build a cover."

"If you're not an actual spy, what is your job otherwise?"

"Using your terms, let's just say I'm in management. My exact role is not important; it is important for you to know only that we are engaged in an extremely important . . . I can't say in English strongly enough . . . this operation is critical to security for both the US and for Israel. I report directly to a cabinet minister almost every day."

Jeremy sat quietly. He felt oddly alert and disoriented at the same time. His heart thumped and he was watching Tzvi like a hawk, but he was thinking slowly, comprehending slowly, reacting slowly. Suddenly he associated it with the accelerated breathing and slow motion of scuba diving, a long abandoned hobby of his youth.

"Also, Jeremy," Tzvi resumed, "this is not going to win a prize because no one is going to know about it, yes?"

"Ah, yes," Jeremy replied. "No one is going to know about it." Pause. "Please remind me again why I'm believing anything you are saying?"

Tzvi was amused, but careful not to laugh. "Here's a starting point. I volunteered to you that I can explain how Evelyn Vaughn came to be on an air taxi last night and not on the commercial flight that was attacked. How could I come to know this information if I'm not who I say I am?"

"Right." Jeremy started to think this through, but the further he went with it the more questions it raised.

Tzvi read his mind. "You are going to have many questions, and we should minimize our time together as much as possible. Allow me to help you out. I've done this before and you have not, so I can tell you about some of the more important things."

"By all means," Jeremy agreed. He suddenly became aware of a deep thirst, and reached for his water glass.

"First of all, you need to tell Vaughn that she is a target. But you can't identify me as the source of the information, so you need to have another source that you can refer to. It needs to be believable." Jeremy nodded his acknowledgment and took a mindless bite of his pasta.

"And you also need to do something about your bugs."

"Changing our security company should be easy enough."

"Definitely, but there's more to it than that. You need to give this to your security director to handle—she will know what to do."

"You don't think I should be holding her accountable for the lapse?"

"That would not be my style. If you fire her the message it sends to everyone else is 'don't say anything when there's a problem; you'll get fired.' Just as important as preventing a breach is handling one once it has been discovered. The woman you have there now will actually be a good person for this." *The Oval Office*'s Director of Security was Amanda Marx, a former FBI counter-intelligence expert whom Jeremy had known for many years through her testimony at various hearings on Capitol Hill. By the time Jeremy hired her in 2016, she had been out of the FBI for five years and was working for IBM managing security for foreign-based executives.

"What do you recommend?"

"You can simply say you've heard through a private source that perhaps Corel has been compromised, and you would like to have their work checked by a private consultant, not another big company. She will not press you for your source."

"Vaughn's situation is different, though. She's going to want to know where I'm getting my information; for her it's a death threat."

"That is precisely correct. It is a serious one as well—she probably has gotten threats before, like any other public figure, and may tend to dismiss them, but this one is very real and very imminent. One possibility is to tell her the information came from an investigation that your own security people were conducting to track down an internal leak." Tzvi paused to let Jeremy absorb the idea. "This has the advantage of being true; she doesn't have to know that the leak was actually discovered by someone else. All she needs to do is be concerned enough to have her own telecom swept. When she finds bugs in her own organization, she'll have her own evidence, and where you got your information should become secondary to her."

Jeremy in the meantime had latched onto a different thought. He looked at his watch, and his tone became urgent. "Tzvi, this all relates to assassination—first Sadat, then Rabin, and now someone is trying to kill Vaughn. You know how familiar this is—this is the kind of thing that happens when we are together. Are we going to trigger Vaughn's assassination just by sitting here together?"

"I have the same concern. Of all the risks we are taking in this operation, your coincidence condition is this factor that most worries us, because we don't understand it. But I started to tell you when we first sat down, about the analysis we have done—"

Jeremy cut him off. "Why don't I just call Victor and advise him to not let Vaughn leave? I don't have to say why."

"I don't recommend this. You must assume that your calls are being monitored. You can't control what Victor's reaction will be . . . he might be stubborn and keep asking why you can't tell him. This would draw attention, especially on a day when Vaughn is visiting your offices. You don't want them—this is very important, the most important—you must not let them know that *you* know. *Fahrshteit?* This is the key to finding out who they are." Tzvi also looked at his watch. "I think the best thing for us to do is to keep our time here to a minimum. When we're done you should return directly to your offices, and make sure when you talk to your security director and to Vaughn that you are in a secure setting."

"How do I know what is secure?"

"Ah, good question. For your most sensitive conversations the safest thing to do is to take a walk outside. Remember, I'm positive only that your e-mail is bugged, but for now you need to assume everything is compromised."

"Should we not just leave right now? Do we have other things we need to talk about?"

"One other thing is very important: we should establish a way to communicate again. We may end up not needing to, but we should be able to reach each other if necessary. Do you agree?"

"By all means." Jeremy was only too happy to keep a line open—but then he quickly caught himself. This was all part of a plan that Tzvi had thought out in advance, and he was agreeing to it on the fly. "As you have said, we are cousins, so can we not e-mail each other without the need for a cover story?"

"Possibly, yes, but like you I am concerned about what happens when we communicate directly. The coincidence thing. So what I have in mind is an intermediary—someone who could be in touch with both of us and buffer our communications."

"No doubt you also have someone in mind," Jeremy said.

"I mentioned we tried to analyze your 'coincidence condition,' as you call it. The person leading our effort on this—his name is Amitai—feels certain that he could make much more progress if he could speak to you personally, and you might be curious to hear what he has to say as well. My plan is to make Amitai your bridge partner. This way you can exchange information freely and directly with no possibility of interception, and if you and I need to communicate on other matters, Amitai can be our messenger."

Jeremy started to ask how Tzvi knew he played bridge, but thought better of it. "This Amitai knows how to play bridge?"

"He has been taking lessons and playing almost every day for the last three weeks to be prepared in case this assignment materializes. He is among the top mathematicians in Israel, and our leading probability theorist, so he should have some capacity to play bridge."

Jeremy now felt like he was being pitched. Tzvi was selling him an arrangement that had been in the planning for at least three weeks. But why should he not stay with the plan, which so far had produced priceless information? "Let's try it. Send him to my regular club in Downtown LA— it's called the Deep Finesse. It's in the basement of the building where Paul Hastings is—the entrance is on South Flower.

You can find them on the Web—Deep Finesse, it's called. How soon is he available?"

"He came with me here to Los Angeles in case this worked out. So he can meet with you anytime."

"Tomorrow is Thanksgiving Day, and Friday during the day I'm going to be working. How about Friday night? All of their evening games start at seven."

"He will be available. Why don't you e-mail him, though, and invite him—that will be consistent with the cover. I'm sure his playing will be fine."

"I have no doubt. I actually don't rate myself a particularly strong player, certainly not compared to the professionals who play full-time. But the King of Spades thing has attracted a lot of attention, so I get invited to play on teams that I definitely wouldn't hear from otherwise. If you know all these other things about me, I assume you know about the singleton king of spades."

"We absolutely know about the King of Spades," Tzvi said. "It is actually the King of Spades data from *Bridge World* magazine that has been the focus of Amitai's work."

In the world of competitive bridge, Jeremy was a reluctant celebrity known as the King of Spades. The nickname derived from what could only be described as his paranormal attraction to the singleton king of spades—a bridge hand of thirteen cards that includes only one spade, that one being the "singleton king." While of no special significance or value to the game, the probability that the king of spades (or any other specific card) will show up as a singleton in its suit is statistically slim—on an average once in every nine hundred random deals. Now documented over a period of a decade, Jeremy encountered the singleton king of spades on an average once in every forty deals. This phenomenon—completely unexplained, and totally consistent over a ten year period—had been picked up in the bridge press, was often referred to in bridge columns and publications, and was eventually written up on the front page of the *Wall Street Journal* in the center human interest column, under the headline "Ten Year Run for the (Singleton) King of Spades."

"Amitai would very much like to speak with you about it all,"

Tzvi continued, "which is why I suggested this arrangement." He pulled a plain white envelope from his breast pocket and held it out to Jeremy. "I have taken the liberty of establishing a cover for Amitai here in Los Angeles. This will explain how he has come to you and what his circumstances are here in the US."

"He couldn't just tell me himself when we meet?"

"He is not a trained field operative, nor are you. Better to have it all written down so that there are no errors—or at least the potential for fewer errors. If you want to communicate with me, ask Amitai for my current e-mail address, which will change frequently. If I need to communicate something to you, Amitai will give you a plain sealed envelope like the one I just gave you, either with my message inside or instructions for retrieving my message on the Web."

"Should I open this now?" Jeremy held the envelope up to the light and tried peering through it. "Maybe I would have questions?"

"By all means." Tzvi signaled to the waiter for a check as Jeremy tore open the envelope and pulled out two sheets of paper. The first was a bridge convention card, meticulously filled out, and behind it was a typewritten note.

Mr. Lerner,

I am member of the mathematics faculty of the Weizmann Institute in Rehovot, and plan to be in Los Angeles for the next six to eight weeks, collaborating with a colleague at UCLA. Your cousin Tzvi Zalmanovitch, whose family I have known for many years, has suggested that my bridge game might improve significantly if I can persuade you to play a few games with me while I'm in LA.

If you are willing, please e-mail to me a date and time when you are available to play. I can meet you any evening at your convenience.

The enclosed convention card reflects the game I have been playing most recently. I look forward to learning what systems you might have a preference for, but wanted to at least show you where I'm at right now.

Amitai Abarbanel
aabarbanel@weizmann.ac.il

There was a brief tussle over the check. While Tzvi was taking out his credit card, Jeremy snatched the slip of paper. "I insist," Jeremy said. "This lunch eminently qualifies as a business expense, and Victor Glade can afford it, I assure you."

"Speaking of Victor Glade," Tzvi said, "my wife Ditza is a huge fan. I'm not kidding—she *does* download every show. She thinks he should run in your real elections next year. Is there any chance that could happen?"

"Hah! For a little while there I was beginning to think you might not ask," Jeremy said. "The answer is a definitive *no*. I spoke to him about it just this morning."

2	November 22, 2019 Downtown Los Angeles

Jeremy sat alone at a corner table in the forty-table main playing room of the Deep Finesse, quite content to be alone with his thoughts, a glass of wine, and a tuna fish sandwich. He had arranged to meet with Amitai at 6pm, an hour before the game, but traffic moved smoothly and he arrived at the club fifteen minutes ahead of schedule. It was deserted except for the club manager and kitchen staff.

From his current mildly buzzed perspective, things were not as bad as he had presumed they might be two days ago. On the way back from his lunch with Tzvi, Jeremy had concluded that his cousin's story had to be true; it was too fantastic to be fiction. But to make sure, he checked with his Executive Assistant to see what he had learned about Vaughn's CAT flight from Detroit. His report: AirShares had flown an empty plane that evening from Detroit to Long Beach, for an *Oval Office* flight scheduled the next morning. But there was no Captain Loughran, and no detour to Burbank with a female passenger.

So Jeremy invited Victor up to their building's rooftop garden and told all. Victor was by turns incredulous, speechless, and furious. Certainly the Administration was no fan of Victor or *The Oval Office*, but why the surveillance, and what was the connection to the 28th Amendment? Were they trying to prevent *The Oval Office* and the 28th

Amendment from joining forces in some way? There were an infinite number of questions, and at that point Jeremy had no answers. In the end Victor's instruction was what Jeremy had expected it would be: use all possible means to determine who was behind the surveillance and why, including maintaining the confidences of an orthodox Jewish Israeli Air Force General-turned-Spymaster who happened to be Jeremy's cousin.

Immediately afterwards, Jeremy spoke with his security director, Amanda Marx, using the script Tzvi had suggested. As predicted, she reacted professionally. Her lips were tight but there was no defensiveness and no questioning of his source, just an urgent new security objective. Within twelve hours she had assembled what she called, disconcertingly, a "recovery team" of internal security personnel and private contractors whose integrity she could personally vouch for. Sweeps were conducted the following day (fortunately it was Thanksgiving and the offices and studios were deserted), and two bugs were found embedded in a gateway firewall; one for voice, the other for data. There were also dozens of cascading sensors at the Long Beach studios placed to relay conversations from various script and conference rooms.

The recovery team framed the immediate decisions that needed to be made and provided briefings to help Jeremy understand the options. Ultimately he decided to leave all of the surveillance untouched, except for one row of the cascading sensors, which they disabled but left in place. Now they would wait to see what would happen next. Would Corel—or whoever was on the receiving end of the bugs—detect the disruption and react in any way? Would Corel try to move up their next sweep, which was scheduled for December 12th? Security logs were scanned to obtain the names of Corel technicians who had previously worked on the premises, and private investigations of each of them had already begun.

After the conversation with Amanda, Jeremy had picked up Evelyn Vaughn at Victor's office and invited her to the roof garden to "see the sights and take in some fresh air." As he soon discovered, Evelyn assumed the invitation to the roof had resulted from Victor telling Jeremy about her dating interest. "*This is my kind of man . . .* " she thought in the elevator going up. By the time they reached the roof and began their stroll, she had constructed a whole future fantasy involving a weekend CAT flight to Cancun.

So when Jeremy, wearing a grim face, told her that the reason he wanted to speak privately was to let her know that someone was trying to kill her, all she could do was laugh. Jeremy, dumbstruck, asked her what she found so humorous, and assured her that he was serious. When she finally regained her composure, she realized the only way to explain why she had laughed was to tell the truth, so she did: the conversation about him at lunch with Victor, her impatience with the dating ritual, the mental trip to Cancun, everything.

When Jeremy finally understood, he burst out laughing as well. "Well if that's the case, let's arrange to go out for dinner one evening, but not tonight. When you know there's a contract out on your date, it dampens the mood."

This provoked more laughter, but Jeremy finally managed to impress upon her the immediacy of the threat. When he suggested that the airliner shot down the previous night might have been targeted because she was booked to fly on it, she focused on it much more seriously, and with some trepidation agreed to accept *The Oval Office's* offer of security assistance while she was in LA and a CAT flight back to her home in Napa County.

If in fact someone was trying to prevent the 28th Amendment and *The Oval Office* from coming together, Jeremy thought, it was satisfying to know that their effort was having the opposite of its intended effect. When Victor learned of the threat to Vaughn, his reaction was to increase his commitment from forty to fifty million dollars, ostensibly to help defray the costs of adequate security. It also precipitated a first date between two of the principals; Jeremy and Evelyn agreed to meet the following week for dinner, when Evelyn was due back in Los Angeles for a 28th Amendment fundraiser.

The elevator chimed in the lobby, and Jeremy looked at his watch. From the corner of his eye he saw a tall, mop-haired man— looking lost—poke his head into the room. "Amitai?" Jeremy asked, pulling back his chair to stand up—but the process of standing seemed to have little effect on his perspective of the approaching man. Amitai was easily six-three or six-four, seemingly even taller as he strode forward.

"Finally, I meet the King of Spades!" Amitai greeted him. His body language exuded childlike delight, as though he had just traveled halfway around the world to get to Disneyland and was now meeting Mickey Mouse. His hair was a pile of random blond curls, unkempt in the style of an absent-minded graduate student, and he thrust his hand forward for an enthusiastic shake.

"And finally I meet Goliath," Jeremy responded quickly, in Hebrew. Expecting English, Amitai at first didn't understand, but was then delighted. "Tzvi didn't tell me that you speak Hebrew," he replied, also in Hebrew. Jeremy motioned to sit down.

"It's quite broken after these many years, but I enjoy making the effort," Jeremy replied, then switched to English. "When we're playing, you know we can speak only in English."

"Yes, of course," Amitai replied. "Did Tzvi give you my convention card?"

"Yes, I have your letter and your card. Please don't worry about the bridge game; you will do fine."

"Should we not review it?"

"I looked at your card, I understand your game. For now that's what we'll play. We can add things later, but better first to find our feet. The key to doing well is not what system we play, it's mental. 'Stay loose and concentrate' is my motto. If you become self-conscious you will tense up and out-think yourself."

"This is all fine with me. We will play using my conventions in the beginning. You are correct. Simple in the beginning is best." Amitai practically buzzed.

"Would you like to join me with something to eat, or drink? They have just put out the buffet." Jeremy pointed to the lounge. "Please, help yourself. I already have," he said, pointing to his now empty plate.

"This would be excellent—I am very hungry. Is there a charge for this?"

Jeremy laughed and waved him off as he reseated himself at the table. "Don't worry, it's all taken care of." Amitai, his shins as tall as his chair, looked like a camel unfolding its legs as he rose. The image was complete when he finally got all of his bones vertically aligned and fairly loped toward the lounge.

Jeremy finished the wine and began twirling the empty glass by its stem. So this camel-colt, whom Tzvi had described as a "young man," was one of Israel's leading mathematicians? He might easily be mistaken for a high school student—there was certainly no hint that he might need to shave anytime soon.

The elevators chimed again. Once. Twice. More players, mostly retirees without pressing schedules, began to stick their heads into the room on their way to the buffet, virtually all of them waving and smiling. Jeremy picked up Amitai's convention card, which he had left on the table, tilted his head, and feigned reading.

Amitai returned with a plastic plate of food and a Corona Light, and placed them with china-like delicacy on the table, as though he expected to trip over himself at any moment. He then released his joints like a string doll and collapsed into the chair.

"*L'Chaim*" Jeremy said, raising his mostly empty wine glass to Amitai, who tipped his beer and then took a long swig. Jeremy resumed his review of the convention card while Amitai ate, and made a few comments to clarify their bidding agreements.

When Amitai finished his sandwich Jeremy changed the subject. "Tzvi tells me that you have taken an interest in my coincidence condition. I'm very curious to know how that came about. Can you fill me in?"

"I'm on the mathematics research faculty at Weizmann," Amitai replied. "Tzvi, who I know through my family for many years, knows about my work in probability theory, and he came to me a couple of months ago and asked me what I thought of your coincidence phenomenon. Some of the stories he told me about when you meet, and these terrible things that happen . . . this is unbelievable."

"Tell me about it."

"Anyhow, I became fascinated with this, and then when I learned that there is *data* about the King of Spades thing, I offered to Tzvi to write it up as a research project and propose it to my department head. The next thing I know—before I write even one word of a proposal—Tzvi's company sponsors the project, and they transfer me and all of my other projects to UCLA for six months. I've got an apartment three blocks from the campus, and a car, and I'm playing bridge with the King of Spades!"

"Tzvi says you've tried to analyze my coincidence condition. What does that mean? What are you analyzing?"

"The King of Spades data that was published in *BridgeWorld* magazine. Your colleague Brian Greene was kind enough to share with me the randomizing algorithms he used in his computer-generated control deals." Greene was a bridge journalist who first publicized the King of Spades phenomenon after playing against Jeremy in a qualifying round for the Grand National Teams in 2005. He subsequently persuaded Jeremy to keep track of his singleton kings over a six-month period, and he recruited a small legion of players through his syndicated newspaper column to act as a control group during the same period. The results showed Jeremy was over ten times more likely to encounter the singleton king of spades than any other player. Subsequent comparisons, including a definitive yearlong study conducted by Greene for *BridgeWorld* magazine in 2013, all returned similar results.

"Here is where I'm at," Amitai continued. "For each instance of the singleton king of spades, we made a record of every factor we could think of. The date and day of the week the hand was played. We noted the board number, and the singleton king's location—whether it was in a North, East, South or West hand. We also developed relative frequency information for each instance; how many days since the previous occurrence, and how many days until the next one."

"Have you found a pattern?"

"I have so far devised and run three different computer programs to test the data for patterns. I have found nothing definitive, but my sense is that somewhere in this data we will find a representation of a differential equation of the second or third order, a dynamic equation like the ones that generate fractals."

"For what it's worth, I agree with you completely. This is all a fractal-esque phenomenon. If you look at it intuitively, it's like a Lorenz Attractor. I'm like a three-dimensional, biologically-powered attractor of some sort."

Amitai nodded his agreement. "I have covered very similar territory. Strange attractors are characterized by patterns that converge on a single point, and the singleton king of spades seems to be doing that with you."

Amitai paused a moment to consider something. "Mr. Lerner, I wanted to—"

"Please call me Jeremy."

"Jeremy, have any spatial experiments been done?"

"What do you mean by spatial?"

"Have you tracked your results when you play with cards that were not shuffled and dealt by you or near you—perhaps not even in the room where the game is being played?"

"Oh, I see what you mean. Yes. That's a question that Greene once asked. He pointed out that the shuffling and dealing is the key to everything, because that's the point at which the singleton king would be fixed in a hand. So a few years ago—many years ago, actually, this was when I was still living in DC—I went for a few weeks without shuffling or handling the cards at all myself, and in most cases I left the room when the deals were being made up; I would go into another room, the kitchen or wherever. This did not seem to make much of a difference—my stats edged lower, but not significantly."

Amitai dusted his hands over his plate and pushed it aside. "I believe this is something that is worth investing more time in. An informal test that you ran for a few weeks many years ago is hardly definitive. Is there a way we can repeat this experiment with stricter standards? If we could confirm that the phenomenon depended on your physical presence at the time the cards are shuffled and dealt, that would be a big clue."

Jeremy considered this. "When I'm playing here at the Deep Finesse we might be able to arrange it to have some pre-dealt boards available. Maybe we could get the daytime directors to deal and set aside twenty-five boards during their downtime."

Other players began moving into the room, finding their tables and setting up shop—pencils, scorecards, side tables for food and drinks. Almost everyone at some point waved or smiled at Jeremy. A couple he had known for many years, the wife a former Congresswoman from California, came up to say hello. Jeremy introduced Amitai by first name only, a friend from Israel, nothing further volunteered. They asked about each other's families, exchanged regards, and the couple departed. Jeremy was relieved that the conversation had not veered into politics. The last thing he wanted to hear was someone else asking him if Victor was going to run for President.

"You are getting this attention because you are the King of Spades?" Amitai lowered his voice a notch. "Or is it because of who you work for . . .?"

"In this particular case," Jeremy nodded towards the Congresswoman, "the connection is through my former job working for the Senate. But most of the attention I'm getting here relates to the King of Spades phenomenon. Everyone knows about it, and at the end of the game my stats will be updated on the results board." Jeremy thumbed over his shoulder to a long computer-generated banner on the back wall of the main card room, and Amitai turned to look:

KING OF SPADES SINCE JANUARY 1, 2019

KOS Total Deals 2,640 - Stiff Spade Kings 68
Control Deals (Live) 2,488 - Stiff Spade Kings 4
Control Deals (Computer) 2,640—Stiff Spade Kings 5

"So am I due to see the singleton king of spades tonight?"

"Statistically, you mean? I don't know . . . let's see." Jeremy craned his neck to see the board behind him. "I think the last time it came up was last Thursday. I've played twice since then, at twenty-four boards per game, so that's forty-eight boards. My average for the past year or so has been about one occurrence in every forty deals—so *that* means statistically that it is likely to appear tonight. It could also not show its face for three weeks and then come up four times in an evening—which is the record here at this club, I think. At the Summer Nationals in 2009 it showed up six times in a twenty-eight-board event."

"It really is the most interesting phenomenon . . . " Amitai started to lose himself in his fascination.

"Let's just bid and play the cards we get," Jeremy suggested, as their first opponents arrived and took their seats. The director walked by and dropped two boards on their table, barely breaking his stride. "Thanks for joining us tonight," he called out as he reached the end of the row. "There are fifteen full tables. Please shuffle and play, and have a pleasant evening."

<table>
<tr><td>

3

</td><td>

JL Coincidence Blog - Entry #1
ca. October 1, 1962
Pickens County, Alabama

</td></tr>
</table>

In an early morning dream, I was preoccupied by some event—I can no longer remember what it was—when a rotating noise began to emerge in the background. It grew louder—whop, whop, whop—at a slow but constant rate. As it came closer, I realized that each "whop" had its own echo: whop WHOP, whop WHOP, whop WHOP. The echoes multiplied, even as the decibels rose, until it all merged into a deafening roar, and I woke up to find the noise was not in the dream, it was right outside my bedroom window. Right on top of my house.

I ran to my window and immediately ducked. Flying low over our yard were at least half a dozen twin-rotor military helicopters. They crossed over the county road and began landing in our neighbor's cow pasture. From my bedroom it was a picture window view.

I remember covering my ears and running, half-crouched, to my parents' bedroom, which was on the opposite side of the house, and it was empty. I then remembered that I was alone: it was Monday morning, my parents were at work, my brothers were at school, and I was at home with the chicken pox—already done with it, but still stranded. My mother had said the night before that she would be going to the factory in the morning and would be back to make me lunch.

I ran back to my bedroom window, dove to the floor, and peered over the sill in time to see the last of the helicopters, like giant steel grasshoppers, touch down on our neighbor's pasture—each one bouncing slightly as it landed. The closest one was half a football field away.

The engines began to idle, and the propellers suddenly became visible and drooped as they slowed. One by one doors popped open and dozens of soldiers in green battle fatigues hopped to the ground. Then they all started tugging at their belts, shedding equipment, unzipping, unstrapping, struggling some more with their trousers, and finally freeing themselves to pee. I could see a dozen or more random yellow arcs spraying into the morning sun.

I remember thinking to myself, this can't be real. This is still the dream. I looked back at my bed to see if I was still there, and I wasn't. Through my bedroom window I could see the soldiers still there, in the sunlight.

I then ran through the kitchen, through the back door to the carport, to get outside. Turning the corner, I could see soldiers gesturing and the scene began to unfold in reverse. Zippers, buckles, helmets, soldiers hopping up, hatches closed. The engines revved, the louder echoing whop WHOP, whop WHOP, returned, and the swarm began to rise. I ran to the end of our driveway, where our mailbox was, and looked up and down the highway, but there were no cars in sight. The noise was like non-stop, close-by thunder.

I watched from there, at the end of the driveway, as the helicopters rose up and skimmed over a stand of trees, headed due West. I remember morning sunlight reflecting off the propellers made it seem like there was a storm in the distance. I remember thinking, right then and there, that no one was going to believe me.

And as it turns out, no one ever did. Everyone knew that the helicopters had come and gone, because they were seen and heard passing over the town, and everyone knew where they were going: President Kennedy had ordered Federal troops to the University of Mississippi. But I never found anyone who saw the helicopters land, and my parents tried to convince me it was a dream that came and went with the helicopters flying overhead. I don't think it was a dream. I think it really happened, but I have no way of knowing for sure.

NOTE: When I started this blog in December 2011, I began

by trying to recall my earliest awareness of a strange coincidence. I'm not really sure what the coincidence is in this story (maybe there isn't one), but it was strange enough to keep popping into my mind, and I had to start somewhere—so I started here.

4	November 24, 2019 ABC News Studios Washington DC

FRIEDMAN: Earlier this week, on Thanksgiving Day, the wealthy technology entrepreneur-turned-movie-mogul Walter Trask announced yet a third career for himself, that of political kingmaker. With twenty million dollars of his own money and apparently no cue or endorsement from any third party—certainly not the Democratic Party—Trask has formed a Political Action Committee that is dedicated to making the writer/actor Victor Glade a candidate in the 2020 Presidential election. For the few of our viewers who don't already know, Mr. Glade has portrayed a fictional US President, Alvin Bosco, in the highly acclaimed and long-running Webcast series, *The Oval Office*, for the past five years. It is also widely reported that Mr. Glade has on numerous occasions denied any interest in electoral politics and has said explicitly that he will not be a candidate in this upcoming presidential contest.

This would appear to lead to a conflict between these two gentlemen at some point in the near future. But in the meantime, we *are* here, and it *is* now, and a fascinating situation it is.

We are fortunate enough to have one of the principal players in this drama with us today in our Washington studio. Victor, thanks very much agreeing to take time with us. We have only a few minutes scheduled here, so I will get directly to the point. What is your reaction to Trask and his Committee that he has named—cleverly, I suppose— "2020 Vision"?

GLADE: Thanks for having me, Tom. My immediate and foremost reaction is that this is an enormously misguided initiative that will go nowhere, and I will re-state for the record that I will not be a candidate in any political party or for any political office, either this year or next year or ten years from now. Everyone who knows me personally knows that I view myself first as a writer, then as an actor, and thirdly as the father of two teen-age daughters. I'm passionate about all of these things, and if you consider how completely incompatible they are with being any rank or level of politician, much less a presidential candidate, it will be crystal clear that I mean what I say.

FRIEDMAN: What factors are going into your decision?

GLADE: Those that I have just enumerated. I'm completely dedicated to my creative work with *The Oval Office*, and whatever time I have left I spend with my family and friends. Electoral politics is simply not in my frame of reference at all now: virtually all of my meager brain capacity is devoted to my writing and acting.

FRIEDMAN: Many of our viewers know that in 1986—thirty-three years ago—you were elected to Congress from the 1st District of Massachusetts, won easy re-election in 1988, and were basically unopposed in 1990—but you declined to run. At the time, your stated reason for not seeking re-election was your conviction that Congress was bought, paid for and owned by special interests that donated heavily to political campaigns. Do you still believe this to be true, and if so is it in any way a contributing factor to your current decision-making?

GLADE: Oh, I think they're even *more* dependent on campaign contributions now than they were thirty years ago. All you have to do is look around you—no one even tries to be discreet about it any more. Any contested Senate campaign is going to cost over $150 million. Politicians have no choice but to be constantly on the prowl for money, and this makes them utterly dependent on their moneyed constituents.

FRIEDMAN: In 1990 you were also convinced that this cycle of campaign finance dependency would never be broken. Do you still hold that to be true?

GLADE: Bless you, I'm so glad you asked that question. Actually, as incredible as it may seem, there appears to be at least some light on the campaign finance horizon.

FRIEDMAN: You are referring to the 28th Amendment?

GLADE: I am indeed. The 28th Amendment addresses the issue of private campaign donations head-on, and to my way of thinking provides a structure for eliminating that influence altogether.

FRIEDMAN: For those of our viewers who are not familiar with it, the 28th Amendment—as it is currently being proposed—would replace private campaign donations with a system of public financing, at the general election level, for all US Senate and Presidential campaigns. And if my information is correct, Victor, it is a cause that you have embraced to the tune of about fifty million dollars.

GLADE: That is correct. That's an indication of how strongly I feel about the 28th Amendment.   Frankly I can't help but ask myself why this solution has never been envisioned—it's not like it's rocket science. Most European countries have had publicly funded elections for decades.

FRIEDMAN: I think it's been in the background for some time, but the notion that it could ever gain the necessary support seemed remote. I for one am fascinated at how this idea has recently taken root in some very unlikely circles.

GLADE: At least some credit is due, I think, to Evelyn Vaughn, the law professor and former prosecutor who has been running the 28th Amendment organization for the past two years.

FRIEDMAN: You've gotten to know her fairly well?

GLADE: Well enough to trust her with fifty million dollars.

FRIEDMAN (laughing): That was fast. Very cute.

GLADE: Well, we want to give your viewers some entertainment too, don't we? It can't be all one long civics lesson or we'll lose them entirely.

FRIEDMAN: I couldn't agree more. Keeping an eye on our time—we have only a few more minutes available—could we return to you, and to Trask and his Committee?

GLADE: By all means.

FRIEDMAN: If Mr. Trask calls you now, will you speak with him?

GLADE: I have not spoken with him, however my attorney has.

FRIEDMAN: Would you care to comment on what transpired in that conversation?

GLADE: Absolutely not.

FRIEDMAN: Can't blame a fellow for asking.

GLADE: No, you can't.

FRIEDMAN: What do you think has motivated Trask to do what he's done?

GLADE: To be candid with you, but not entirely modest, I think he has been motivated by the superb job we do with *The Oval Office*, portraying competent public servants who work very hard to consider and advance the interests of average Americans.

FRIEDMAN: Yes—Trask argues in his statements that your qualification is your track record with the Bosco Administration. Quoting Trask, ". . . the policies of the fictional Bosco Administration are still policies. Someone, somewhere, is responsible for articulating these policies. The fictional integrity they portray is still integrity—at least they know what it is." Close quote.

GLADE: It's easy to portray success for the Bosco administration because our writers can get the characters to do whatever we want them to do. As you know, in real life, things don't work that way. The great irony here, as I see it, is that the Grove Administration believes that it *can* get people to do whatever they want, and it is this arrogance that is the fatal flaw in their own policy thinking.

FRIEDMAN: Could you give one example?

GLADE: The notion that we can force democracy on the Arab Middle East; just because democracy works for us doesn't mean it's right for every society. Democracy might be something that can only successfully emerge through a process of social evolution that these nations have not yet gone through.

FRIEDMAN: I understand we need to wrap it up. Do you have any general comment you'd like to make to our audience about 2020 Vision, the Committee that has been established to draft you into the 2020 presidential race?

GLADE: Only that if any of your viewers are contemplating making donations to Trask's Committee, they are throwing their money away— they might as well flush it down the toilet. If they would like to see some actual change in the political environment in this country, my advice is for them to send their money to the 28th Amendment. Through the end of this year, all donations the 28th Amendment receives from individuals, up to maximum of five thousand dollars per contributor, are being matched two-for-one by my private foundation, which is sponsoring its own separate PAC in support of the 28th Amendment effort.

FRIEDMAN: Thanks very much for taking the time to be with us and for sharing your thoughts.

GLADE: Thanks for having me, Tom. I appreciate the opportunity.

*   *   *   *   *

Irving Liman was waiting in the studio's wings when the interview was finished. At ninety-one he was far and away the best known campaign consultant in the world of Democratic politics. An economist-turned-political strategist who had dozens of wins to his credit, his time and attention were sought by virtually every Democrat in Congress. On his ninetieth birthday he reduced his schedule and gave notice to many of his clients, but still rode the Hudson Line three days a week to his office in midtown Manhattan and was gearing up for the 2020 Elections.

Jeremy first met him in 1997, when he was working for the Foreign Relations Committee, and over the years they developed a close relationship. When Jeremy left the Senate to work for *The Oval Office*, Liman offered to join as a script consultant but insisted that the relationship be unofficial and off the record. Jeremy and Victor therefore did not call on him very often, but did so frequently enough over the course of five years to conclude that Liman's analytical powers and general acuity were improving as he got older, not tapering off.

No stranger to broadcasting studios, Liman strode out onto the set to greet Victor as soon as the OFF AIR light blinked green. A small man in his younger years, he had by now settled down to a diminutive 4'11", so for Victor, who was 6'1", a conversation while standing in a brightly lit studio was not a practical arrangement. Liman's highly polished pate, the color of waxed pine, reflected the bright lighting upwards and gave Victor's aerial view a shimmering quality.

Victor reached down and gave Liman a kind of vertical hug. "My friend, my friend, I can't tell you how honored I am that you would make this trip."

"It was not a big deal," Liman said, holding Victor's hand and patting it. "Don't let it go to your head. I needed to be in Washington tomorrow, so I just came down a day early." When Liman learned that Victor was taping the Friedman interview in Washington, he arranged to meet him at ABC's studio on 17th Street and accompany him back to Washington National, where his plane was waiting for the flight back to Burbank.

"For the conversation I wanted to have," Liman continued, "in-person is much better anyhow. But I've gotta tell you, before anything else, I am absolutely enamored of your show. Especially recently, I think it's been fantastic. Where do you come up with this stuff—whose idea was it to send an ex-President out as an emissary to Muslim clerics? I want to know *whose idea that was!*"

"Irving, Irving, I love your enthusiasm. I'm honored that you watch the show, truly. We'll talk, but not here . . . let's go back to the car. We've got half the world staring us down."

"Yes, by all means," Irving readily agreed, and in fact noticed as he looked around that almost everyone in the studio was nonchalantly watching Victor's every move.

"I left my driver speaking with your fellow with the British accent . . . what is his name, Grainger?"

"Right, Grainger is my number one man. He's the guy who keeps me alive—or at least he has up until now."

As they began to walk Victor noticed a little hesitation in Liman's gait, and extended his arm.

Liman waved him off. "Thanks, but I'll be fine. The jerkiness comes from my new knees . . . they're too tight."

"I thought you already *had* artificial knees. And hips too, don't you?"

"Indeed I do, or did, but the last set of knees wore out. They were twenty-two-years old—can you believe it? These new ones are adjustable, they're much better. The Doctor set them so I gained a whole inch! But they're a trifle too springy, as you noticed."

Victor stopped in his tracks. "What are you, the Bionic Man? You are truly amazing. "

Liman motioned to him to keep walking and recited cheerfully,

I wake up each morning and dust off my wits,
Open the paper and read the obits.
If I'm not there, I know I'm not dead,
So I eat a good breakfast and go back to bed.

"That hardly describes you," Victor protested, "but it's very funny."

"That's from an old song by the Weavers—do you remember the Weavers? They were probably before your time."

"Sure I know the Weavers. I seem to remember there was a Weavers reunion concert at Carnegie Hall."

They arrived in the front lobby and were greeted by Grainger. "Mr. Liman, Grainger Wells here." He lowered his hand for a gentle handshake. "If you don't mind, you'll make the trip to DCA in Victor's car—it's comfortable, and it meets our security requirements. Your driver will follow in your car and you can change back at the airport."

"Whatever you need. We certainly want to keep Victor safe."

"Thanks very much," Grainger replied. "Please come with me this way," and he led them to the exit where they were joined by three additional bodyguards. When the doors were pushed open, they were greeted by a thunderstorm of applause, boos, ululations, epithets, whistles, howls, and group chants from a waiting crowd. They started down a roped-off gauntlet lined on both sides by ABC security guards, toward the sedan waiting at the curb. The crowd's electricity surged wave-like as they passed. The majority appeared to be *Oval Office* fans and "Victor Glade for President" supporters, but there were also anti-abortion and pro-choice activists, anti-war and anti-gun control protesters, and crusaders for animal rights, gay rights, Muslim women's rights, and prisoners' rights. The last few yards had been cordoned off for the press, where the cacophony included unintelligible questions shouted over the hum of dozens of camera shutters. Victor ignored it all and focused on Liman's legwork, poised to catch him if he stumbled. This would be an awkward place to take a spill.

Once they were seated in the back of the car, Victor apologized. "I'm sorry to have put you through that. I honestly didn't expect this kind of crowd. It's the Sunday after Thanksgiving, for Pete's sake—don't these people have anything else to do? They're Americans, why aren't they out shopping or something?" Victor had grown very impatient with the trappings of fame.

Irving waved him off. "Don't worry about me. I've been through worse."

"I'm sure you have." Victor remembered that Liman had managed Kaspar Randall's Senate bid several years back. It was hard to imagine anything more contentious than an openly gay woman running for the US Senate in Michigan, and then winning in a recount!

The opaque partition that separated them from the driver suddenly clicked and began to retract into the seat. The driver peered over his shoulder. "Good morning, sir, William here. Just confirming that we're going to DCA."

"That's my understanding, thanks for checking," Victor replied. He had once commented to Grainger that he sometimes felt anxious about being driven away in a car where he had never even seen the driver. Since that time, his drivers always made a point of introducing themselves, and confirming their destination.

"No problem. Sir, it's going to be another minute or two before we pull away. If you wanted to get something to drink now would be a good time."

Victor nodded acknowledgment and the divider whirred upward, emitting a quiet hiss after locking into place. It was darker in the car, and it took a few moments for Victor to re-focus on Liman, who despite having gained an inch with his new knees was virtually swallowed by the leather upholstery. The soles of his shoes just barely scraped the floor. "Would you like something to drink?" Victor asked. "We have lots of soft stuff, and hard things also if that's your Sunday morning taste."

"Nothing at all for me, but please help yourself." Liman's spoke in a patient-sounding tenor, with the cadence of someone who has all the time in the world.

Victor pulled a small container of milk from the refrigerator, peeled off the plastic top, and took a swig. "I was a Tums addict for years. My doctor suggested drinking a glass of milk three times a day to suppress the acid, and lo and behold . . . it works!"

"Your health is okay otherwise?"

"I'm as fit a sixty-six-year old as you're likely to find—unless you know something that I don't know."

"No, no, I'm just being solicitous. Or maybe getting even. Everyone's always asking me how I feel, how's my health—as though they can't believe I'm still ticking. So after they ask me how my health is, I've taken to asking them the same thing. I've lived long enough to know how fickle life—and death—can be. I've just been lucky."

"Well you are not your average ninety-one-year old, I'm sure you know that."

A single, gentle chime sounded from a console above their heads, and the car pulled away smoothly. The noise from the outside crowd faded away.

"So, Irving, who's going to go first? I know you wanted to speak with me, and I know what you wanted to speak about. But I also have some questions for you."

"I'll go first," Irving jumped in, "because I think I can save us some time. You are right, I did want to try and convince you to run for President—you could win, by the way—but I heard your interview with Friedman just now and I can see that you really, truly don't want to be President of the United States."

"That is the absolute, God's honest truth. Who in their right mind would want to be?"

"Well, unfortunately, that's the problem." Liman wore the face of a man who has just learned of a close friend's death. "The environment has become so poisonous that no one who possesses both integrity and common sense will get involved. So the people who *do* get involved are lacking in either or both. And we've already arrived at the logical extreme of that formula with the Grove Administration." He fixed Victor with lamenting eyes.

"I thought you weren't going to try to persuade me to run," Victor moaned.

"I'm not. I told you, your interview with Friedman convinced me."

Victor paused, and Liman made no effort to fill the void.

Finally: "Irving, do you believe there is a moral or ethical dimension to my decision here?"

"What am I, your Rabbi?"

Victor smiled. "In a manner of speaking, you are." Jeremy, in fact, privately referred to Liman as their "Jewish Yoda."

"Well, put your emphasis on 'manner of speaking.' Your question is for a *real* rabbi."

The car accelerated onto a highway and then plunged into a tunnel. "Computer, turn on the lights, please," Victor said quietly, and an indirect glow slowly rose up from the recessed edges of the ceiling. The car zipped out of the tunnel moments later.

"Melissa, my wife, bless her heart, never stops being my conscience. On one hand she says she doesn't want me to run, but she also believes that there is a moral issue that I'm hiding from and she doesn't see any conflict in holding both of those opinions!"

Liman stood his ground and contributed nothing. Victor now had one eye glued to Liman's hands, which remained motionless in his lap, not having moved so much as an inch.

"Well, I have no intention of running for President. If I change my mind you'll be the third person to know—after Melissa and Jeremy."

Liman nodded his acknowledgment. "Assuming you don't change your mind, I wanted to ask you to consider endorsing another candidate, and perhaps actively supporting that candidate. If you decide you do have some type of moral or patriotic obligation that you want to respond to, an endorsement would be a material contribution to the cause, but would not require you to take up an unwanted or overwhelming burden. This is called 'having your cake and eating it too.'"

"I have of course thought about this. This is a possibility, but to tell you the truth there's no one on the horizon who I can get excited about."

"Excitement you're looking for?" Liman was incredulous. "If you want excitement, get in the race! Otherwise, back the person who you think has the best chance of beating Grove, and offer your services for the campaign. If you did even one ad it would have a tremendous impact—it would take you all of an hour to do."

"Is there anyone you have in mind?" Victor asked.

"Not yet. We'll talk after the first of the year."

"Good, we don't even have to go into it now. If I decide I want to do this, will you help me with the pick?"

"Absolutely. Without question. I would be honored." Liman bowed his head appreciatively, and then they both peered out into the speeding marble cityscape through one-way, bulletproof windows. There was very little traffic and Victor could see they were already approaching the Potomac River Bridge.

"So, Irving," Victor picked up, "what is your take on the 28th Amendment? We've not discussed this. What are your thoughts about it?"

"I'm ecstatic about it. And in the Friedman interview, your tactic of trying to re-direct money and support from Trask to the 28th Amendment was a brilliant stroke. If the 28th Amendment were somehow ratified, it could bring about a fundamental change in the system—no offense, but something that would endure long past your presidency."

"No offense has been taken, I assure you. And I'm encouraged to hear your reaction. That is certainly the position that I take—this could change everything. What do you think its prospects are?"

"Infinitely better than they were before you put fifty million dollars into it."

"I should hope so," Victor replied. "Seriously, is there a winning scenario for this thing?"

"I believe there is."

"Could you enlighten me at all?"

"Here's my reading of it. As you know, it's a two-stage process, so the first thing we're looking for is two-thirds of the Senate. I'm hard pressed to believe that your friend Evelyn Vaughn could pull this off with today's Senate. But there are five Republicans up for re-election whose defeat next November could tip the balance. They are all uphill battles, but absolutely winnable. If you wanted to render the greatest possible service to the 28th Amendment, you would support the Democratic candidates in those races."

"And those candidates would be . . .?"

"I'll send you an e-mail. Let's not go into it here—it doesn't matter who they are, it matters who they're replacing."

"Okay, send me the list. I don't know if I can campaign for them, but I can certainly lend them financial support."

"In-person campaigning, in your case, makes the biggest difference."

"I know that, but I also know that my security situation makes it a very cumbersome proposition."

Liman nodded. "I can see. You know I had never thought about it, but now that I'm with you I understand why you need it."

"There's nothing like reading an internal security memo and finding yourself referred to as a 'high risk profile.' Why don't they dispense with the niceties and just call me a 'likely target'?"

"Maybe they're trying not to alarm you?"

"Hah! If that's their intention, they've failed completely. Every public appearance I make I'm sure will be my last. But enough about me. I have another question for you that's related to what we've been talking about."

"Shoot." Irving unfolded his hands and briefly pointed an index finger at nothing.

"I am not a candidate, and have just reaffirmed that I'm not a candidate, but apparently I'm still the most potent domestic adversary the Administration has. Even an endorsement, as you have pointed out, could have a huge impact on the outcome of the race next year."

Liman nodded.

"So assume as a starting point," Victor continued, "that we are already a big thorn in the Administration's side. Then add to that our portrayal of a successful Middle East initiative, which of course was picked up by the media and compared to the Administration's recent results, . . ."

"I'm well aware of it."

" . . . which made them look even worse. And now Trask comes out with this insane draft idea, and it's like pouring gasoline on a fire. Even though I'm not running, the Administration doesn't necessarily know or believe that. One reason I went for the interview today was to send as strong a signal as possible to the Administration that I really am not a threat."

Liman's head bobbed. "So what's you're question?"

"So my question is, what do you think of the idea of running an ad campaign to assert my non-candidacy? The objective would be to put up obstacles for Trask, *and* to placate the Grove Administration."

"You mean actual ads on TV or the Web?"

"Maybe print, I don't know. The *Wall Street Journal,* the *Washington Post.*"

"You're serious. You would spend money to do this?"

"Money is not high on my list of concerns. The Administration trying to close down *The Oval Office* is on the TOP of my list of concerns."

"Pheww. I gotta think about this one for a minute." He paused several moments. "You really think the Administration wants to close down *The Oval Office?*"

"Our security people—who seem to have their shit together, if you'll pardon the expression—have this whole big operation dedicated to assessing threats, and they are saying that the Grove Administration, by some high order of probability, is very likely to attempt to shut down *The Oval Office* and/or neutralize the perceived threat that I represent. Sometime before I can have any impact on the elections."

"That really seems so implausible," Liman said cautiously. "What are they going to do, assassinate you?"

"Well, that's one of the scenarios I'm protected against, but let's skip over that one—which is not one of my favorites anyhow—and go right to the idea that our people think is more likely, which is a lawsuit or arrest, maybe with some help from the Homeland Security Court."

"Oh!" Liman's eyes widened and he shifted in his seat.

They both sat quietly for a moment. Homeland Security District Court had classified dockets and its own separate bar, the membership of which was also, of course, classified. Even the number of people with access to the dockets was a secret. Accountable only to the Supreme Court, HSDC had become the kangaroo court of choice for the Grove Administration.

"Without going into details"—Victor knew not to disclose the eavesdropping that had been discovered in their offices— "let's just say we have indirect evidence that a move like this is at least being planned for."

"So your question again is . . .?" Liman asked, looking a little dazed.

"So the question is: the ads. If I were to run ads denying my candidacy, would they have the intended effect, to placate the Administration?"

Liman put his hands back in his lap and thought for a few moments. "I don't see why not . . . but it would be the only time, in my lifespan at least, that anyone has ever run ads to stay *out* of a political office."

"Jeremy pointed that out. It gives a whole new meaning to the term 'negative campaigning.'"

"Hah! I love it!" Liman was delighted.

The car exited off the highway and turned onto a local road. "God bless you, Irving. You really are amazing. You look terrific. But I won't ask you about your health."

"Good. Because I still have a question for you."

"Shoot." Victor tried out Liman's earlier finger gesture to see how it felt.

"Whose idea was it to have an ex-president train to become an emissary to Muslim clerics? I just want to know whose idea that was."

"I'll tell you, but why do you want to know?"

The sound of a jet flying low overhead prompted them both to look out their windows. They were approaching the General Aviation terminal.

"I want to know because I think it's brilliant. I'm not talking about the acting or the writing or the directing, I'm just talking about the idea, the concept. It came from somewhere. Who's making this stuff up?"

"Most of these things are dreamed up by our writers. This particular one was my own."

"I knew it! I was sure of it! And I want to tell you, it's an indicator of how *in some respects* you would make a great President."

"You think?"

"Yes, I think."

"Well then, think about this. I came up with that idea one

night when I was stoned."

"You mean on grass?"

"I mean on the kind of marijuana that only a billionaire can buy."

William's voice came through an invisible speaker. "Sir, we'll be there in a minute or two. I have been told there is no press or public at all."

"Thanks," Victor called back.

Liman was giddy. "That is absolutely the funniest thing I've heard in months. You still smoke grass?"

"Like clockwork, a joint every night for the last forty years. Whether I need it or not."

"Well, from my perspective you're now an even more appealing Presidential candidate! That's exactly what this country needs, a President who knows how to loosen up a little."

"That's very funny, your perspective. Here's my perspective: I should give up my cannabis nightcap so that I can become the sober, twenty-four-hour-a-day caretaker of ten thousand plutonium warheads? What is it, exactly, that I'm supposed to find so appealing about this proposition?"

5 | December, 2019

Two weeks after the surveillance was uncovered, the key questions all remained unanswered. The first was who—who was behind it? The working assumption was Homeland Security, or more likely the White House under the cover of DHS. The second was why the Administration would want to eavesdrop on *The Oval Office*. The assumed answer was that they were gathering "evidence" that would be used to neutralize Victor in some way. But no direct or even indirect link had yet been found between Corel's technicians and DHS or the White House, and they were treading lightly in order to avoid detection.

Fortunately, the number of *Oval Office* personnel who knew about it had been limited to nine (Jeremy recalled Tzvi's valuation of the risk he was taking by revealing his spymaster identity to an 18th person). Among this group, designated Team 9, a third question was also discussed: How did Evelyn Vaughn and the 28th Amendment fit into the picture? It did not take a great leap to imagine that the Administration could have learned via eavesdropping of Evelyn's plan to visit *The Oval Office*, and that the attack on the airliner in Detroit was an attempt to prevent that meeting from taking place. Many Republicans, including President Grove, were vehemently opposed to the 28th Amendment, but could they feel so threatened by it that they would resort to violence?

To Jeremy this sounded very far-fetched, but he was determined to protect Victor and *The Oval Office*. He read every Team 9 briefing paper as soon as it was released, and met at least twice a week with Amanda to get updates and discuss options. When possible he also liked to drop into the early morning security briefings that Amanda held with her various section heads and project managers, ordinarily just listening in and making no comments.

One project was the maintenance of an enemies list, and the compilation of dossiers on the individuals who represented the greatest potential threat to Victor and *The Oval Office* as measured by two factors: means and motivation. Since two of the people at the top of this list Jeremy knew personally from his years in Washington, he submitted to interviews about his experiences with them. When he read the completed dossiers, their conclusions only reinforced what he already knew to be true: White House Chief of Staff Morley James was driven by a Christian moral certitude that was both absolute and above the law. To him, someone like Victor Glade was Satan in the flesh. Any means to Lucifer's end would be justified.

*   *   *   *   *

In mid-December Jeremy and Amitai began to meet at the Deep Finesse four and sometimes five times a week, playing bridge hands that had been shuffled and dealt two days before they arrived.

Jeremy had spoken with the owners of the Deep Finesse about Amitai's proposed experiment with pre-dealt hands, and they were only too eager to help. Jeremy was far and away the club's most celebrated regular, and the source of a lot of indirect publicity in the bridge world. With cooperation established, Jeremy left the rest of it to Amitai and the game directors, who recruited daytime players to shuffle and deal an additional two rounds of twenty-four boards every day before the afternoon game. Once these pre-dealt hands were slotted into their rectangular boards, they were placed in a locked, glass-front cabinet against the back wall of the main playing room, under the King of Spades banner where Jeremy's cumulative and year-to-date stats were displayed. Whenever Jeremy showed up for a game, the cabinet was unlocked and the game director arbitrarily chose one of the two sets of boards that had been assembled two days before, and those cards were used in Jeremy's game.

As explained by Amitai, the object of the experiment was to determine if Jeremy's physical presence was somehow associated with the singleton king of spades. If he was nowhere near the cards when they were shuffled, dealt, and tucked in their boards—the point at which the singleton would get fixed—and the phenomenon then ceased, that would strongly suggest a spatial connection, and the solution to the mystery could be pursued within a classic Newtonian framework of time and three dimensional space. If, however, after all the remote shuffling and dealing the singleton king still persisted, Amitai's theory was that it must be a quantum phenomenon that was somehow manifesting itself in everyday Newtonian reality.

The plan was to play fifteen hundred deals, which was the equivalent of about sixty games, but by the end of December the singleton king of spades had not shown its face once. As the effect of the experiment became increasingly evident, Jeremy noticed that some of the club's long-time players had come to see Amitai as a spoiler of sorts. He was the one who organized the pre-dealing, so it was he who was responsible for the King's demise.

Jeremy didn't quite understand how anyone could ascribe such Rasputin-like qualities to Amitai, who had the physical presence and persona of a Muppet. But there was no mistaking the hostility. When they arrived to play at certain tables, gregarious, witty people whom Jeremy had known for years were suddenly struck humorless, while Amitai was met with narrowed eyes and almost invisible nods. The King of Spades thing was all in fun, but it was *their* fun.

Jeremy thought about taking aside a couple of key people and suggesting they lighten up, but there was no point. Amitai was oblivious to it all, and in general, Jeremy observed, as socially tone-deaf an adult as he had ever met. Jeremy wondered, *Does above-average height correlate to social isolation?* His background processor whirred, and the question was stored.

6	January, 2020 North American Bridge Championships Las Vegas, NV

At the end of their dinner date in early December, which included an introductory bridge lesson diagrammed on the tablecloth, Jeremy had impulsively invited Evelyn to join him for a weekend in mid-January at a Las Vegas hotel, where he was playing in a team event at the North American Bridge Championships. "It's not quite your Cancun scenario," he said, "but maybe we can do that another time." She readily agreed, and was delighted to learn that there would also be lessons and games for beginners.

So after work on the 17th, instead of driving downtown to his regular Friday night game, Jeremy boarded a helicopter at Century City and flew to the Van Nuys airport where Evelyn's CAT flight from Napa was due to pick him up at 7:00pm. Looking out the porthole window of the chopper, he saw traffic on the 405 flowing smoothly southbound and completely blocked northbound . . . *certainly room for greater efficiency there.*

Suddenly his heart skipped a beat. He tried to remember, and couldn't, the last time he had had sex. If he had thought this out at all he would have called his doctor to get a PriaPatch, or whatever it was that men were using nowadays to get it on. There must be whole ad agencies by now, he thought, that specialize in pushing erections. At *The Oval Office*, erection drugs accounted for more ad dollars than any other product category except automobiles.

The helicopter banked steeply to the right and Jeremy rolled his eyes. Maybe it will be all over right now, he thought. But it wasn't; they were landing in Van Nuys. *Let yourself go!* he admonished himself, using his ex-wife Samantha's favorite phrase, and then he berated himself more for thinking of her. *Oh, the hell with it.* He finally gave up, ducking his head as he rushed out from under the still-whirling blades. *S'iz ba'shert.* This is the way it was meant to be.

Evelyn's plane was already there, and he was met at the top of the stairs by a bodyguard who, wired for sound and soulless behind reflective sunglasses, looked to Jeremy like an evolved, bi-ped insect. The insect politely offered to take his travel bag and briefcase, however, and then directed him into the rear compartment where Evelyn greeted him from her armchair with a glass of champagne and a carefree smile. "Please join me." She handed up a fizzing goblet, which turned out to be plastic. "I'm about six hundred miles ahead of you."

Jeremy relaxed. This was making it much easier. He took the goblet and lowered it to hers for a toast. "Well, here's to your continued safety. I'm glad to see you've got some security in place."

"Thanks to Victor Glade . . . this toast is to Victor," she said with genuine appreciation. Jeremy suddenly realized that the woman he was looking at was transformed completely from the all-business version he had dined with four weeks earlier. She was relaxed. Her hair was longer, seemingly darker, and somehow now framed her face differently, making her features rounder. She was wearing slacks, a gray cashmere-like pullover, and a simple string of pearls. Her brown eyes were inquisitive and eager and mischievous. She was turning him on . . . something he hadn't felt spontaneously, outside of a movie theatre, in nearly twenty years.

He swallowed some champagne, handed the goblet back to Evelyn, and got himself settled. He took off his jacket, hung it up in the closet, loosened his tie, and slung himself into the seat opposite Evelyn by gripping an overhead handle. She handed him back his champagne, and he was sipping it when the cabin door was closed and the outside airport noise faded away. The pilot appeared at the front of the compartment.

"I'm Sally Harper," she said with some authority, offering a casual salute in lieu of trying to shake left hands. "Thank you for choosing AirShares this evening, folks. Am I correct in understanding that I'm taking you to CAT Strip NV57, which is the Grand Mirage in Las Vegas?"

"That's where we're headed," Jeremy replied.

"Well then, you know to keep your seat belts buckled at all times when you are seated, and please use the hand-holds when you move about the cabin. I have to run the video, but you can turn down the sound if you like. The flying time is forty-four minutes, and I expect to be airborne in about five." She smiled and left, closing the compartment curtains behind her.

"I'm not finding CAT travel is a taste that's difficult to acquire," Evelyn said, raising her glass and taking a sip. Since her meeting at *The Oval Office* she had flown only on CAT's, both for security reasons and because the 28th Amendment organization—thanks to Victor Glade—could now afford it. "But I'm always going to feel guilty about it."

Jeremy laughed. "I don't think the combined guilt of *all* ambivalent CAT customers, including my own very weighty contribution, will have any impact on the growth of this business," he said, referring to the Co-Operative Air Taxi industry, which had quintupled in size, to ten thousand aircraft, since the missile attacks on airliners started in 2016. "It's human nature. People aren't going to risk their lives if they don't have to. Money quickly becomes a secondary thing."

During the short flight they also exchanged their respective divorce stories, and told each other what is was about them that drove their ex-spouse batty. "I'm very blunt," Evelyn volunteered first, "and I have a natural tendency to home in on people's weak spots."

"No kidding. I've seen some of your appearances on the Sunday morning shows."

"Well, as you can imagine, this is a style that many men, in particular, find threatening. I think most men believe, either subconsciously or otherwise, that theirs is the naturally dominant role in a relationship, and I don't function from that premise at all. So I speak my mind, we clash, game over."

Jeremy countered with his own self-diagnosis. "After our kids left for college, my wife became frustrated that we didn't have many other common interests. She was heavily involved in her academic career, which took up numerous extra-curricular and evening hours. I had my career in the Senate, and I played a lot of bridge, which took care of many of my evenings. I thought it was working for both of us, but she wanted more than that; she was looking for something we could both be passionate about. So we split. Since then I've gone through one or two cycles of dating, but there were no sparks, and I guess I convinced myself that I would be happier living as a bachelor—not having to account for my time to anyone. I play *a lot* of bridge. The only thing that's missing is the sex, and I *remember* being frustrated about that, but it doesn't occupy me as much as it used to."

"Well you've got your priorities all wrong there," Evelyn said.

That answered any lingering doubts in Jeremy's mind about how many rooms they were going to take. Minutes later they were at the hotel's check-in desk. (The Grand Mirage, built on the edge of the Las Vegas Strip, had its own 2,500-foot CAT runway.) The plane taxied under a broad canopy adjacent to the lobby, and bellhops dashed out to retrieve their bags and check them in.

He registered at the desk and ordered a bottle of champagne for the room, ASAP. They went directly upstairs and by the time the champagne arrived, Evelyn had gotten his shirt and belt off. Interrupted by the room service, they took a break and restarted the champagne. Jeremy raised a toast to Evelyn, and they clinked glasses. "What fun!" he said. "I really had completely forgotten what this was all about."

"I'm glad you like it. I do know when I'm attracted to a man, and I'm attracted to you." She sipped.

"Is that so?" Jeremy replied. "Since you are so articulate, why don't you tell me what is it about me that attracts you?"

"Your sense of humor . . ."

"Aaaahhhh." Jeremy nodded.

" . . . and, now that I see it, your hairy chest." She came over and began combing it with one hand while fumbling with the other to set her glass down.

"Hmmm." Jeremy took her glass and his own, placed them

on a table, and rejoined her, running his fingers through her hair and gathering in her odor. "I really did forget what this was like, and you are doing a great job of reminding me."

*   *   *   *   *

The following morning they were eating breakfast on the balcony of their hotel room overlooking the desert. Jeremy thought hard, and couldn't remember the last time he felt this content. He was now completely sober, but his inhibitions somehow remained suppressed.

"I have not felt like this for years," he said, stretching and moaning. "Actually, I'm pretty sure some of those things I've *never* felt."

"Hey, I'm just doing what I like to do." Evelyn smiled and poured herself more coffee. "You should do the same."

In other words, Jeremy thought, *I should let go*—his ex-wife's old refrain.

"I can tell you're not really letting go," Evelyn continued.

This kind of coincidence happened so frequently to Jeremy that he barely took note. This was actually more like the kind of coincidence that anyone could encounter—they had, after all, just spent a dozen hours together in bed.

"What are my telltale signs?" Jeremy asked.

"None that I can express in words," Evelyn answered. "It's a sixth sense."

Jeremy stared at her.

"Really, that's all it is. Believe me, if I could describe it to you, I would. I don't even know how to be coy. I wish I did."

"It's a thing my ex-wife used to say about me."

"What, that you don't let go?"

Jeremy nodded.

"Well then, there you have it, Counselor," she said, smiling, stretching her hand out for the jam, which Jeremy handed to her.

"Your Honor, I move to re-direct. Are you usually this forward with men?"

"I just don't have the patience, or the time, or whatever it takes, to go through a long dating ritual. When I meet a man I usually have him pegged in a few minutes, and I know what I'm looking for. So you tell me—how often am I going to meet a single man, in my age bracket, in good physical shape, who has a sense of humor, and is confident enough not to be intimidated by me? I mean, what are the odds? They must be astronomical! So when these planets suddenly align themselves, my instinct is to *carpe* the *diem* while it's *carpable*."

Jeremy laughed. "Well, the appeal to me—aside from the fact that you re-introduced me to sex—is that your approach is *efficient*. Efficiency is a kind of hobby for me, so I appreciate it in all of its forms."

Jeremy related to her his earliest recollection of his "hobby," when, as a young boy, his mother handed him a spoon to scoop the seeds from five halved "muskmelons," as cantaloupes were known in rural Alabama in the nineteen-fifties. He recalled waving the spoon away, and instead pulling open the big chest-high kitchen drawer to choose *the best utensil for the task*, eventually selecting an aluminum measuring cup with a beveled edge. His favorite childhood book was Dr. Seuss's *Cat in the Hat* . . . he spent countless hours poring over the pictures of the multiple-armed cleaning machine that the Cat rode in on at the end.

By the time he had reached the working world, this focus on efficiency had become second nature—as invisible and pervasive as gravity. As a bachelor in Washington in the 1980's, cleaning his own kitchen late at night after a party, he would automatically choreograph his movements to finish the task in the least amount of time, taking the fewest possible steps. Inevitably the refrigerator door would open only once, after the leftovers had all been wrapped and stacked on an adjacent shelf for quick loading. This so that the smallest possible volume of cold air would escape, and the least amount of energy would be needed to restore the fridge to its thermostatic equilibrium. These thought processes and calculations were executed continuously in the remotest corners of Jeremy's mind, with no conscious mental effort and virtually no self-awareness.

At the conscious level, his pre-occupation with efficiency manifested itself as abundant curiosity; in order to know how to make things more efficient, you first have to know how they work. So over the years, in pursuit of innumerable questions about how things work, Jeremy had acquired varying levels of knowledge in physics, chemistry, linguistics, biology, botany, electricity, metallurgy, genetics, astronomy, fluid dynamics, hydraulics, chaos, glass manufacturing, heuristics, optics, magnetic imaging, aeronautics, geology, and a host of others. In the early years of the Internet, when Google was a novelty, he would spend endless late-night hours researching his curiosity *du jour*, whatever it happened to be. A seemingly simple question—"how do differential axles work?"—might trigger a cascade of related searches: "How do ball bearings work? How are they made, and how many are manufactured annually?" (Tens of millions worldwide every year, was the best estimate he could arrive at).

At *The Oval Office*, Jeremy found the ultimate outlet for his curiosity—an unlimited budget. He kept half-a-dozen Executive Assistants occupied with his various queries and research projects. It was also the ultimate efficiency challenge—producing four new one-hour segments every week, continuously, indefinitely.

"Victor mentioned this to me," Evelyn commented. "He called you an 'organizational genius.'"

"What he's referring to is our production schedule," Jeremy explained, "which I have to say I'm proud of."

"May I ask you something?"

"Go for it."

"Does *The Oval Office* as a whole—I mean all the segments combined—make money? When I was reading up about Victor, before I met him—and you—I remember seeing an article that suggested you had to be losing money, with all of the production overhead and everything."

"I can answer off the record. Victor has certainly invested far more in it than it has returned in net profit, but not in any amount that is material to him. The direction, however, is up, not down. We have a huge audience and revenue is now starting to pour in, especially from things like product placement. We'll be breaking even very soon."

"You spend a small fortune on security, and I now know from my own recent experience how expensive it can be. Does Victor really have that many enemies?"

"Victor for some reason attracts a lot of threats, far more than your average celebrity actor. But that's actually the least of it—he's well protected against those kinds of threats. Our bigger concern more recently has been the Administration."

"The Grove Administration? What do you mean?" Evelyn asked.

"Even though Victor has been absolutely definitive about his non-candidacy, the Draft Campaign that Trask started has the Administration looking at Victor as a political opponent. If he were to run, as you know, he could be a big threat."

"What could the Administration do about it? He's free to run for office if he wants."

"Our concern is that they would arrest Victor on some made-up charge, and use that as an excuse to close down the entire show."

"You can't be serious," Evelyn said. "You think Grove would engineer something like that?"

"No, but we think his Chief of Staff, Morley James, might. Our security people have been building a dossier on him for the past couple of years—they've done a whole psychological work-up on the man. Think of James as a Mullah—he's America's Christian version of an Iranian Mullah. In his moral order, he is bound to a higher authority than President Grove or the US Constitution, and that is his Christian God. Civil legalities and short-term casualties are only transient concerns for him, and only to the extent that they might impact his ultimate goal."

"How we ended up with this cast of characters is still beyond me. How could we have elected yet another Republican Rambo?"

"Well, if you look back, that also has James's fingerprints all over it. He is an absolute master when it comes to using fear as a political weapon," Jeremy said, "so when al-Qaeda shot down an airliner a month before the 2016 election, Grove knew exactly what to say. The rest is history. American voters have a notoriously short memory."

Jeremy's phone beeped from inside their room, which he took as a most unwelcome sound. His phone was turned off; the only beep that could get through was from his emergency channel. He pushed his chair away from the table and stood up. "I should at least take a look at that," he said, and followed the beeping sound to his nightstand.

When he returned to the balcony and sat down, he continued in a subdued voice. "You were noting how much we spend on security. The call was from *The Oval Office*'s Security Director, Amanda Marx. She called to tell me that the hotel here is under surveillance by DHS agents."

Evelyn almost yelped. "Jeremy! *Jesus, what's going on? What's this all about?*"

Jeremy remained calm, taking a sip of his tea. "Evelyn, at this point you're a major national figure. Knowing that DHS is here doesn't necessarily make me feel any *less* safe. Andrea points out that it could also have to do with Bill Clinton being here."

"President Clinton is here? At the hotel?"

Jeremy nodded. "I actually don't know if he's staying at the hotel, but he's playing in the tournament. I'm hoping to have a chance to play against him at some point; we have scores to settle from last year." He explained that at the same tournament the previous year, he had been on a team, captained by veteran teacher and theorist Rick Seeger, that lost by the smallest of margins to Clinton's team, popularly known as the "Million Dollar Bills." In addition to four "Bills"—Bill Gates, Bill Clinton, Bill Monteverde, a Bear Stearns executive, and Bill Baron, a retired Vero Beach stockbroker—the team also included two professional players, hired guns for whom the first name requirement was apparently waived. "I'm on Seeger's team again this year. A head-to-head rematch is just what we're aiming for."

"If you do play against them, will it be possible for me to watch?" Evelyn asked.

"I thought you were going to be playing novice games with Amitai." Jeremy had asked Amitai to come to Las Vegas to try and maintain the pre-dealing experiment they had been running at the Deep Finesse. Since he was already here, Jeremy had also asked him to play in some beginner games with Evelyn and provide some tutoring.

"Oh, I have it all arranged with Amitai—we are playing in several games. I have them all circled on the schedule." She pointed toward a desk in the inside room. "But if you end up in a showdown with the Million Dollar Bills, I won't want to miss that."

*   *   *   *   *

Evelyn was not disappointed. Both Seeger's team and the Million Dollar Bills arrived at the quarter-finals of the Senior Swiss Teams event, and the stage was set for their showdown. Four rounds of play—112 deals—were to begin Sunday morning and end Monday afternoon. Evelyn, Amitai, and a few dozen other spectators watched the play on a Vu-Graph projector in a darkened banquet room down the hall from the actual match.

Jeremy was scheduled to play in the third round, partnered with Seeger himself. This sparse contribution was perfectly fine for Jeremy, who knew that he was the weakest player on the team, and did not like the feeling that he might be the cause of its demise.

At the end of round two, the Million Dollar Bills were ahead by eight International Match Points (IMP's)—a marginal lead that could easily be overturned in one deal. When it was time for the third round to begin, Jeremy headed off to the hotel's mezzanine, and Amitai sat in for him at the table to help shuffle and deal out the cards. Opposite Amitai, sitting North, was Seeger, an aging hippie who still wore his hair in a two-foot-long ponytail. East and West were Clinton and Gates, who had been ardently discussing their bidding agreements until the boards arrived. Each of the four players then took one of the aluminum racks, removed the cards from their four pockets, and quietly began shuffling.

Clinton glanced at Amitai and then asked Seeger, "Where's my friend Mr. Lerner? I thought we were playing against the King of Spades!"

Seeger began explaining the pre-dealing experiment they were doing to test for Jeremy's physical connection to the king of spades, but fumbled and tried to pass the question to Amitai. Amitai did not pick up on it, however, having become distracted in the presence of the ex-President and Bill Gates, who, despite his homespun bridge manner and rampant philanthropy, was still one of the wealthiest men on the planet.

Clinton held up his hand and called out loudly for the tournament director.

"You've got a problem with this?" Seeger asked Clinton incredulously. "What possible objection could you have?"

"I don't know. If I understand this correctly, you believe you are having some influence over the cards by virtue of who's shuffling and dealing them. As absurd as that sounds, you evidently believe it, and I'm left wondering what it all means. Why should we even be left thinking about this?"

The director arrived, but Seeger waved her away. "We have it settled. Thanks. No problem. Amitai, call Jeremy and tell him to come down." Then, turning to Clinton, "This is silly, but if you've got a problem with it, we won't do it."

Amitai tried objecting, but Seeger cut him short. "We're in the quarter-finals of a national tournament. Call him and tell him to come down now. So he'll play some hands outside of your experiment—so what?" Amitai pulled out his phone and called, and Jeremy appeared a minute later.

The shuffling and dealing resumed. When all of the boards had been made up, the Director reviewed them and placed the first one in the middle of the table to begin the play. As they reached for their cards, Clinton laughed and said to Jeremy, "It's very funny that you think the singleton king of spades is really tied to your physical presence in some way."

"I don't necessarily think that," Jeremy replied. "I'm actually trying to find out. The experiment we're doing with the pre-dealing is to try and determine just that."

"Well I'd like to propose another experiment. Could I interest you in a wager of say, twenty thousand dollars? Twenty K says the singleton king of spades will not appear in any of the deals we just made up."

Jeremy was not the betting type, and the odds here were very poor that his singleton king would show up in a short-term sequence of eight deals. But twenty thousand dollars was an immaterial sum to him, as it was to Clinton, and he greatly valued his relationship with the former President.

"I'm in." Jeremy stuck out his hand and locked eyes with Clinton. Seeger, who worked long hours teaching and writing for a modest income, was horrified. Gates, who loved a good show at the bridge table, was delighted.

"Let the games begin!" Clinton announced as he finished arranging his cards.

The first four deals were all played for partial contracts—meaning no game bonuses were won, so there was less potential for a significant shift in score. When the fifth deal was put up and everyone began arranging their cards, Jeremy, out of habit more than anything, glanced around the table. Gates seemed fussier than usual, and then was suddenly still, staring at his cards. Clinton, sitting on his right, opened the bidding with one spade, and when Jeremy looked at his own hand, where he held five spades to the ace-nine, he was sure that Gates must be holding the singleton king. Between Clinton's five spades (he had to have five spades for his opening bid) and the five spades in his own hand, there were only three spades outstanding—greatly increasing the odds of a singleton in one of the other two hands. Jeremy passed, holding only a few other high cards, and Gates bid one no-trump—certainly plausible with a singleton king holding. Clinton then bid two clubs, a second suit, and everyone passed. Jeremy was on lead against two clubs, played by Clinton.

N-S Vulnerable
Dealer – East

                          North – Seeger
                          ♠ 5 2
                          ♥ A Q 6
                          ♦ A 7 6 2
                          ♣ J 8 6 5

West – Gates   East – Clinton
(Dummy)   *(Declarer)*
♠ K   ♠ Q J 10 8 6
♥ K 5 4 2   ♥ 10 9
♦ K 9 4 3   ♦ 8 5
♣ 9 7 3 2   ♣ A K Q 4

                          ♠ A 9 7 4 3
                          ♥ J 8 7 3
                          ♦ Q J 10
                          ♣ 10
                          South – Jeremy

Should he lead out his ace of spades—which he would ordinarily never lead against this contract—just for show? He could kill the singleton king in the dummy, in full view of everyone, on the first trick! Jeremy could barely restrain himself—he was a ham at heart—but it wasn't likely to be the best defensive play, so he led his singleton trump, the ten of clubs. Gates laid down his cards as dummy: four clubs, four diamonds, four hearts, and then . . . from an exaggerated height he launched the last card so that it landed spinning on the felt: the singleton king of spades.

"Holy Toledo!" Clinton looked like he had just emerged from an air raid shelter. "How do you do that? How is that possible?!"

Seeger, who had seen this many times, whooped with laughter, and even Gates, Jeremy thought, looked impressed.

The Director came over to see what was happening, and when Jeremy pointed to the singleton king she smiled and joined in the fun for a millisecond, then reminded everyone that they were in the middle of a game and had twelve minutes left in the round.

A flustered Clinton played out the two club contract, going down one with the bad trump distribution and the ace and queen of hearts both off-side. As soon as the cards were tucked away, he said to Jeremy, "I want you to know, I am now a true believer," and he bowed his head briefly. "We'll settle at the end of this round. Unless you would like to go double-or-nothing on this next hand."

Jeremy tried thinking this through but there was no time, and actually he was unable to resist. Clinton had the same effect on Jeremy that he had on everyone else; he projected an invisible force—an ether, maybe—that made one feel privileged and grateful just to be a Friend of Bill. Jeremy had no intention of taking the money anyhow; he planned to forward it to a charity of Clinton's choice. So he fed his hand to Clinton's massive paw—enlarged and muscle-bound from decades of handshaking and golf—and smiled with genuine fondness. "All that's important is that you believe," Jeremy said.

Clinton laughed uproariously, and the final board of the round was put in front of them to be played. They pulled out their cards, and here the king of spades not only turned up singleton *in Clinton's hand*, it was also the only spade missing from the combined twelve-card trump suit held by Jeremy and Seeger.

N-S Vulnerable
Dealer - South

North — Seeger
♠ Q J 10 8 6 5 2
♥ A Q 6
♦ A 6
♣ 5

West — Gates
♠ - Void -
♥ 10 4 3
♦ K Q 9 8 2
♣ J 9 7 3 2

East — Clinton
♠ K
♥ 9 5 2
♦ J 10 7 5
♣ A 10 8 6 4

♠ A 9 7 4 3
♥ K J 8 7
♦ 4 3
♣ K Q
South — Jeremy
(*Declarer*)

To his credit, Clinton kept a completely straight face up to the point where Jeremy played his ace, dropping the king. Then he glared at Jeremy like a madman. There was silence at the table at first, but three seconds later a muffled cheering penetrated the carpeted walls as the play was replicated for the Vu-Graph audience down the hall.

At the end of the round, Clinton (looking as dazed as Jeremy had ever seen him) came up to Jeremy and promised to send him a check for forty thousand dollars. "Make it out to Seeds of Peace," Jeremy said, which was an organization that they both supported. "I'll forward it to them under both our names."

Scores were tallied, and the winner of the round was announced—Seeger by nine!—giving a one IMP lead going into the final twenty-four-board match. In the last round Seeger gained another three IMP's, and in the end took the national title by four.

<table>
<tr><td>7</td><td>JL Coincidence Blog - Entry #37
August 1971
Eilat, Israel</td></tr>
</table>

During the summer between my senior year in high school and my first year in college, I traveled with two friends to Israel where we backpacked around the country for three weeks. We spent a several days snorkeling in the Red Sea off the occupied Sinai Peninsula, near Dahab and Di'Zahav, and became stranded in Eilat over the Sabbath, when buses didn't run. By late Saturday afternoon we were stir crazy, sweltering hot, and numbingly bored, so we stood at the northernmost road intersection in Eilat and began thumbing for rides. In an hour we saw a total of two cars heading north, both of which were going to Yahel, the Kibbutz a half-hour up the road. Then a white van stopped, a windowless panel truck with no commercial identity.

The driver spoke no English, and his Hebrew was heavily accented, but with some back and forth we established that his name was Rami. He was driving a private ambulance to the airport at Lod, and we were welcome to climb in the back and sit on the fold-down bench, but there was a corpse on the floor.

We asked all of the usual questions you ask someone who offers you a lift while ferrying a corpse to the airport, such as "who is it?" and, "did you kill him?" After getting reasonable answers to most questions, Rami opened the back door for us to see. There was in fact plenty of room—the sheet-wrapped body lay on a very uncomfortable-looking canvas stretcher that separated it from the corrugated steel floor, and the side bench left plenty of clearance. "Is it going to smell?" I asked him. Rami said he didn't think so, and then whipped out a canister of air freshener like it was a six-shooter. "If it does, I've got this"

We piled in and he set off northward along the older Beersheba highway. I took the front passenger seat since it was available. A full moon, which appeared as a giant silver-white disk hovering on the Eastern horizon, cast an eerie array of moving shadows across the desert landscape as we drove. The setting could not have been more surreal.

The unfortunate soul in back turned out to be an American teenager from outside Chicago, one Eliezer Sperling, who had been killed in a car crash in Sharm el-Sheikh earlier in the day. A name tag was pinned to one of the straps keeping the body wrapped. Rami, who did appear somewhat saucer-eyed, soon volunteered that he had been driving for ten hours straight when he was called to go down to Sharm, so he was now wired on uppers. He then asked me if I wanted to drive, suggesting maybe it wasn't the best thing for him to be doing.

So I took over the driving, and Rami goes into the back and lies down right alongside the corpse, stuffing my rolled sleeping bag under his head for a pillow. In no time he fell asleep, and I ended up driving all the way to Lod, where we woke Rami up, bought him coffee and bagels, and thanked him for the ride.

Two weeks later, I arrived at Brandeis as a freshman and discovered that I was the only one on my dorm floor who did not have an assigned roommate. When I checked with the Resident Advisor, I learned that I would have a single for the time being: the roommate who had originally been assigned had been killed two weeks earlier in a car crash in the Sinai desert. His name was Eli Sperling.

By February, Jeremy and Amitai had worked out an excellent partnership and were beginning to win some games. Jeremy was pleased because he liked to win, but also because Amitai had made himself such a likable and interesting partner. Aside from his social naiveté, which Jeremy found refreshing, Amitai was thoroughly devoted to investigating his coincidence condition, and was a continuous source of new ideas and observations about it. Jeremy was therefore caught off guard one evening when Amitai greeted him at the Deep Finesse with a grim look and handed him an envelope from Tzvi:

> *11.02.2020*
> *I regret I am not able to maintain AE's assignment with you past the end of this month. As interesting as his research is, it is veering off target for our purposes and absorbing resources that we need elsewhere. I will be notifying his Program Director early next week.*
> *I regret any disruption, and I will make arrangements for us to communicate through a different channel.*
> *Alpha03*

"What does Tzvi mean?" Jeremy asked, "when he says the research is veering off target? How is anything different now than it was two months ago?" He was watching Amitai closely. They had taken seats at an unoccupied corner table in the main playing room of the Deep Finesse. Amitai was looking distraught, Jeremy thought, but not surprised.

"It's complicated," Amitai replied.

"I went to college," Jeremy said. "Try me out."

Amitai smiled weakly. "Of course. This is the issue. The experiment we've been conducting definitely suggests that your physical presence is somehow tied to the appearance of the singleton king. Which means, as we have discussed, that the answer to the mystery must somehow be in the Newtonian world, in the world of three dimensional space and time."

"Okay," Jeremy said, "I'm with you so far."

"Well, there are two problems with that. The first one is that all of the theories I have proposed about your coincidence condition relate to a quantum solution—or at least a quantum *description*. So the results of our pre-dealing experiment are basically invalidating all of my theories, and it's like I am starting all over from the very beginning."

"All right, so you're starting over at the beginning. Scientists do that all the time. So now you examine it as a Newtonian phenomenon— maybe you'll come up with a solution in that realm."

"That's the other problem," Amitai said.

"What's that?"

"I have *no idea* how this could be happening in regular space-time, nor does anyone else on my faculty. If you think about it, what possible physical explanation could there be? Do you think your brain or your body is producing a wave or a chemical or something that is affecting how playing cards get ordered when they are dealt? Any explanation like this you try to come up with is too crazy to be taken seriously. I have no problem starting over, *but I have nowhere to begin.*"

"Oh." Jeremy sat quietly for some moments, staring blankly at the back wall where the King of Spades statistics were posted. Finally: "So you have no idea where to go with this from here?"

"No. No idea at all. The only thing to do now is to finish the

experiment, stop the pre-dealing, and see if the king of spades comes
back. You don't need me to do that."

"What happens if it does come back?" Jeremy asked.

"That supports the Newtonian premise even further."

"And if it doesn't come back?"

"I don't know what that means, if anything. Maybe it would
mean that your ten-year run with the king of spades was one extremely
long-term coincidence that is now over. Maybe your absence from the
dealing disrupted the vortex. Do you understand how ridiculous it feels
that I am even talking like this?"

Jeremy looked up at Amitai to catch him in the eyes. "I would
like to have your analysis continue—whatever direction it takes, even if
it goes nowhere. If I take over your contract, would you be willing to
stay on?"

Amitai's could not conceal his excitement. "Of course I would
be happy to stay on—are you kidding? With my apartment and car and
everything? We would continue to play bridge?"

"Everything."

"I would be very happy to continue. But I want to make sure
you understand, I am very doubted—doubtful—however you say it—I
want to make sure you know that I don't think I will come up with even
a *theory* about why you attract the singleton king of spades."

"Okay, your reservation is noted. Regardless of that, it's worth
it for me to have someone at least trying to understand it."

That night after the game, from the small tablet he kept in his
bedroom, Jeremy responded to Tzvi:

11.02.2020
*"With regard to AE's assignment, for my own reasons
I have an interest in continuing his work. If you are
amenable, I would like to assume responsibility for his
contract starting March 1, and will commit to six months
of full funding. I have discussed this with AE already and
he has readily agreed to continue with it.*
*I would appreciate it greatly if you could make this
accommodation.*
JL

The following Saturday when they met for their game, Amitai, grinning broadly, handed Jeremy an envelope. Jeremy knew why, but he opened his pocket tablet and retrieved Tzvi's message just to confirm:

> *15.02.2020*
> *"You will receive a call from Dov Szulkin, who is Amitai's Program Director and the head of Weizmann's Mind Sciences faculty. He has agreed to your request to extend AE's assignment, and will give you the particulars."*
> *Best regards.*
> *Alpha03*

After the arrangements had been concluded with Szulkin, Jeremy decided it wouldn't hurt to thank the Weizmann Institute for their help. He arranged for Victor's private foundation (with his assent) to make a three million dollar unrestricted donation to Weizmann, stipulating only that the funds be directed "where they are needed most," and that the donation not be publicly acknowledged in any way.

In lieu of taking a required history course as a senior in college, my academic advisor arranged for me take on a small research project for the American Jewish Historical Society, whose archives were located on the Brandeis campus. The assignment was to review all of the historical records and documents associated with the long-defunct National Committee for the Relief of Sufferers by Russian Massacres, an organization founded in 1903 by the railroad baron Jacob Schiff that was dedicated to raising funds in the United States for the victims of pogroms in Russia. I was given three large Redweld folders containing original correspondence, accounting records, minutes of meetings—everything that was extant at the time the organization was disbanded in 1914—and asked to catalog the materials and write a short history of the Committee.

One of the three folders contained letters sent to the Committee in response to a telegram that Jacob Schiff had dispatched to every Western Union office in the country addressed to "Rabbi or Other Prominent Jewish Citizen" (Schiff had been a Director of Western Union). The telegram was a solicitation for funds for the Committee, and there were over 400 responses in the archive.

I began cataloging these letters, reviewing each one and making notes about where it came from and how much that community contributed.

They were mostly dated 1903—the latest ones came in early 1904.

From this batch, I picked up a letter that was written in a very lavish European handwriting that looked familiar. Moments later I realized the writing was not just familiar, this was someone I knew. This was someone I had corresponded with before.

Someone I knew from 1903? I raced through the three pages, the hair already standing up on the back of my neck, to get to the end. The letter, dated October 15, 1903, was signed by Rabbi Louis Kuppin, the leader of the Jewish community in Youngstown, Ohio.

I recognized the handwriting because it was the same Rabbi Louis Kuppin, living in Columbus, Mississippi in 1965, who came out of retirement to train me for my Bar Mitzvah. When I researched it further I found that the date of my Bar Mitzvah had been October 15, 1966, the 63rd anniversary of Rabbi Kuppin's letter to Jacob Schiff.

The date that I made this discovery in the Historical Society's archive was October 15, 1974, the 71st anniversary of Kuppin's letter to Schiff.

10 | March, 2020

The 28th Amendment, or rather its fictional equivalent, first surfaced in an episode of *The Press Room* on March 3. Thinly disguised as a constitutional amendment to impose Term Limits on Congress (five terms for Representatives, two for Senators), Press Secretary Pfieffer is asked about it by a reporter in one of her daily briefings. Soon afterwards, the issue is taken up in two other segments: *Dunmorgan*, where the conservative Senator rails against it, and *The Oval Office* itself, where the President and his advisers wrestle with the implications of the amendment. Serialized through several episodes, the debate is voiced through two White House advisers who clash about whether or not the President should be taking a public position on this issue.

His chief political strategist sees it as a lost cause that will never be ratified by three-fourths of the state legislatures, and opposes expending valuable political capital for causes that are dead on arrival. The White House Counsel believes the principles at stake are too fundamental for the President to remain silent, even if there is a political cost. She argues that since Congress set term limits for the Executive Branch, in the form of the 25th Amendment, the President should support term limits for Congress in order to restore parity to the Constitution's system of checks and balances.

After seven weeks of various renderings of this thread in three different *Oval Office* segments, an internal compromise is reached. The Chief of Staff recommends to the President that he publicly support the Term Limits Amendment, but only in the form of a statement, and that they avoid giving it any sustained communications focus. The President agrees, and in an episode of *The Press Room* on April 2, Pfieffer reads the President's statement:

> "President Bosco favors enactment of the recently proposed Amendment to the US Constitution that would place term limits on Congressional office holders. The President will support any effort to re-introduce competition into an electoral marketplace that has become increasingly monopolized not by one political party, but by a clique of self-enriching, self-perpetuating Congressional incumbents.
>
> The President substantiates this claim with the following facts:
>
> Since 2008, over 95 percent of all Congressmen and Senators seeking re-election, on average, have been returned to office.
>
> Since 2008, 77 percent of all Congressmen and Senators seeking re-election have been re-elected without any substantive opposition.
>
> Since 2008, incumbent Congressman have raised, on average, six times more campaign contributions than their challengers, and Senators raise nine times more than their challengers. As a result, by last year about two-thirds of each house—seventy Senators and 310 Representatives—had served twelve or more years in the same Congressional seat.

It is difficult to claim that members of Congress are enriching themselves through their offices, because over 90 percent of all members are multi-millionaires *before* they take office. However, during the period from 2008 to 2016, the mean personal net worth of senior Congressional staffers increased by 175%. This is compared with a 1.5% increase in net worth among the general population, and a 19% increase in a random sampling of white, college educated males, who occupy 81% of all senior Congressional staff positions.

Not surprisingly, considering how profitable incumbency is, Congress has gone to great lengths to shelter itself from competition and place every conceivable obstacle in the path of would-be opponents. This is all in the finest tradition of Congressional self-serving, which in modern times includes, among other things, exemptions from Social Security and DC Property Tax, free TSA passes for all members of Congress, their extended families, and their staffs, and hundreds of billions of dollars in ear-marked appropriations directed towards major campaign contributors.

President Bosco believes that these facts speak for themselves. Congressional incumbents have arrived at a *de facto* electoral monopoly, and they are enriching themselves and their staffs through their public offices.

The President therefore supports any *bona fide* civic initiative that will help re-open Congressional elections to true competition and valid political discourse. The President supports a Constitutional Amendment, in particular, because he believes it will restore a parity of checks and balances between the Executive and Legislative branches that was altered when Congress passed the 25th Amendment, imposing term limits on the Executive Branch only.

The President, in consideration of his other responsibilities, has concluded that he will not himself devote any substantive time campaigning for the Amendment; he has made his view known, he knows that others have views that deserve attention, and he would like this initiative to succeed on its own merits."

By the end of the month, Kramer's projection—that *The Oval Office*'s portrayal of a term-limits amendment would boost support for the real-life 28th Amendment by as much as 8% in key contested states—had largely held up, and a plausible scenario for ratification by the state legislatures began to materialize.

11 | April, 2020

After four months of intensive investigation, Team 9 had made almost no progress in determining who bugged *The Oval Office's* communications systems and studios. The only potential clue came from their surveillance of the two Corel technicians suspected of having planted the bugs: they had each, separately, on several occasions, met with the same unidentified man in conspicuously public places like parks and shopping malls. But there were no leads on who this third party was, and otherwise the two technicians' activities were unremarkable.

It was a surprise, therefore, when all questions related to the bugging were answered for them one Sunday morning in April by Morley James himself. The White House Chief of Staff appeared on CNN's Sunday morning *DC Week*, and let loose with what could only have been a carefully rehearsed barrage of attacks on *The Oval Office* and Victor Glade.

James accused Victor of deliberately scripting *Oval Office* episodes to embarrass the Grove Administration, or even to sabotage their foreign policy initiatives. He cited several examples, and wondered out loud if Victor's overt support of the 28th Amendment and other liberal causes wasn't making *The Oval Office* look more like a political party than a television show. He also rattled off the names of several

Oval Office script consultants—a revolving cadre of real-life, mostly Democratic politicos and issues experts who advised the show's writers on various policy matters—and characterized them as Victor's "shadow cabinet."

"Despite his denials," James speculated, "Glade is a man who looks like and acts like he's running for President. For all we know his insistence that he won't be a candidate is a ruse; why should he announce his candidacy now, when he can continue to rack up hours of broadcast and Web exposure every week through his television shows? It's the ultimate free ride: he's making money from his shows, and incurring none of the costs or obligations of a political campaign. In my mind there really is a question as to whether or not *The Oval Office* should be required to comply with the same regulations that govern political activity."

Aside from validating Jeremy and Victor's general concern about the threat the Grove Administration posed to *The Oval Office*, James's comments also had the effect of proving that it was the Administration that had planted the bugs. Two of the script consultants named by James—Irving Liman and Gordon Kramer—were working for *The Oval Office* on a strictly unofficial, unpaid basis. Their names were not listed on any *Oval Office* rosters of personnel, and there were no financial or other records of their engagement. In Kramer's case, in particular, the relationship had been carefully kept under wraps. The only reasonable explanation for how James could have obtained the names was through eavesdropping or interception of e-mails.

Jeremy spent hours with Amanda Marx and Team 9 reviewing a videotape of James's performance. Victor's security protocols underwent substantial revision, and a decision was made to extend twenty-four-hour personal protection to several other *Oval Office* employees, including Jeremy, Gordon Kramer, and thirteen other actors, writers, and production executives. When Jeremy told Victor the expanded security would cost an additional two million dollars a month, Victor's instruction to him was plain: do what needs to be done to protect us, regardless of the expense.

*   *   *   *   *

A week later, at the end of their game one evening, Jeremy asked Amitai for Tzvi's current e-mail address. When he got home, he dispatched his message:

> *I am in need of services similar to those you demonstrated last November, when you picked up our mutual friend in Detroit and brought her to us in Burbank with no trace of a flight plan. Would it be possible for my organization to acquire such a capability for international transfers?*
> *JL*

When they played again two days later, Amitai gave Jeremy a plain white envelope with a link address for Tzvi's response:

> *You will receive a call from a representative of AirShares, who will identify himself as a Special Projects manager. Meet with him privately in a secure location. He will offer you his business card. If the telephone extension printed on it is x613, feel free to speak with him as you would speak with me about your needs.*
> *Alpha03*

Our family was traveling south on Interstate I-81, on the way to our annual camping expedition in the Great Smokey Mountains. After having just stopped to get gasoline at an exit off the highway, our youngest son, Joseph, announced from the back seat that he had to go to the bathroom.

Everyone booed and hissed, but at the next exit I left the highway again and at the top of the ramp encountered no fewer than five gas stations and convenience stores to choose from. I randomly chose one, and guided the car into a parking space in front of the store, away from the gasoline pumps. Another car, coming from another direction, pulled into an adjacent space at the same time. The other driver opened his door and got out of his car in perfect unison with me, like a ballet that had been rehearsed to perfection, and we looked at each other.

Facing me was my older brother Paul, who was driving with his son Stephen in the opposite direction, from Atlanta to New York. As was soon revealed, they too had stopped only a few minutes earlier for gas, and were making an annoying second pit stop out of sudden necessity. Somehow they chose the same exit, the same gas station, adjacent parking spaces, and arrived at precisely the same time, to address the exact same need.

13	May, 2020

At noon on a cloudy, threatening Sunday, Jeremy got into his Volvo convertible and headed south on the 2 toward LA for the afternoon game at the Deep Finesse, doing his best to ignore the armored sedan shadowing him on the freeway. The towering cumulus clouds rolling eastward dwarfed the downtown skyline, casting it as a luminous, distant Oz. The building's valet took his car, but he waited in the main lobby for his bodyguards to catch up—Serena, whom he knew, and another woman Jeremy had never seen before. She was about two inches shorter than his six feet, probably in her late twenties, and undoubtedly capable of wrestling him to the ground inside of five seconds. She thrust her hand forward and introduced herself as Valerie.

"Did you read this morning's *Times?*" Jeremy asked, whimsically deciding to demonstrate that he read his security briefings.

"I prefer to wait for the afternoon papers." She responded with the correct recognition phrase, delivered with no loss of tempo and no change in expression. He noticed a slight accent—Eastern European, probably.

The elevator chimed and they filed in. When the doors opened again downstairs, Amitai was waiting for him in the elevator lobby, alive with excitement.

"Come with me," he said eagerly, "there's somebody here who wants to say hello to you." He gestured for Jeremy to follow him down a narrow hallway that led to the bathrooms, the owner's office, and several smaller, private card rooms.

Valerie leapt forward and planted herself between Jeremy and Amitai. "Where does this go?" She nodded toward the door-lined hallway. "What is down there? Who is it that wants to meet him?" On cue, Serena quickly took up a position guarding Jeremy's rear, where the closest threat was a klatch of retirees waiting in line to pay their card fee for the afternoon game.

Jeremy waved to Amitai to come back. "Amitai, you need to tell me who it is you want me to meet. Otherwise my bodyguards will have a problem."

"Of course, of course . . . I'm so sorry." Amitai rolled his eyes. "I forgot about your bodyguards. I didn't realize these are your guards."

"Aren't they cute?" Jeremy said, regretting it as soon as he did. Valerie scowled.

Amitai stared at Jeremy, clueless.

"So who's here?" Jeremy repeated. "You want me to meet someone."

"Tzvi is here. He wants to spend a few minutes with you before the game."

"Tzvi is here? Now?"

"That's what I'm trying to tell you. And Szulkin too. I arranged with Sa'id to use one of the private rooms for a few minutes before the game." Sa'id was the club's weekend manager, an Egyptian ex-pat whom Amitai had befriended employing a seemingly competent Arabic.

Valerie kept an eye over her shoulder, waiting for a signal from Jeremy, but none was forthcoming. Something wasn't right. Why would Tzvi would show up for an in-person meeting like this at all, much less unannounced?'

Amitai gestured to Valerie to come with him, and Jeremy nodded his assent. If Tzvi was in fact here, perhaps it was out of urgency.

Valerie followed Amitai into the first of three private rooms on the left side of the corridor, and returned ten seconds later thumbing "all clear." Serena signaled and broke away to do a quick circuit of the rest of the club. "Are there other entrances to these rooms?" Valerie asked as he stepped through the door.

"I know there are not," Jeremy replied, having spent many an hour playing high-stakes money bridge in each of the club's three private rooms.

At the last of six single-file card tables stood Amitai, Tzvi, and Dov Szulkin, Amitai's Program Director, whom Jeremy knew via the Web but had never met in person. Amitai loped forward to greet him, but Valerie was tugging at Jeremy's sleeve. "Sir, you're okay with this?" she asked, pointing to an alcove in the corner, where two men were hovering over two open briefcases brimming with electronics.

Jeremy nodded. "I'm sure the room is very secure. Do me a favor and let the game director, his name is Bill Pullman, let him know that Amitai and I will be a few minutes late. Ask him if he can find a pair to fill in for us for the first round. Got that?"

"Yes." Valerie's annoyance did not register with Jeremy, who had already broken away and joined Amitai on his way to the back table.

Tzvi, as far as Jeremy could tell, might be wearing the exact same clothes he had worn as their last meeting in the Beverly Hills restaurant. A day's worth of gray stubble completed the effect. But he extended his hand formally—precluding the bear hug that Jeremy might otherwise have offered—and they shook hands. Jeremy then saw there was no toothy smile; Tzvi was suddenly all business—a face he had never seen before.

Tzvi introduced Szulkin, and they shook hands. He was younger looking in person—the alternating shocks of dark and silver hair had seemed oddly contrived, almost painted on, over the Web, but in person it was a distinguished and seemingly natural mane that would have been the envy of Einstein. Szulkin then invited them all to sit at the table. "B'vakasha," he said, spreading his arms, and took his seat. Jeremy loved the word for "please" in Hebrew, which could mean anything from a courteous "after you" to a subtle "I'm in charge."

Jeremy took the seat opposite Tzvi, and Amitai and Szulkin sat across from each other. As they sat down, Jeremy thumbed over his shoulder to the men in the alcove. "They are yours?" he asked Tzvi in clipped Hebrew.

Tzvi nodded, but volunteered nothing further.

"Tzvi, I'm surprised to meet like this. You didn't want to discuss this first?"

"All will be explained," Tzvi replied impassively, and nodded to Szulkin.

Szulkin picked up in his clipped British English. "Tzvi is here as part of an experiment, one that we intentionally did not discuss with either of you in advance."

"What experiment is that?" Jeremy asked, also switching to English.

"You have described how dramatic events always seem to unfold when you and Tzvi get together. The experiment we want to conduct recreates this condition in the presence of some very sensitive and specialized monitoring equipment." Szulkin pointed to the two technicians who Jeremy assumed had been packing up their counter-surveillance gear. They had instead conjured up from the two open briefcases a small forest of miniature antennas, coils, and dishes.

"We want to see if there are any unusual electromagnetic or other spectral phenomena that might be detected when the two of you are together. Will you consent to have us conduct these scans?"

Jeremy felt dizzy. He looked at Tzvi. "You knew about this?"

"They say this is the only research path open to them, and I have no better alternative to suggest. I'm thinking, let's do it and be done. The longer we sit here together, the more likely it is we'll trigger a coup somewhere, *God forbid.*"

"Why didn't you just tell me you wanted to do this, we could have scheduled it?"

"It's a control factor in the experiment," Szulkin said. "It precludes any physiological response that might have built up in anticipation of a meeting with Tzvi."

Jeremy didn't want to go there, so he shifted. "What are the scans you are running?"

"We are running a Virtual Directed MRI (VD-MRI), two different PET-based scans, and two classes of electromagnetic sensors. They are all standard diagnostic and research tools that have been used clinically for years. If you are willing to wear a few dermal monitors, we can also run continuous EEG's and EKG's, and a related test called a Synapse Trigger Array. This would be most useful."

Jeremy looked at Tzvi again, who shrugged and stood up to take off his jacket. Jeremy did the same, and Szulkin waved the two technicians over. In less than two minutes they had planted seven wireless electrodes each on Jeremy's and Tzvi's head, neck, ankles, and hands.

As bizarre as it all was, Jeremy at this point was also beginning to feel pleased. He was in fact getting what he had indirectly paid for, which was a seemingly thorough scientific analysis of his coincidence condition.

The technicians returned to their station across the room, donned headsets, and began twisting dials. Szulkin turned to Tzvi and Jeremy: "We are going to run two identical sets of scans. Each sequence will go for about four minutes and forty-five seconds. Only one scan will be running at any given time, except your EEG's and EKG's will be recorded continuously.

"And," Szulkin continued, "it is important to be engaged in some consistent mental activity while the scans run, so that there is a constant background against which any unusual readings will more readily stand out. To produce this effect, we are going to play a couple of hands of bridge: one with pre-dealt cards, and another with cards that are shuffled here. We're covering a lot of bases."

Jeremy squinted across the table at Tzvi, and then at Szulkin. "You both know how to play?"

"We have learned enough from Amitai to play two hands," Szulkin said. "Let's begin, shall we?" He raised a thumbs-up to the technicians, received one in return, and then reached for his cards. The others pulled their cards from the tray and began arranging their hands. "You've played bridge before," Jeremy said, eyeing Szulkin. "I can tell from how fast you are at organizing your hand."

"You are correct, very observant." Szulkin offered not even a hint of a smile. "I played at Oxford a fair amount while I was in graduate school, but never picked it up again in Israel. Amitai has brought me up to date, though, and we've played a few hands together, so we're ready for you. *Bring it on,* as you Americans say."

The aluminum board marked Amitai as the dealer. There were bidding boxes mounted on the corners of the table, and the bidding proceeded silently. A competitive auction resulted in a three-spade contract, which Szulkin proceeded to play with all of the cadence and confidence of an experienced player—in the end making four.

Jeremy bore down on him with narrowed eyes: "Played a *few hands* with Amitai, have you?"

Szulkin didn't respond. He looked at his watch again and called out, "We're finished with the first hand here. Everything go okay over there?"

"One hundred percent," a voice came back from the alcove in Hebrew. "Ready again in one minute."

"Let's get the cards shuffled," Szulkin said, passing his cards to Amitai and motioning to the other players to do the same.

Amitai reassembled the deck and began shuffling, counting each dual-stroke under his breath in Hebrew. Tzvi pushed back his chair, stood up, and twisted a phone-set into his ear.

"What are you doing? We'll be ready in less than a minute!" Szulkin scowled at Tzvi, who raised his index finger and then turned away to continue his whispered conversation.

"Can I deal out the hand?" Amitai asked Szulkin.

Szulkin reached over and cut the cards. "It's okay to deal, but let's not start the bidding until the scans are running."

"Proceed," came a voice from the alcove. "We are starting now."

Amitai began dealing the cards.

"Tvzi," Szulkin hissed. "Please. We are ready to go."

Tzvi finished his call just as the last card landed on the table in front of Amitai. Jeremy, arranging his own cards, kept half an eye on his partner as Tzvi pulled his earphone out and sat down again. Tzvi's expression was different; Jeremy could see that the phone call had done something. Something had happened.

Amitai started the bidding by pulling the one diamond card from his bidding box and placing it in front of him. Jeremy put out a green Pass card. Szulkin bid one spade, and the focus shifted to Tzvi, who stared at his cards momentarily, and then folded them face down and turned to Szulkin.

"I have learned that fighting is underway in Saudi Arabia. Oilfields are on fire, and the Muslim Brotherhood is claiming a *coup d'état*. Putting us together like this was not a good idea, and we should end it right away."

Jeremy's adrenalin shot in. *Boom!* In the microsecond it took to trigger the chemical release, he marveled at the adrenalin's instantaneous effect. It was something he had researched before, so his awareness had a slow-motion feel to it.

"You just said something a few minutes ago about triggering a coup!" Jeremy said.

"I am aware. I knew nothing about Saudi Arabia when I said that."

"This is really happening?" Amitai asked. "There is fighting in Saudi Arabia?"

"Apparently so. What I just told you is all that I know." Tzvi turned back to Szulkin. "Unless you can think of a reason to stay, I plan to leave now."

"Doc," a technician called from across the room in Hebrew, "both of their heart rates are up. Way up."

"Continue the scans," Szulkin called back, twirling his index finger in the air. "Continue until I say stop!"

Szulkin turned back again to Tzvi, lowering his voice and speaking in rapid Hebrew. "Whatever is happening in Saudi Arabia is already happening, nothing you do here now is going to change that. If proximity to your cousin is related in any way to events elsewhere, running scans like these while it is actually happening—while you are together—could give us a big clue."

Tzvi hesitated, but Szulkin did not. He pushed Tzvi's cards back up toward his chest. "Pick up your hand, please. It is your bid. Please play the game. Please focus on the game, we're talking about four minutes here; stay with this for four minutes more. We have hundreds of hours invested in putting this together."

Tzvi rearranged his cards, reviewed the bidding cards that were on the table, and pulled out a Pass card. Amitai and Szulkin continued the bidding, their opponents passing at every turn, and arrived at a game contract of four spades with Szulkin again playing the hand.

Jeremy was on lead. He gave it some thought and led a trump, his lowest spade. Szulkin played the spade queen from the dummy. Tzvi was now due to play, but was instead squinting at his cards, as though they were hard to read. After some moments he tilted his head up slightly and directed his still-blank gaze across the table to Jeremy.

"Look at this," he announced calmly, pulling the king of spades from his hand and dropping it onto the table. He then lowered the rest of his hand for all to see: five clubs, two diamonds, five hearts, and *no more spades.*

N-S Vulnerable
Dealer - East

North – Amitai
(Dummy)

♠ Q J 9 5 2
♥ K
♦ K Q 7 6 2
♣ 8 6

West – Jeremy

♠ 8 6 3
♥ Q 6 5
♦ J 10 8
♣ A Q 7 5

East –Tzvi

♠ K
♥ J 10 9 4 2
♦ 5 3
♣ K 10 9 4 2

♠ A 10 7 4
♥ A 8 7 3
♦ A 9 4
♣ J 3
South – Szulkin
(Declarer)

"This is unbelievable!" Amitai was ecstatic.

"Please, Tzvi, pick up your hand!" Szulkin pleaded. "We must play this out! The scans are capturing all this!" He played the Ace from his hand, taking the trick, and led another spade. Jeremy was thinking about the coup in Saudi Arabia—a blow to the Administration for sure. "Mr. Lerner"—Szulkin waited not a second—"please follow suit. Please keep the tempo."

Jeremy jokingly protested. "You've seen three hands! You know where everything is!"

"My dear sir, please just humor me by playing a spade."

There were still three cards left to play when the technicians announced that the scans were done. Everyone threw in their cards and Szulkin waved the technicians over, but Tzvi had already started peeling the adhesive tabs from his ankles and neck. "My dear cousin," Tzvi said as stood up and put his jacket on. "I hope we learn something from this, because it's going to be an expensive lesson."

*   *   *   *   *

Expensive it was. Over a period of eight hours an elaborate sabotage operation staged by the Muslim Brotherhood had disrupted about a third of Saudi Arabia's oil production, probably for the better part of a year. World energy markets were roiled, and in some countries fuel was not available at any price. In the US the price of gasoline had risen forty percent in a week, until President Grove announced that he would open the Strategic Petroleum Reserve (which had grown to two billion barrels) and keep it open until Saudi production was back on-line.

The following Tuesday, Jeremy received a call from Lester Hammill, the ranking Democrat on the Senate Foreign Relations Committee, who asked if he would be willing to come to Washington on Thursday to sit in on an unclassified briefing about the events in Saudi Arabia, and provide them with his impressions. When Hammill explained that the presentation was being made to the Subcommittee on International Operations and Terrorism, by a team from the State Department, Jeremy understood immediately why he was being asked to attend; many Senators simply no longer trusted any information they received from the Executive Branch, especially concerning the Middle East. Even the secret Congressional intelligence watchdog

committees had been gerrymandered to ensure their concurrence with
the Administration's policies.

Jeremy readily agreed to make the trip. It's not as though he
wasn't qualified; he had an insider's familiarity with Middle East politics,
was fluent in Arabic, and had extensive experience with these types of
crises through his previous tenure with the Committee. Especially
considering the jeopardy he felt *The Oval Office* was in with the
Administration, it was important to maintain his "wiring," as he called
it, with his former colleagues in DC.

The presentation lasted for forty-five minutes. According to
State, the attack had begun the previous Saturday, May 16, with the
planting of a computer virus in a master control system that regulated
the flow of oil into the giant Abqaiq facility from numerous pipelines,
and out to loading platforms in Ras Tanura and Ras al-Ju'aymah. False
sensor readings triggered shutdowns of five key pumping stations,
where Brotherhood agents, posing as emergency computer specialists
and sensor technicians, gained entry. Over the course of twelve hours
they placed dozens of small, lightweight BMTP explosive charges in
carefully selected locations throughout each station, and the devices
were detonated simultaneously by radio-transmitter just before dawn
on the 17th.

The Saudi Army had several different well-rehearsed responses
to oil field sabotage scenarios, all of which involved sending commandos
via helicopter to secure the facilities. Fifteen minutes after the last
commando touched down at the last pumping station, two additional
helicopters arrived at each, but instead of landing, they attacked—
first destroying the commandos' helicopters on the ground, and then
firing rockets and rocket propelled grenades into targets carefully
selected for their explosive potential. All five of the substations were
completely destroyed, and ninety-seven people, including fifty-five army
commandos, were killed.

Simultaneously, with inside assistance, the Brotherhood
managed to hijack the studio facilities of Channel 2, a fledgling
commercial Webcaster that had only the previous year commenced
operation under strict government oversight. From Channel 2's studios
the Brotherhood claimed responsibility for the oilfield attacks, reported

that a coup was underway, and urged army and police units that were "loyal to Allah" to join the battle.

With oilfields in flames and still no real information about what was happening, the government and military were in a state of near panic. Officers in key commands who were sympathetic to the Muslim Brotherhood apparently had received untraceable e-mails only minutes before the first detonations, advising them to "watch for a sign from Allah, and to open a window to Channel 2."

Efforts to retake the Channel 2 studios were slowed considerably by the terrorists' careful planting of mines and booby traps on their way into the building, but the Webcast itself was terminated inside of an hour by a helicopter, dispatched from a nearby Palace, that fired rockets into the antennas and transmitting arrays on the studio's roof. This action, taken independently by a duty officer in the Palace Guard, appeared to be a pivotal move that stabilized the situation. It also appeared to be a pivotal career move for the officer, who two days later was promoted from Captain to Brigadier General.

The helicopter squadron that joined in the oilfield attacks had been led by a renegade army colonel who had his own score with to settle with the Saud family. The Webcast itself, for the fifty-one minutes that it lasted, contained stock stuff — a suitably inflammatory appeal delivered by a suitably attired defender of the faith. The rhetoric was all *jihad* and mayhem, but the message was carefully crafted, and spoken slowly enough to be clearly understood and not sound hysterical.

The prevailing assessment at CIA, according to State, was that the attack was staged by the Muslim Brotherhood and probably organized in Egypt. There was no apparent organizational connection to Al-Qaeda, although they both benefited from the action. The very latest news, just now coming out on the wires, was that the wife and children of the newly promoted Brigadier General had been slain in an attack on their car in suburban Riyadh.

Jeremy spent the entire day with the Committee, helping to frame questions and trying to project the ramifications of different responses. When they were done he had a half-dozen invitations to dinner, desert—even a bridge game. He actually had hoped to spend some time with Senator Arnall of Georgia, whom Victor was

considering endorsing in the Democratic Presidential primary, now
in full swing. But he was exhausted and had to be in Long Beach the
following day for lunch, so he passed.

Two hours into the flight, his pilot came back into the cabin to
suggest that he check the Web: at least fifty small BMTP explosive charges
— seemingly very similar to the ones recently used in Saudi Arabia—had
gone off simultaneously in public places all over Washington DC. At
least three people were reported dead so far. The Mayor was on the Web
pleading with people to get off the streets so that emergency vehicles
could respond. A curfew had been announced for 10pm.

Jeremy turned on his tablet, which he had sworn he would not
open during the flight, and watched the panic unfold.

14	July 4, 2020 Washington, DC

Victor woke up in a drape-shrouded hotel room having no idea where he was. Even after sitting up and laughing at himself—thinking, *this is ridiculous, how could I not know where I am?*—he still couldn't get his bearings. He knew *who* he was, which he took as a good sign, and he knew he had been on the road for several days campaigning for Democratic Congressional candidates. But he had no immediate recollection of where he had been, the number of stops he had made, even the names of the candidates. He hadn't a clue as to where his biological clock was at, or what time zone his watch was set to. The red LED clock on the nightstand said 5:30am.

He got out of bed, wearing only his boxers, padded over to the window and drew back the thick curtains. Outside was a sea of black punctured by haloed street lamps, but no recognizable skyline. He found the phone book in a desk drawer and reality came flooding back. He had made it to DC! Today was Saturday, July the 4th. He was speaking at a rally in Dupont Circle for the 28th Amendment at 11am, and that was it! His campaign nightmare was almost over—by the afternoon he would be headed back to LA.

He opened the door to his bedroom, continued through the suite's living room, and opened the front door, startling the two bodyguards stationed in the hallway.

"Everything okay, sir?" Serena called, getting up from her chair.

"Fine," Victor said, waving her away, vaguely wondering if he should be embarrassed, and then remembering how old he was. "My time is all screwed up," he said, looking dazed. "There are no newspapers yet." It came out as a statement, but he had meant to inflect it as a question.

Serena converted it for him. "I'll see what's available," she said, but Victor had already turned and was closing the door. He showered and shaved, and then ordered breakfast in, which arrived with a *Washington Post* and a *New York Times*.

Ah, yes, the hot water for the tea was actually still hot. He poured it over a tea bag. Lead story: the Grove Administration defending its nuclear weapons "modernization" program, which was recently discovered to include almost twenty billion dollars for developing and testing small tactical nuclear warheads suitable for obliterating individual Afghan mountain cave networks. That was supposedly classified information that a reporter had found on the Web, in the published minutes of a House Oversight Subcommittee! One run for the good guys!

Homeland Security maintaining orange level security . . . . *gotta keep the population on their toes.* Saudi Arabia to remain under martial law for three more months. Nation's 244th birthday celebrated under a cloud of anxiety . . . blah, blah, blah. He remembered that the *Times* on July 4th always reprinted a full-page facsimile of the Declaration of Independence, and he found it on the back page of the first section. He tested his recollection of the names of the signers—doing worse, he judged, than he ever had since 9th grade.

Now it was 7am on the clock. He opened the drapes. The room, facing west, was flooded with a grayish illumination. His body was awake, but his mind was completely fatigued. Too early to call Melissa, who was at home in La Cañada Flintridge with their younger daughter. His older daughter, Andrea, was probably awake, in bed, having all-night sex with some intellectual-affecting UCLA sophomore, in a painted cinderblock dormitory room. *Do all daughters' fathers have these fantasies?* he wondered. This was the kind of question, he reckoned, that Jeremy would actually get an answer to.

He got dressed, poured more tea, brought his tablet over to an armchair with an ottoman, and sat down to read scripts. This worked, and he began to feel productive. At 9:30 the phone rang, and a minute later Jeremy and Evelyn, who had been in a suite down the hall, knocked on the door.

"You make such a charming couple!" Victor said warmly. Jeremy shot him a *spare me* look. "I'm being serious, that was very genuine," Victor protested.

"I will acknowledge your very thoughtful words." Evelyn tipped up on her toes to plant a kiss on Victor's cheek.

"Well I missed where that was going," Jeremy said. "I stand corrected. I shouldn't be so cynical. Thank you for your kind sentiment." Victor and Jeremy ground their fists together.

"You know, of course," Evelyn said to Victor, "that you are credited with introducing us. You are the *shad-chan*.

Jeremy was impressed. She might have heard him use that Yiddish term once or twice in the whole eight months of their relationship, and she nailed it perfectly, with the a hard accent on the first syllable.

"Which means?" Victor inquired.

"Matchmaker," Evelyn replied, but then looked at Jeremy for confirmation.

"Absolutely. It makes you, like, the godfather of the relationship."

"*Vey iz mir!*" Victor gripped his head, imitating Jeremy perfectly. It took Evelyn a moment to see it, but then she too laughed.

"Please come in," Victor said, motioning them inside. "Are you here to collect me, or are we all waiting for our own details?"

"I don't know myself, actually. I haven't spoken with Charles or Grainger yet," Jeremy replied. Charles Witt, a so-far humorless former Green Beret and West Point running back, had been hired as Jeremy's Personal Security Manager—the corporate euphemism for chief bodyguard. "As far as I know we're leaving about the same time, so we thought we'd hang out here and bother you."

"Actually," Evelyn cut in, "if we're not going to be in same car, then the next time I see you will be on the podium, so I thought we might just compare notes here for a minute."

Victor led her over to a sitting area, where she handed him a printed schedule and reviewed the various cues. Jeremy stepped into the hallway to assess the departure time, and came back in almost immediately. He called out from the doorway, "Grainger is ready when you are." Victor and Evelyn joined him in the well-guarded hallway, and they piled into an elevator that a bodyguard had been holding open for them.

"As it turns out," Jeremy said to Evelyn as they rode down, "our respective security people have worked it out for you to ride with Victor. Which makes sense—his car will be going directly to the podium gate. I will take a separate car to the Washington Club, which is where you'll both exit to when you're done. We can meet there and then head back to the airport together."

*   *   *   *   *

It was a sultry, hot morning. The sticky heat began to wear on Victor's mood as soon as he stepped from his car. The speakers' podium had been set up in the Dupont Circle roadway itself, built up on scaffolding, and a secure path had been established between it and the Washington Club, a hundred-year-old, marble-clad building of classical Greek lines that stood on the eastern edge of the Circle. Evelyn, who had preceded him out of the car, was immediately swallowed up by her staff, and Victor was escorted backstage by four seemingly hyper-alert bodyguards.

Even sheltered from the sun, the weather sapped Victor's energy. His mind wandered to the question of why there was a need for a continuous, seven-foot tall transparent security window along the entire length of the stage's apron. What was it about him that triggered such virulent and obsessive hatred, among young men in particular? According to his security briefings, the threats he received, which were numerous and never-ending, were all—one hundred percent of them— made by young white males between the ages of eighteen and thirty.

Over the years Victor had acquired a fatalistic attitude about public appearances, and as a matter of policy he kept to a minimum the number of friends and relatives accompanying him into the "red zone" that was established for every public event. In particular he was careful to keep Jeremy out of his danger zones; he did not want to unnecessarily jeopardize his old friend, and he also saw Jeremy as the key to an orderly continuation of *The Oval Office*, should something happen to him.

From Jeremy's vantage point, which was a large, west-facing window in the ornate marble lobby of the Washington Club, there was no direct view of the stage; if there were, it would have put him in Victor's red zone. He did have a good view of the crowd, which had been estimated at about seventy thousand, and the left wing of the sound stage. He pulled a small tablet from his side pocket, rested it on the edge of a lamp stand, unfolded the keyboard, and opened a connection to the Web. From the 28th Amendment's main Web site he found a link to the live video.

The speaking program had not yet begun, but the crowd was being chatted up by Mickey Freeman, the blues singer, who had made several guest appearances on *The Oval Office* over the years. Three minutes before the speakers were to due begin, the news helicopter that had been hovering high over the crowd was joined by two much louder, lower-flying helicopters—one from the DC police, the other having no insignia, but Jeremy assumed it to be Homeland Security. Ostensibly there to protect the crowd, everyone on the ground saw it as an intentional disruption of the speakers. When Earth Day organizers in 2017 sued to block the helicopters on the grounds that they were interfering with their 1st Amendment rights to free speech and free assembly, the Supreme Court quickly sided with the Administration's argument that the helicopters were actually protecting the 1st Amendment rights of the organizers, and that the speakers could be heard via podcast and other electronic media, and their speeches could be read afterwards.

So Jeremy twisted his earphone into his ear and was linking it to the audio from the Web site when Charles strode up to him. "Sir, Amitai is here. He says that he must speak with you, that it's an emergency. Very insistent. Do you want to see him?"

"Amitai is here now?" Jeremy was surprised, and glanced

around the lobby, which was sparsely populated. He had invited Amitai to join him on Victor's campaign swing, thinking it would be a good distraction—and relaxing—to play some bridge while they were on the road, and in fact they had had several very spirited games on the plane playing against a pair of European journalists. Amitai, for his part, had been quite content to tag along, viewing it as a unique (not to mention free) opportunity to visit a number of American cities that he might otherwise never see.

"He's in the next room," Charles said. "This is a secure area. But he knew you were here and apparently came from the hotel to track you down. He said he tried to reach you by phone."

Jeremy changed the mode on his tablet to check, and saw Amitai's calls there—both within the past half-hour. This was not typical of Amitai at all, and then Jeremy suddenly realized that this wasn't about bridge at all—more likely he had a message from Tzvi. "By all means," Jeremy told Charles, "please send him in."

By the time he arrived, Jeremy had re-established his video link and was listening to Evelyn's introduction of Victor to the crowd outside. "I have message from Tzvi that he said is very urgent," Amitai interrupted.

Jeremy held up his index finger to Amitai as he listened to Evelyn's remarks through his earphone. He pointed to his tablet, which he had rested on a lamp table, so that Amitai would see what he was listening to. Amitai danced with urgency, but then restrained himself and waited until Evelyn had completed her introduction. Jeremy had already read Victor's speech, so he pulled out his earphone and turned to Amitai, who handed him a heavy, full-size tablet with the screen open. "This came into my e-mail for you," said Amitai. "I didn't have a way to print it." There was a roar of applause in the background as Victor took the stage.

04.07.2020
15:07:05 GMT
Advise you to activate Magic Carpet immediately.
My current e-mail is below, and you are welcome to contact me, but I regret I cannot disclose the reason for my recommendation.
Alpha03@ppo.net

Suddenly Jeremy was in a position where he had to bet the farm. *The Oval Office* might well live or die with this decision, but oddly there was no adrenalin. This was a possibility that had been foreseen, discussed, analyzed and planned for, so for him it was just a matter of what their options were.

Operation *Magic Carpet* was the massive overnight removal of all *Oval Office* operations and key personnel, for all segments, to a back-up production facility that Jeremy had acquired the previous summer in Bulgaria and had been upgrading ever since. It was designed to be invoked in a limited number of circumstances: major earthquakes and other natural disasters, a nuclear detonation anywhere within a one hundred mile radius of Los Angeles, or a move by the Administration to close down *The Oval Office* or arrest Victor. Tzvi knew about *Magic Carpet* because, as Jeremy had come to learn, the CAT airline AirShares was owned by an Israeli company that was apparently controlled by the Mossad, and it was AirShares that would be providing the bulk of the transportation and logistics for the plan. Considering the amount of Victor's money he had invested in *Magic Carpet*, and the fact that it was being executed largely by Israeli Air Force veterans, Jeremy had a high level of confidence in its success.

The question was whether or not to invoke it. What had happened, exactly, that was making this decision necessary? He had gotten a vague, mysterious warning from an Israeli spy who happened to be his cousin? Was this the same as an earthquake? He quickly calculated when the message had been sent: 15:07 Greenwich time, here Greenwich time was minus five . . . Tzvi had sent the message less than an hour ago.

"Amitai," Jeremy said, throwing some urgency into his voice, "can you establish a secure messaging link to Tzvi?"

"I can, but don't you want to use the e-mail address? That's the usual procedure."

"There is no time. Can you set up a link or not?"

Amitai nodded again, looking to Jeremy as nervous as he had ever seen him.

"Amitai, Tzvi knows this is urgent—please just do it. Set up your tablet on the windowsill there and try and get him on-line. This is secure, yes? This is encrypted?"

Amitai nodded and took his computer over to the window. Jeremy returned to his tablet and reset it to the video feed of the rally. Victor was speaking now. Jeremy looked around and found a printed program on a nearby side chair, and then checked his watch. He would be speaking only for another five or six minutes at the most. Maybe Victor should be the one making this decision, Jeremy thought.

Amitai called out. "I'm ready, let me know when."

He looked beyond Amitai, and through the window saw the crowd in the background, thousands of heads all tilted upward at the same slight angle, in rapt attention.

"Okay, Amitai, since you are familiar with your equipment, please just type for me what I say. I will read over your shoulder to confirm, and then click 'Send' only when I say. *Hay-vanta?*"

"Understood," Amitai replied.

"Please type this: 'Tzvi, this is Jeremy here, together with Amitai. Please confirm that we have reached you.'" Amitai typed, and Jeremy read it. "Okay, click send, please."

After a short delay, the reply message was posted. Amitai bumped up the text size a notch, and Jeremy read over his shoulder. "Yes I am here, and I will save you the trouble of authenticating. One half of the loan was given to a *Rebbe*."

Jeremy smiled. "Type this please," he instructed Amitai, speaking slowly, "'Nothing has happened here that would justify *Magic Carpet*, and know of no pending threats.'" He paused to let Amitai catch up with the keyboard. "'What is the probability that the event you anticipate will occur within the next 24 hours?'" Jeremy paused. "Okay, let me read this," and he bent down lower over Amitai's shoulder to get his view. "All right, send it." The message blinked, and was gone.

The reply came back almost immediately. "Extremely high."

Jeremy for some reason then noticed that the crowd outside, which had faded from focus when he was concentrating on the screen, was now looking up at a different angle; everyone was now looking straight up, above their heads. Following their gaze, Jeremy saw that one of the helicopters—it wasn't clear which one—was in trouble.

Smoke was pouring from the rotor hub and it was wobbling in the air. He looked back at the crowd, which had now started to stream from the square, in all directions, en masse. For far too long—Jeremy later blamed himself relentlessly—he stood watching the scene as it unfolded through the window, the helicopter gyrating wildly and losing altitude. Three or four billion nanoseconds later he finally put it all together and fumbled with two fingers on his pocket array to open the emergency channel. After another interminable pause he heard the double beep in his earpiece. "This is Jeremy Lerner," he said quietly but distinctly, "authorization Alpha Charlie 7747. Run *Magic Carpet* now! I repeat, Operation *Magic Carpet* is in effect. This is not a drill. Please acknowledge."

"We copy sir," his audio crackled. "Acknowledge *Magic Carpet*. *Magic Carpet* is in effect, no drill. All forward personnel—" Jeremy tapped his chest to close the channel, and started to retrieve his own tablet from the lamp table. "Amitai, pack up your things." He spoke quickly. "We must leave right away"—and as he turned he saw Charles sprinting toward him from across the lobby. "Move away from the windows!" he called out, "Amitai, away from the windows, heads down!"

At the same moment, the helicopter hit the ground right in front of the soundstage, no more than fifty yards away, and there was a thunderous, booming explosion. Amitai had just closed his computer, snapping shut the full-size screen. Maybe if he had left it open for another three seconds, or maybe if he wasn't 6'4", he would have survived, but as it was, when the shock wave blew the window in, he was virtually decapitated by flying glass.

Jeremy had been tackled to the ground by Charles, who then spread himself over him. They were sprayed by glass, but Charles's Kevlar deflected much of it, and they were flat on the floor, ten feet behind where Amitai had been standing.

Now there was a screeching, metallic crunch that continued unabated for many seconds as the wreckage outside settled. Then another smaller explosion. Charles kept Jeremy pinned until the only noise they could hear was screaming and sirens.

       *   *   *   *   *

President Grove, addressing the nation in a live Webcast, confirmed initial reports that the helicopter had been hit by armor piercing bullets fired from a high-powered American-made "Slam" rifle that had both civilian and military versions. There were leads, and the perpetrators were "on the run." As of that hour, twenty-eight people were confirmed dead and thirty others hospitalized. He praised the DC police officers who were piloting the helicopter and lost their lives in the line of duty, and mourned the loss of so many innocent bystanders. The terrorists learned that they could expect a swift and sure punishment, and he then announced he was invoking the Special Executive Powers of Patriot Act III. Congress, which was in a scheduled recess until the following Tuesday, had been recalled and would meet in special session to ratify this action as provided for in the law. This would give the government the tools it needed to battle these "evil purveyors of terror and anarchy."

As he spoke from the *real* Oval Office, another cluster bombing with dozens of simultaneous detonations erupted all over downtown Washington DC—one less than a thousand yards from the White House. It was the seventh such attack in the US since March, and the third one in the Capital.

15	July 5, 2020 Tenerife, Canary Islands 08:15 GMT

As soon as his plane landed for refueling, Jeremy called Szulkin in Rehovot to tell him about Amitai. He already knew; Tzvi, who according to Szulkin was devastated, had called to tell him. The entire Institute was in mourning.

"Fortunately," Szulkin said, "his parents are no longer alive. He has a brother and a sister, but they have not yet been located."

Jeremy was stricken and streaming with tears. He made Szulkin his confessor, and explained how he was responsible for where Amitai had been standing, for ordering him to make the connection with Tzvi, for failing to act when he first got Tzvi's warning. And stupidest of all, he put himself in direct communication with Tzvi, and didn't once consider the possibility that this might have the same effect as meeting with Tzvi in person.

Szulkin listened in silence. When Jeremy was spent he remained quiet for some moments before responding. "Jeremy," he said, "I can't say anything that's going to make either of us feel any better. But as an Israeli I have been through these things before—random, meaningless violence kills someone who is close to you. And I can tell you that there is one perspective you have that is inaccurate."

"What is that?" Jeremy asked somberly.

"The idea that you are the only one who should have done something differently. What about Amitai . . . did he know the helicopter was crashing?"

"I assume so. He was right at the window."

"And he is not responsible for protecting himself by taking cover? Only you are, for not telling him to?"

Jeremy didn't respond.

"Doesn't Amitai know what happens when you get together with Tzvi in person?" Szulkin pressed on.

"Yes."

"Of course he knows, maybe more than anyone. He had been studying your coincidence condition for months! He was with us in LA when the attack in Saudi Arabia happened. Why didn't *he* see any danger in the communication with Tzvi?"

"I think he might have been trying to steer me away from it, but I insisted that he set up the link. I definitely pressed him to do it, and I instructed him to stand at the windowsill!"

"When some time has passed, hopefully you'll be able to see that you alone are not responsible for these events."

*   *   *   *   *

Southern California
8:30am Pacific Standard Time
16:30 GMT

Dozens of Federal agents arrived at *The Oval Office*'s facilities at Olympic Boulevard and Long Beach, and at Victor's home in La Cañada Flintridge, presenting a Homeland Security Court warrant for Victor's arrest on a single charge of failing to register *The Oval Office* as a political action committee. They also presented a temporary restraining order barring the production of any further episodes of *The Oval Office* or its segments, and subpoenas for all "printed, written and electronic information contained within the warranted premises." All voice and data communications were cut, and computer servers and hard drives were tagged and secured by latex-gloved technicians. Employees were directed to company cafeterias, where agents had set up shop to interview them. Newly arriving employees were greeted and identified by FBI agents, and then escorted to the cafeteria.

Being so well organized, it did not take long for the agents to realize that the raid had been expected, and that *The Oval Office* was just as well organized as they were.

The first hint came when very few people showed up for work: by 10am only seventeen people had arrived at Long Beach. Then they learned that everyone who was at work had been trained to say absolutely nothing other than their name. Even the cooks in the cafeteria refused to answer questions, asked for attorneys, and demanded to know if they were free to go. Finally, as technicians began to gain some access to the computer system, they realized that the main servers had been wiped clean; a thousand terabytes of disk storage available, with not a single datafile to be found. Even the applications were gone.

*   *   *   *   *

Plovdiv, Bulgaria
6:54pm Central Balkan Time
16:54 GMT

Jeremy had been at his desk in *The Oval Office*'s new twenty-acre campus outside of Plovdiv, Bulgaria, for all of three hours when he learned that their facilities in Long Beach and LA were being seized, and that arrest warrants had been issued.

"Do you want to call Victor yourself, or shall I let him know?" asked Leslie Graev, *The Oval Office*'s Director of Communications, who had brought him the news. She, at least, was keeping her eye on the ball, thought Jeremy. It was important that Victor be notified.

Victor was in Sofia. He had arrived first, on a 747 that carried mostly creative-side personnel (including all of the segments' leading actors and almost a hundred writers), and his own family. By prior agreement he was supposed to be greeted at the airport by the (real) President of Bulgaria, Amman Tikhanov, in the presence of the press. Under these circumstances, however, that agreement needed to be altered; Victor did not want to reveal his whereabouts just yet, and in theory the US authorities should still be under the impression that he had flown back to the West Coast and was at home with his family.

So when he telephoned President Tikhanov from the plane to notify him that *The Oval Office* was exercising its option and in fact moving all of its operations to Bulgaria, he asked for a delay in any public announcement. As expected, Tikhanov was so stunned that it was actually happening, he relented immediately. For his country, the arrival of *The Oval Office* was an enormous boost in prestige and a major economic coup. They were expected to employ over seven hundred Bulgarians in production and administrative jobs, and the newly arrived Americans would themselves be pumping millions of dollars into the retail and service sectors.

By the end of the conversation, Victor had agreed to stay in Sofia, with his family as guests of the President, until a press conference could be arranged. Everyone else, except for his security detail, boarded helicopters at the Sofia airport that ferried them a hundred miles south to *The Oval Office*'s new home outside of Plovdiv, Bulgaria's second largest city.

Jeremy had been on one of the two Airbuses that had refueled in Tenerife and then flown directly to Plovdiv. The two planes carried a total of 591 *Oval Office* production and administrative personnel— all of whom, he hoped, were now working non-stop to prepare for a resumption of taping no later than Monday.

This latest news about the raids in the US vindicated Jeremy's decision to invoke *Magic Carpet*, and he would have been relieved, and perhaps even proud, were he not so tired and so numbed by Amitai's death.

"Please, you make the call," Jeremy answered, breaking his trance. Too much was happening for him to do it all.

"Is there anything else you want me to relay to him?" Leslie asked.

"Just that he should feel free to call me if need be. I don't envision being able to sleep any time soon." Jeremy had dark crescents under his eyes.

"Why don't you *try*, at least, to get some rest?" she ventured.

"Why don't you, on your way out, *try* and get Evelyn Vaughn on a secure line for me?" Jeremy tended towards snippy when he was tired.

*   *   *   *   *

7:15pm Central Balkan Time
9:15am Pacific Standard Time
17:15 GMT

"Thank God, thank you for calling!" Jeremy had never heard Evelyn so distraught. "Are you okay? Where are you?"

"I'm okay, I'm fine, please don't worry. I called you as soon as I could. Are you okay?"

"I'm fine. I'm fine." Her voice was still quivering. "Now I'm okay."

"Amitai is dead," Jeremy said. He had closed his door and was sitting alone in his office with the lights dimmed and his speakerphone on.

"Amitai your bridge partner? Is dead? He was killed in Washington?"

"He was standing right next to me in the lobby of the Washington Club. A window blew in when the helicopter hit, and he was killed by flying glass."

There was long pause.

"Amitai is really dead?" she asked, stunned.

"What do you think, that I would kid about this? He is dead, dead, dead! I saw it happen and as far as I'm concerned it was my fault."

"What do you mean?" Evelyn asked.

"I mean what I said. He was following instructions from me when he was killed. There were a half-dozen reasons I should have seen what was coming."

"How can you even say that? Jeremy, where are you? Where are you calling from?"

"Bulgaria. A city called Plovdiv."

"What? You are where?"

"You heard me. Evelyn, nothing I say in this phone call will be in jest. Assume that my humor is turned off."

"But you are okay?"

"Physically I'm fine. I'm just overwhelmed about Amitai. What an unbelievable waste, what a fucking disaster."

"Is Victor okay?"

"He's fine. He's not here with me now; he's in Sofia. Meeting with the President of Bulgaria."

"The last I saw him, he was surrounded by bodyguards in the basement of the Washington Club. How did he get out? How did you get to Bulgaria?"

"How we got here will have to wait, but I can tell you what happened in Washington," and he related briefly the events that had been documented in a security report that he read on the plane. A downed helicopter, as it turned out, was one of several threat scenarios that had been anticipated by *Oval Office* security, so as soon as Victor's detail saw that the chopper was in trouble, a rehearsed operation was executed. Both Victor and Evelyn were escorted off the stage, and immediately an agent, who was later seriously injured in the crash, picked up the microphone to try to guide the panicking crowd. Once off the stage, Victor and Evelyn were rushed into the basement of the Washington Club, which is where they were when the helicopter hit. The next move was being weighed when *Magic Carpet* was called in, and a whole different operation unfolded.

Because of the fleeing crowds and the incoming emergency vehicles, it was impossible to leave by car. A team of bodyguards surrounded Victor—Evelyn had been retrieved from the basement by her own personnel—and they began walking East on P Street. As they walked, one of the guards put on a "double" mask of Victor, and Victor assumed the Nordic-looking face of Armin von der Liethe, *The Oval Office* make-up artist who was also their mask-maker. Then identical Detroit Tigers baseball caps were donned by everyone.

When they reached the corner of Ninth they turned south and were soon overtaken by an armored sedan that had been kept in reserve at the hotel. Victor's double got in along with one other agent, and they sped off to DCA, where Victor's private Airbus was waiting for him for the flight back to Burbank. The remaining agents spread out and shadowed the real Victor as they all continued walking south on Ninth at a normal pace. They reached K Street and turned west. In pairs the agents then began to hail cabs and leave the scene. Victor and Grainger got in the third cab and took it to Union Station, where an unmarked livery sedan was waiting for them. This car took them to a CAT strip in suburban Eastern Maryland.

"Can you at least tell me *why* you are in Bulgaria?"

"I can tell you a little bit—enough so you'll understand. But let me ask first, where are you? What time is it where you are?"

"I'm in my office in San Francisco. It's a little after nine in the morning."

"Good. And your encryption light is on?"

Evelyn paused as she looked at her phone. "The encryption light is on."

"This isn't about trust, it's about this new wireless private network we've got here that I'm not too sure about."

"Okay."

Jeremy closed his eyes momentarily just to wet them, but then realized they felt better closed. "What were you saying? What was the question?" He could tell now, he was slipping.

"Why you are in Bulgaria. Why are you there?"

There was a long pause. Jeremy kept his eyes closed. Finally he connected. "We have moved everything to Bulgaria. All of our production, actors, everything. We're going to be producing the shows here from now on."

Evelyn couldn't think of any stranger conversation in her entire life. "Jer, I know you're not joking. I understand that. But think of how weird that sounds. Why would you move everything to Bulgaria, and how could you even do that?"

Jeremy was now asleep, but in one distant corner of his mind things were still processing, processing, processing, and finally an answer came back. Not an answer, but an awareness. Of course she thinks it's strange, because she doesn't know yet that they are closing our offices there. Nothing has been announced. He summoned his voice but it did not answer.

"Jeremy, are you still there?" Evelyn asked. "Are you sure you're okay?"

"Yes, Evelyn, I'm fine. It feels so good to me that you're concerned. I can tell you're concerned. Don't be."

"Jer, are you awake? *Are you falling asleep?* We didn't just have sex, you know."

His eyes popped open. "I'm sorry, I dozed, I was dozing for a second. I'm in Bulgaria. It was a long flight."

"Jeremy, why are you in Bulgaria? You were going to tell me why you are there!"

"Yes. I am going to tell you. But you won't know why. Yet. Here it is, let me just spit it out."

"Please do."

"You don't know it yet, because it hasn't been announced. But the Grove Administration is shutting us down. Or rather, they're trying to shut us down. They've indicted Victor, and they are in the middle of closing down Olympic Boulevard and Long Beach."

"Indicted Victor? On what charge?"

"On a ridiculous, contrived nuisance charge of failing to register *The Oval Office* as a political party. Or so I've been told. I haven't seen the warrant."

"You are sure about all this?"

"It's already begun. At both locations they've taken everyone into custody. But when they find out that they haven't shut us down, and that Victor is not at home but in Bulgaria, they may try to backpedal very fast." Jeremy was now thinking out loud. "But the raids took place, the press have arrived in Long Beach. It's going to be very hard for them to put it back in the bottle."

"Whoa," Evelyn said with something of a whistle. "Wow!"

"Wow is right," agreed Jeremy.

"But they're not going to succeed, because you've moved everyone to Bulgaria? In one night? How in heaven's name did you do that?"

"I can't tell you that now. So far we have about eight hundred key people here including all of the actors and most of the writers. Several hundred more will make their own way here over the next few days, and we'll be hiring a lot of local people as well."

"Where are you working from? Where are you getting your equipment and soundstages and everything?"

"We bought a big production studio here last year as a back-up facility for just this kind of thing. There's a lot to be done, but we have enough in place to make it work."

"So they're not going to be able to shut you down?"

"I don't see how. More importantly, they're not going to get Victor. Not unless the long arm of the Grove Administration can somehow find its way into south central Bulgaria."

"Can they block your Webcasts?"

"They might be able to block our domestic feed on NBC, but there's nothing they can do about the downloads."

"Holy Moses, the shit is going to hit the fan on this one. This is going to be some showdown. Do you think Victor will run for President now?"

"I haven't discussed it with him." In fact, he had not even thought of it, and quickly filed it away for tomorrow.

"One more question, and then I'll let you go—you should sleep. But the question is, can I come see you in Bulgaria?"

"Give us a week to get things going here, and then you come anytime you please. We're not far from the Black Sea resorts. Let me know when and I'll make the travel arrangements."

"Good. Get some rest."

"Okay. Thanks for offering to come over. I would love to see you."

"I do miss you," and she blew a kiss. Jeremy listened for another few moments until he heard the connection click off—about the same amount of time, he thought, that he hesitated before making his move in DC. It was also about the same amount of time he had had to see Amitai's shredded, blood-gushing torso, before Charles forcibly hauled him away. That image, he knew instantly as soon as he saw it, would haunt him for the rest of his life.

He put his feet up on a wastebasket and fell asleep wondering if there wasn't some moral equivalent to the tort concept of contributory negligence.

*   *   *   *   *

Washington, DC
3:00pm EDT
20:00 GMT

At the beginning of the regular afternoon briefing, Deputy Press Secretary Gale Rose announced that an arrest warrant for Victor Glade had been issued, and that the offices and production facilities of *The Oval Office* had been closed pending a resolution of the charges. The press room erupted. To get them quiet, she simply stood by the microphone looking bored. When it finally subsided she paused longer, waiting for complete silence.

"We are aware of the controversy that this action will generate," she spoke quietly, "and we know what your questions will be. But your howling will not get you any answers." She paused, like a mother stopping to make sure that her children were still listening to her lecture. "The only answers I have for you on this matter, at this point, are those that are included in the statement I'm about to read, copies of which are being distributed to you now. I will have no further comment afterwards, and we have a lot of other ground to cover, including new information about the attack in Dupont Circle yesterday."

*   *   *   *   *

Plovdiv, Bulgaria
10:43 pm Central Balkan Time
20:43 GMT

Leslie Graev knocked on Jeremy's office door, paused, knocked again, and then came in and shook him awake.

"I feel terrible waking you, but you wanted to know if there was any news out of the White House."

"What do you have?" Jeremy pulled his legs off their perch and sat up in his chair.

She handed him a copy of the Administration's statement. "Would you like me to read it to you?"

"Yes, please. Thank you. No, actually, I changed my mind."

Jeremy shook his head to wake up. "Computer, turn up the lights. Oh, right, there's no . . . do me a favor . . ." he gestured toward the wall switch. "And do we have any coffee?" The lights came up. "See if you can get me some coffee. Please. Where are my glasses?" He realized he wasn't sure whether he was thinking or talking. He found his glasses next to the telephone and was reading through the statement a second time when Leslie returned. An EA followed behind her with a thermos of coffee and mugs on a tray.

"What time did this come in?" Jeremy asked. "Or rather, when was this released—how much time has elapsed?"

"This was the first item at the regular afternoon press briefing at the White House. It was read by Gale Rose, a Deputy Press Secretary, about fifteen minutes ago, and she took no questions. She said the only information she was authorized to give right now was contained in the statement."

This confirmed Jeremy's sense of what had happened. He took a sip and then a swallow of coffee, which seemed to course through his veins.

A disaster was unfolding for the Administration, and they were doing the best that they could to manage it. The statement read "the warrants are in the process of being executed"—i.e., *Magic Carpet* had gone undetected; they still didn't know where Victor or anyone else was. The "blurring of lines between entertainment and the serious business of national security" language was old, recycled. They said that *The Oval Office*'s facilities had been closed, but there was no mention of the Temporary Restraining Order halting production, a facsimile of which they now had in hand. That might mean they had by now deduced that *The Oval Office* was going to resume its production elsewhere; if they couldn't stop it, they certainly didn't want to announce that they were trying to.

And the whole thing was organized so that the Deputy Press Secretary who read the statement wouldn't take any questions about it, which meant that all of the questions would end up being asked and answered in the media—by the Administration's well-greased network of *spinmeisters*. For this kind of thing Morley James probably had his entire bullpen out in the field.

It didn't matter; the best it would do was buy them some time. When Victor held his press conference, arm-in-arm with the President of Bulgaria, and announced that *The Oval Office* had relocated to a country where artistic freedom and free speech were still protected—the White House would then have its hands certifiably full. *Couldn't happen to nicer people.*

"I will be happy to let Victor know, if you'd like," Leslie offered, trying to keep it on track. "There are bedrooms in the commissary, you know . . ."

"Nope, I've gotten a couple of hours of rest, and caffeine is just amazing. I've got a few things I want to cover with Victor besides this . . . but first, do we even know if he's awake? If he's not, I'm not sure I want to wake him. I'll think about that, but find out for me, please, what his status is?"

Leslie left and almost immediately Charles Witt stuck his head inside the door. "He's asleep. Victor and Melissa turned in about an hour ago . . . how are you doing?"

"I got three hours' sleep and a shot of caffeine. I'm better. It really is amazing which drugs are legal and which ones aren't. I'm still haunted by the thing with Amitai."

"As am I, sir, as am I. Is there anything I can do for you now—you're not planning on going anywhere are you?"

"*Are you fucking kidding?*" Jeremy looked at him, wild-eyed.

"Okay, got it. Well, good night, sir. Try to get some rest. Door open?"

"Closed, door closed, thank you." Jeremy raised his voice so everyone in the adjoining office would hear. "Jesus, everyone's a mother!" he shouted. "I'm sixty-six years old!"

He logged onto his computer and began another draft of the statement Victor would release tomorrow.

16	July 6, 2020

6:30am Central Balkan Time
04:30 GMT

As soon as he woke up, Victor called Jeremy from Sofia. "How are you feeling?" he asked.

"I'm fine," answered Jeremy. "I got some rest, how about you?"

"I'm fine, and I'm not in jail in the United States. You may not be in a position to recognize it—I understand you're upset about Amitai—but to me you are a fucking *hero*. I have you and only you to thank for this brilliant piece of foresight and planning."

This did make Jeremy feel a little better. At one point while they were in the Puerto Vallarta staging area, Victor made a point of telling Jeremy how distraught his younger daughter was at being removed from her blossoming high school social life, which was his indirect way of saying "I hope you're right about this." Just as easily as this was turning out to be a disaster for the Administration, it could also have been a disaster for Jeremy and *The Oval Office*, had he been wrong.

"You're welcome. You're right, I'm not in a position to appreciate it."

"So how are you holding up, I mean in terms of Amitai? Is

there anything we can do?"

"Not unless you can bring him back, or get my memory erased, or send us back in time."

"Ahh, yes. All those things that money can't buy. The list is a lot longer than you'd think."

"You've made such a list?"

"No, I haven't. It's just a billionaire's random thought—but it seems like a good idea. Rich people should keep a list like that taped to the frame of every mirror in their home." Jeremy's background processor was virtually audible as the entry was recorded: *Compile list of things money can't buy.*

Victor continued: "So I read the Administration's statement. What do you think?"

"I think they don't know what's happening, and they're trying to buy time to find out." Now he was feeling clear-headed for the first time in thirty-six hours at least.

"Can you think of any reason why we shouldn't let them know now where we are? I'm anxious to get back to work."

"No, I think we can go ahead and make our announcement. I have taken the liberty of drafting a statement, which I'll send to Grainger and he'll get it to you. But I can think of a good reason why you should not come to Plovdiv right away."

"Pray tell what is that?"

"I recommend that you fly to Athens—or at least offer to—to meet with Paulous and solidify our relations there." Victor had been made an honorary citizen of Greece after *Demosthenes* was published, and the new *Oval Office* facilities in Plovdiv were, by no coincidence, a 30-minute helicopter hop to the Greek border. "I have made an inquiry and found that the timing is good. He is in Athens now and doesn't have other things on his plate that would make it difficult."

"Jesus, are you a diplomat too? How do you know all this?"

"It's my job," Jeremy said. "Keeping you safe is part of my job—that's why you pay me the big bucks, right?"

"So explain to me why it is so important for me to go to Greece right now?"

"Bulgaria was our back-up for the US, and now Greece is our

back-up for Bulgaria. You always need to have an exit plan."

"What do I do there, just *schmooze?*"

"You need to balance things out for Paulous. We've just moved everything to Bulgaria, there's going to be a lot of regional publicity about that. Everyone in Greece thinks of you as their national godson, so the question in their minds will be—why didn't he move back to Greece? It makes the Prime Minister look like he failed to bring you home. You need to appear in public with him and take him off the hook."

"Well I've gotta tell you I'm exhausted, and I think my family would be very unhappy about a trip to prop up a head of state somewhere. Now it's beginning to look like I'm the *real* President—which is what we are trying to avoid, right?"

"Speaking of which,"—Jeremy thought this was a good a time as any— "has this changed you ideas about running for President at all?"

"No, it has not, but it has made me decide that I'm going to endorse a Democrat to run against Grove."

"I thought you didn't like any of them."

"I'm not *excited* about any of them, but, as Liman said, if I wanted excitement I should run myself. I now agree that it doesn't matter who it is who gets in; we've got to get this idiot out of the White House before he blows us all up. What a fucking loose cannon. The electorate in this country is so unbelievably stupid."

"I beg to differ. The electorate in *this* country is Bulgarian. It's the American electorate that is so unbelievably stupid."

"You know what I mean," Victor said.

"The Democratic Convention begins in a month—less than a month—and you're here in Bulgaria. How do you plan to work that?"

"Even if the indictment thing went away, I don't want to attend the convention myself. I don't want to be a center of attention there. It would make it look too much like I'm really trying to slide in myself at the last minute."

"I agree with you there—in terms of how it would be perceived. So what do you propose to do?"

"I wanted to ask you and Liman to pick five Senators, not

Senators who are running for President, but Senators whose judgment
you value and respect, and line them up to meet with me via the Web
on the first day of the convention. Invite Bill Clinton too; if he'll take
the time to attend, I'll listen to what he has to say. Can you put that
together?"

"I don't see why not. And it doesn't matter to you who the
Senators are?"

"It matters a great deal. Aaron Stewart is an example the kind
of Senator I have in mind . . . you know much more about these people
than I do, and I know what your criteria are, so I'm going to go with
your call."

"Should they know what the purpose is?" Jeremy asked.

"Absolutely. Tell them I'd like their input on an endorsement.
In fact, my idea is that we should announce now that I will make an
endorsement at the convention. That will build up some "Who Shot
JR" pre-publicity and it will keep the Grove camp on edge. What do
you think?"

Jeremy considered that for a few moments. "I can get behind
that," he said. "I'll need to rewrite the statement a little, but I think
announcing it now will maximize its effect later. Your political instincts
are still very sharp—you'd make a great President."

"Don't even go there."

"I'm just kidding! Take it easy."

"Okay, so you'll put that together—at the convention? Let
Caroline know as soon as possible so that it's on my schedule."

"I will take care of it. Will you go to Athens? I strongly advise it."

"Okay, okay. Make it so. But I think my family is going to
want to settle somewhere. You can get them to Plovdiv without me,
right?"

"Just let Grainger know what your travel needs are and he'll
arrange it. I'll call the Prime Minister's office to get the meeting set
up."

"So I'm now going to do my press conference with Tikhanov
here, and then fly directly to Athens?"

"That's what I'm thinking. Give me a half hour to get language
about your endorsement in the statement, and then you can do your

thing with Tikhanov. When you're done with that, Grainger will get you to Athens, and from Athens back to Plovdiv. We're not going to be ready to start taping until Monday anyhow, and you'll be back Sunday afternoon."

"I'm grateful to you, my friend, for arranging it so that I can go back to work on Monday."

*   *   *   *   *

10:05 am, Central Balkan Time
08:05 GMT

Speaking from the ballroom of the Presidential Palace in front of 100 journalists and a dozen Webcams, President Tikhanov welcomed *The Oval Office* to Bulgaria, praised himself for bringing this good fortune upon their small country, and praised Victor for his excellent judgment in choosing Bulgaria as his new home. Victor, who could barely understand the translator, made his reciprocal thanks and said a few more words for the domestic audience, but then looked straight into the Reuters Webcam, made his trademark eye contact with his Oval Office audience, and read a prepared statement.

"As many of you already know, yesterday—July 5th—the Grove Administration obtained a Homeland Security District Court warrant for my arrest, on a fantastic charge of failing to register The Oval Office *as a political action committee, and attempted to arrest me at my home near Los Angeles. The Administration also sought and obtained from the same Court a Temporary Restraining Order halting any further production of Oval Office programs, and early yesterday morning, California time, our offices and studios in the LA area were seized by hundreds of Federal agents.*

"Because of security precautions that had been activated after Saturday's terrorist attack in Washington DC, where I was present, I was out of the country when we learned of the Administration's actions. Even more fortunately, The Oval Office *last year purchased a back-up production facility that was intended to be used in the event of a major earthquake or other catastrophe, but it serves equally well when the President of the United*

States decides to go trampling on the First Amendment—a disaster of no lesser consequence.

"Therefore it pleases me to notify our viewers that despite the Grove Administration's best efforts, The Oval Office will maintain its regular production schedule. New episodes in each segment are expected to be released every week at their regular times, although this week they may be delayed somewhat. If the Grove administration blocks our live feed through NBC, our broadcast viewers can download our programs through any major non-US Web distribution portal.

"I have been asked many times in the last 36 hours if the Grove Administration's actions—or attempted actions—have caused me to reconsider running for President. The answer without hesitation has been a consistent and immediate 'No'. I will not be a candidate for President, for reasons that are all on the record.

"However, the Administration's latest actions have convinced me that I must actively involve myself in the upcoming election. Although I may yet endorse a candidate prior to the Democratic nominating convention, I'm now announcing my unqualified support for the Democratic nominee, whoever that turns out to be. At this point I'm more concerned about the immediate need to remove Burton Grove from the White House. If it weren't so close to a regular election, I would actively support a drive for impeachment.

"I am not making these statements outside of the context of today's dangerous world, as the Grove Administration and its media allies will surely argue. I was a personal witness to the attack in Washington DC on July 4th, and a dear friend of our General Counsel was killed in the crash. The cluster bombings that have been terrorizing our cities must be stopped—but kangaroo courts and assaults on the First Amendment will not stop them. I would argue instead that the Grove Administration's policies are a major contributor to world terrorism. As long as we continue to kill scores of people in our drive to impose our notion of democracy around the World, there will be an endless stream of terrorist recruits making their way to our increasingly undemocratic shores."

*   *   *   *   *

11:47pm Central Balkan Time
21:47 GMT

"Doc, I'm returning your call," Jeremy said to Szulkin. "Our inbound communications are still not secure, so I had to call you back."

"I understand. Thank you for responding so quickly." Szulkin's British accent and diction were still crisp, even at midnight. "I'm sorry the hour is so late, but something important has come up."

"Are you calling with a message from Tzvi? If you are, I advise against it. The last middleman to get between us didn't fare so well."

"I understand your concern, but don't you want to keep some form of communication open with him?"

Jeremy thought about this. The answer was, of course, that he did; without Tzvi's advance notice, it was certainly possible that *Magic Carpet* would not have succeeded, or may never have gotten off the ground at all.

"We have worked out a way to make the connection even more indirect," Szulkin continued. "I will not communicate with Tzvi directly in any form, either by e-mail or telephone. His communications will always go through a third-party—an analyst in his office who has security clearance. I am communicating with her by e-mail only, and with you by telephone only."

"Maybe I should add someone on my side," Jeremy ruminated. The conversation was so preposterous anyhow, it seemed like the right thing to suggest.

"By all means, I think you should," Szulkin said. "It insulates *me* more."

"My communications will go through Charles Witt, he's my security manager. I will give him your contact information. In the meantime, I'm returning your call."

"Indeed. 'T'is a brief but important question. Did you by any chance see what happened to the tablet Amitai had when he was killed?"

"You've got to be kidding!" Jeremy blurted out, horrified. He wanted to tell Szulkin what he *had* seen, but then thought better of it.

"No, I didn't see what happened to his tablet. I think it's likely that it was damaged or destroyed in the blast."

"It actually was a military-issue encryption tablet that was built to withstand far more impact than that."

"I assume you have tried to recover it through regular channels?" Jeremy asked.

"We have. And we certainly had no expectation that you would know anything, but the device is missing, and we thought you should be aware of that. No crucial information has been compromised, but it does establish Amitai as a common link between you and our mutual friend Tzvi."

"Thanks. I will pass this information on to our security people here. In fact, this is something Charles would handle, so it will give him another reason to be in touch with you."

17	July 15, 2020 Musala Palace Hotel Varna, Bulgaria

In his dream Jeremy was walking somewhere with Evelyn—he couldn't remember now where it was, but it must have been a beach, because he was barefoot, and wearing only shorts. It was a pleasant walk, and Evelyn was being very playful with him. He was getting turned on. But then his left foot began to drag like it was getting stuck in the sand, and he started to hobble. And then his right foot suddenly hung on something and he fell backwards, smoothly, slowly, landing on something very soft, and woke up.

Evelyn saw him awaken, scooted up to the top of the bed, and tried to distract him with her smile.

"What are you doing?" he asked. "Why are my legs tied?" He might have panicked, except that Evelyn was completely naked and now half on top of him, one leg thrown over his, her hand roaming over his chest. She nuzzled her head in the crook of his neck.

"Let me tie you up," she whispered to him. "Have you ever done it before?"

"No, I haven't, and I'm not sure I want to start now."

"You are afraid?"

"Well, what happens when you tie me up? I'm not into pain if that's where you're headed."

"It's not about pain. I'll tie you up and turn you on very slowly. It will help you let go."

"How do you know?" Jeremy tried shifting his legs and found they were well anchored.

"You can say stop anytime you want." Her breath was warm. "Just say stop and I will, but try this out with me. You'll see what I mean." She rested her head on a planted elbow, grazed his chest, and gave him an encouraging "trust me" look that he accepted with a nod. This was Evelyn at her kinkiest by far, but he trusted her and had no reason to stop doing so now.

"What do I do?" he asked.

"Nothing. That's the point." She was delighted, and scrambled over him, slipping soft, looped ropes over his wrists.

"What if it doesn't turn me on?" He was wearing loose boxers, and at this point they were still feeling quite roomy.

She was concentrating on securing his wrist ropes to the frame of the bed. "What if tomorrow doesn't come?" she finally responded, testing and adjusting her work, and then returning to his legs to make sure things were still secure. "One of the rules of the game is: no thinking. Don't even bother to think, or plan, or anticipate, because there's nothing you can do about it anyway. If it doesn't turn you on, it doesn't turn you on." She ran fingernails up the soles of his feet to see how secure things were, and he wiggled but went nowhere. She then tried the same thing under his arms and got even more thrashing. This added some slack to his ropes, which she rapidly took in, making them even tighter.

"I can see you've done this before," Jeremy said, trying to sound casual. "Where did you learn?"

"If you can see I've done this before, you're seeing too much," she replied, and proceeded to blindfold him using one of his socks as a mask, and one of her stockings to tie it on. "Do you want to guess what happens if you keep asking questions?"

Jeremy was now quite immobile. Evelyn got up onto the bed, sat astride his stomach facing his chest, and began a slow massage from his shoulders down. She felt his boxers stiffening behind her, so reached back with one hand and guided his quickly stiffening cock through the fly of his shorts. She then began a coordinated slow stroking, his chest with one hand and his now throbbing cock with the other.

Sooner than he ever thought possible he arrived at a point of no return, but at the penultimate moment Evelyn released her grip and he was left dangling breathlessly from the edge.

"What? What?! Don't stop, please don't stop!" Jeremy desperately tried to find her hand by pushing his hips up. "Why are you ... don't, please, don't."

"Oh, I'll get around to it. But you can speed things up a bit if you answer a question." She reached down and gave his cock a couple of slow squeezes, but then let go.

Jeremy turned his head as if he could see her. "What, what?" he moaned. "What is your question?"

"Tell me how you were able to get eight hundred people out of the US, undetected, on short notice, in one night."

"Ahhhh," Jeremy suddenly saw the true game revealed. "Now I understand." She had already asked him this once over dinner, and he had declined—politely, he thought—to give specifics. When she pressed further, he had answered, perhaps a trifle too patronizingly, that it was better for her not to know. "You didn't like my previous answer, I gather. Why is it so important for you to know?" Jeremy asked.

"You are thinking," Evelyn said. "Thinking is not an activity that is rewarded in your situation." She got out of bed and walked around to all four corners of the bed to tighten things up. "Thinking will just slow things down."

At the foot of the bed she discovered Jeremy's shoes. "Oh, how convenient!" she said, and picked them up and began extracting the shoelaces. Jeremy could not see what was so convenient, but soon felt her tying the shoelaces to his big toes. His ankles were anchored two feet apart, but she pulled the laces together as closely as she could and then knotted them, so that his toes were being pulled together while his ankles were being pulled apart. She then ducked into the bathroom and returned with a small pair of nail scissors. "Your shorts have got to go," she said. "So now would not be good time to squirm around," and she proceeded to snip them off. When she was done she dropped the scissors on a night table and joined him back in bed, lying next to him with her head on his shoulder. "This is much better," she whispered into his ear as she pulled him erect again. "'Now you are all mine," and she began a slow, rhythmic stroking as she breathed in his ear. Jeremy moaned and thrusted.

In less than a minute she had brought him back to his failsafe point. "I'm about to stop again," she whispered, "unless you have something you want to tell me."

"What do you want to know? It would take twenty minutes to tell the whole story."

"I've got some time on my hands. Do you have an appointment somewhere?" She stopped her movements but kept her grip on him.

"What is it you want to know? Ask me a question!" He was breathless.

"How did you get three big airliners out of the country on short notice without anyone knowing?"

"We didn't leave the country on big planes. We left in CAT's."

"How did you get that many CAT flights out of the country without anyone knowing? Jesus, eight hundred people must have taken over a hundred flights!" The government's $160 billion overhaul of the nation's traffic control system was supposed to detect any and all aircraft coming into or leaving the continental US at virtually any altitude.

"That part is complicated. I'll tell you that later."

"Where did the CAT flights go to, Canada?"

"Mexico."

"And you transferred to large planes there?"

"Yes."

"And you had all this worked out in advance?"

"Yes."

"This was your idea?"

"Not exclusively mine. But I approved it all."

"How much money did you spend on it?"

"I don't know, forty million dollars. Sixty million including the studios in Plovdiv."

"Oh, you are my kind of man!" she exclaimed, and kissed him on the cheek. "You promise to tell me the rest of the story?"

"I promise."

"When will you tell me?" She squeezed him to get an immediate commitment.

"Before you leave. I'll tell you at breakfast. Will you please make me come? Please?"

"I can never resist a helpless man," she said, and resumed her stroking with one hand as she peeled back his blindfold with the other. She counted a few slow strokes until his body began to shudder, and she sped up—watching his eyes as they rolled upward and froze in a catatonic half-smile.

18	JL Coincidence Blog - Entry #125 April, 2009 Guilin, China

While accompanying several Senators on a junket to China, I ended up playing bridge for two consecutive afternoons in the city of Guilin, partnered with the local American Consul, playing against a pair of high-ranking Chinese trade officials. They all knew about the singleton king of spades, and eagerly awaited its appearance, but in the 100+ deals we played it did not show up once. After the last game we headed on foot to a restaurant for dinner about half a mile away from the hotel where we had been playing.

On the way it began to rain heavily, and we dashed from block to block, trying to take cover while waiting for traffic lights to change. At one corner we stood under the massive pillared canopy of the Nikko-Doh Department Store. While waiting for the light to change, I glanced inadvertently to the side, and at exactly my eye level, plastered to the massive concrete pillar next to me, was a miniature decal of the king of spades. About the size of a small postage stamp, it was just there, by itself, with no other decals or markings of any kind near it or on any of the other pillars nearby. Just that one tiny image, on that one pillar, in that one spot where I happened to look. I brought it to the attention of my colleagues, who were suitably impressed and took pictures, one of which I have retained as an attachment to this journal.

19	August, 2020 Democratic National Convention Atlanta, GA

By the time the Democratic National Convention convened in early August, the 28th Amendment had become as important an issue to the Democratic Party as was their choice of Presidential nominee. In the absence of some type of campaign finance reform, Democrats had little hope of overcoming the inherent fundraising advantage held by the Party of the "Have More's."

The Amendment was therefore given a prominent spot in the Convention's agenda, and Evelyn, who had emerged as a Joan of Arc figure among many despondent liberals, was invited to deliver the opening night keynote address. Her humor won the audience's rapt attention immediately, and eleven minutes later she had so deftly and logically gutted the arguments against the Amendment that it was hard to see how anyone could not be convinced.

"Our proposed Amendment," she concluded, "is ultimately a referendum. It's an opportunity for us to decide whether the Founding Fathers of this nation intended for ours to be a government by and for the *people*, or a government for sale to *the people who can afford it*."

A burst of applause started out, but Evelyn waved it down.

"My friends, we all know that our Founding Fathers *never* intended ours to be a government for sale to the highest bidder.

Nonetheless, 244 years later, for reasons beyond anyone's prediction or control, we have arrived at a point where political representation in this nation is purchased like a commodity, and the price has become so high that only the wealthiest among us can afford it." Now the cheering rose in a swell and Evelyn raised her voice over it to finish up. "I therefore call upon all Americans, regardless of their party affiliation or economic status, to join with us in our effort to restore our Founding Fathers' vision for this Nation. I urge you to support and vote for candidates who . . ."

If she finished her last sentence, it was not heard by anyone. The floor erupted in a thunderous symphony of cheering, clapping, drum beating and horn blowing that did not abate for five minutes. Jeremy, who had read Evelyn's speech the night before, and had seen and heard all manner of oratory during his years in Washington, still felt a tingle in his spine, and then he was up on his feet cheering and whistling along with everyone.

*   *   *   *   *

"When you're done with the 28th Amendment," Jeremy said after she arrived at their suite, changed into a hotel bathrobe, and opened a bottle of wine, "you really should consider going into politics. I have a lot of experience with this, and I'm telling you, you're a natural."

"You have got to be kidding!" Evelyn sounded horrified. "Why would I ever want to do that?"

"Because you're very good at it. A lot of people enjoy working at things they're good at. Success is a great motivator."

Evelyn thought about that, sipping her wine. "I don't know, the 28th Amendment is a single-focus effort. No matter what I'm doing I always feel like I'm advancing that cause. Elected politicians deal with issues that have two or more sides—it's just a lot messier. Too many variables up in the air at one time. It would be very different, I think, from what I'm doing now."

"Well if I were you I would start thinking about your next career move, because the way I see it, the 28th Amendment is going to happen—it may happen sooner than any of us ever expected."

"You are being overly optimistic," she replied. "I agree that we could have Congress nailed down next session if we make some modest headway in the elections, which we should be able to do. But the state ratification is a completely different matter—it could take years and years."

"Maybe so, but I also see the potential for the domino effect that you experienced in Congress taking hold with the state legislatures. Each state that comes on board adds more critical mass, making each subsequent state easier. It's exciting to think it could really happen."

"Thanks to Victor." She raised her wine glass and came over to Jeremy. "The exposure we got from *The Oval Office* has been a huge boost."

"Don't sell yourself short." He set his own glass down and pulled her onto his lap. "*You* are the person that has made this happen. You are very, very persuasive—not to mention charming and intelligent and sexy."

"I'm so wired," she said, standing up. "I just spoke in front of twelve thousand people."

"More like fifty million."

"Jesus, it's a good thing I wasn't thinking that when I was speaking." She drained her wine glass. "Give me a while to unwind here."

"Let me know if there's anything I can do to help. If you're going to save American democracy, I'll contribute any way I can."

"Just talk to me." She wandered toward the window overlooking nighttime Atlanta and its array of illuminated geometric forms mounted on shadowy skyscrapers. "What's going on with the nomination? Who's the current favorite—has Victor endorsed anyone yet?"

"He is committed to supporting the nominee, whoever it turns out to be, but he is also considering endorsing someone before the balloting begins on Saturday night. I've set up a Web meeting tomorrow morning for him, with Liman and a group of Senators—Senators who aren't running for President. He invited Clinton, too . . . maybe I'll be able to collect my forty grand."

"He still hasn't paid you? That's scandalous!"

"D'ya think?"

"I don't know. Really, I'm buzzed and at this point just rambling."

She put her glass down on the windowsill. "So who do you think he'll endorse? Victor, I mean."

"I have no idea. He's mentioned Arnall to me, but my gut says that he won't endorse anyone before the nomination. He said he's not excited about any of the major contenders, and I'm hard pressed to think that these Senators tomorrow are going to succeed in suddenly getting him excited about any one person. They're not even going to agree among themselves."

"Do you have someone you are trying to point him to?"

"No. When he asks me my opinion, I'll tell him—because it's the truth—I'll tell him that he's the only person I can think of who I would feel strongly about."

"Now that's something to get excited about: Victor Glade vs. Burton Grove! Whew! I wonder, actually, what the legal issues are: can someone who's under indictment run for President?"

"I wouldn't spend any time researching it. The odds of Victor running are about the same as the NRA backing a Democrat."

*   *   *   *   *

"I'm ready now, are you?" Evelyn whispered into Jeremy's ear.

"What?" At 2:15 am, Evelyn had gone into the bathroom to take a bath. He had stripped down to his boxers and sat with his tablet in the bed trying to catch up on *Oval Office* business, but dozed off after a few minutes.

"I'll make it worth your while." She closed the tablet that had slipped from his lap, put it on the floor, and sat up in bed next to him.

Jeremy shook his head to wake himself up. "Why couldn't I have known you when I was twenty-two?"

"Oh, my dear, but you can, you can."

"Hmmmmm . . ." Jeremy inhaled her scent and exhaled slowly. "I get it. In addition to bondage, you also do time travel? Now *that's* kinky."

"See, that's what I love about you. It's three o'clock in the morning, you're in the midst of being seduced, your wits are still about you."

"Hah! You call waking someone out of a deep sleep at three in the morning seduction?"

"You were sitting up in bed with a tablet beeping on your lap!" She began running her hands through the hair on his chest. "If you want I'll give you your tablet back, or we can try this out."

"Try what out?"

Evelyn didn't answer, being fully occupied in extracting his penis through the fly of his boxers before it became too stiff to maneuver. She then pulled him down from his sitting position, made herself comfortable amid-hips and began an oral exploration that any passing third party could easily conclude was a favorite pastime.

Jeremy melted, as always, and began emitting moans that guided her to his preferred destinations. Then through the carnal fog he realized she was taping something around the base of his penis.

"It's a patch," she said. "You don't take any heart medications, do you?"

"No, no, but do I need it? I think I'm supposed to be insulted or something."

"Don't think about it." She resumed her leisurely blowjob. "If it bothers you, tell me and we'll take it off."

Ten minutes later he was inside her, being guided by *her* moans and cues. When they arrived at a point where he knew she was close, he suddenly stopped his thrusting on a down-stroke, leaving her deeply impaled, but remaining motionless.

"What? What?" she opened her eyes, reluctantly coming back from another place. "Is something wrong?"

"No, nothing's wrong." He wiggled inside her.

"Why did you stop?" she asked, practically breathless.

"I wanted to see if stopping had the same effect on you that it did on me. When you tied me up."

"Oh yes, yes, it does, it does!" she said earnestly, pumping herself up to try and get re-started.

"So you want me to continue, or to stop?" He added a few strokes to keep her on edge.

"Jer, please, please don't stop."

He stretched out his arms, pinned hers beside her head, and

lowered his head to whisper in her ear. "What if there was something I wanted to know?"

"Oh, Jer, I'm not prepared for this. Fuck now, ask later. Really."

"I'm fucking, what do you call this?" He resumed some modest strokes.

"Oh, YES, YES. PLEASE DON'T STOP. I'M BEGGING YOU."

"All right, okay, hold your horses," and he started up again with some apparent end in mind, and brought her very close, but then slowed again. "You could help move things along faster," he whispered, "if you would just answer one question for me."

"OKAY, okay! What is it?"

"Will you marry me?" He stared into her desperate eyes.

"YES, YES, I'll marry you if you'll fucking finish me off right now. Otherwise FORGET IT!!"

Twenty seconds later, riding the throes of her run-on orgasm, Jeremy suddenly realized why erection drugs were *The Oval Office's* second largest source of ad revenue. He felt like he was 22 again!

*   *   *   *   *

As the invited senators arrived at the hotel conference room for the Web meeting with Victor, the small hallway outside quickly filled up with various aides and adjutants. When they asked how long the meeting was going to be, all Jeremy was willing to say was "at least half an hour, maybe longer," an ambiguity that seemed to stump most of them, and provoked a lot of muttering and hasty text messaging.

Liman arrived and Jeremy immediately stood up and came around the table to escort him in. The Senators all rose as well, greeting him warmly as Jeremy helped him into a chair next to his own. Liman beamed with appreciation and offered brief waves as he made eye contact with each one. Senators Stewart and Wellesley he had known for more than thirty years, and he had probably advised all of them at one point or another in their numerous re-election campaigns.

Next to arrive was Carla Sanders, the DNC Chair, who, to

Jeremy's knowledge, had not been invited. No one else knew that, however, so everyone pushed back their armchairs and stood up to greet her as well. When she got to Jeremy she explained that she had spoken with Victor yesterday—she had called to ask him one more time if he would allow his name to be put into nomination, and after saying no, he had invited her to stop by if she could.

"It's nice of you to make yourself available on short notice," Jeremy said.

"Are you kidding? If Victor Glade is going to endorse someone, I want to know about it."

"Everyone wants to know about it, as do I. I have no idea what his intentions are."

"Jeremy, I assume this room has been swept?"

Jeremy nodded. "By the hotel, and then by my own people. If you want to have your people do it, call them in, but we're about to get underway."

"No, that's good enough for me. I just wanted to make sure it had been done." She gave him a small wave and took a seat at the end of the table next to Senator Stewart.

Last to arrive was Clinton, whose presence caused everyone to stand up yet again.

"It's like a Bar Mitzvah service in here," Liman grumbled out of the side of this mouth to Jeremy as they got up yet again and waited their turn to greet the ex-President.

After Clinton took a seat, Jeremy stood up. "Gentlemen, ladies, please finish up your conversations," he announced. "Everyone is here, and I will get the connection together with Victor. He will be with us momentarily."

Thirty seconds later the test pattern on the overhead projector flickered off and Victor appeared. The audio blasted for a second unintelligibly, but the volume came down quickly.

" . . . for taking your time to lend me the benefit of your individual and collective wisdom. Two of you—Senators Wellesley and Graham—I know personally, and I send my best wishes to you and your families." He nodded to them, and they nodded back. "Needless to say, I regret that I can't be there with you in person but, as you know, circumstances don't permit it."

"Victor, Aaron Stewart here."

"Greetings to you, Senator."

"I just wanted to say that even with the Supreme Court that we have, I'm simply not able to conceive that Grove's direct assault on the First Amendment will be allowed to stand. History will shed a very harsh light on this Administration."

"Senator, I hope and pray you are right. But in the meantime I want to do what I can to help remove Grove from office before he does even more damage."

"Should we all assume here," asked Jeremy, "that your help will not include your own candidacy?"

"That's correct," Victor responded right away. "I spoke with Carla Sanders about this yesterday—hello, Carla—and thought it might come up here, so let me be quick to squelch it. This is not something we should spend any time on."

"Acknowledged," Jeremy said. "Moving on to endorsements, then . . . ," and he left off for Victor to pick up.

"Well, as I've announced, I will endorse whomever the convention ultimately nominates, and I will support that person in whatever way I can, including financially. But the reason I have asked for this time with you all now is because I'm considering endorsing a candidate before the balloting begins, and I hope to hear your most candid and forthright thoughts about the individual I have in mind. I'm concerned about two things: suitability, and electability. I'd like to hear whether you think this individual is qualified, and if he is, could he win."

There was a flurry of hushed conversation. Jeremy spoke out over the buzz. "I don't think anyone here realized you had someone in mind. We thought you were looking for a recommendation."

"No, I've had this person in mind for several months now, and in fact I have gone to the trouble of producing a five-minute video endorsement. I'd like to run this video for you now. That will identify the candidate, and will explain why I think he's our best shot."

Jeremy was stunned. Victor had gone for months with a particular endorsement in mind and never mentioned it to him or Liman? Previous conversations with Victor flooded back into his mind .

. . could he have missed something? What he did remember was Victor, on numerous occasions, saying he "couldn't get excited about anyone."

The projected image of Victor reverted back to a test pattern, and then quickly to the video, which started out with Victor standing on the set of *The Oval Office* with the mechanics of production—cameras, booms, stagehands—all visible in the background.

Many of you know me as President Alvin Bosco, the character I portray on the NBC series The Oval Office. *My real name is Victor Glade. In real life I am a father, husband, writer, actor and entrepreneur.*

Many of you may also know that our nation's real President recently sought and obtained a Homeland Security Court order to halt production of The Oval Office *and its companion programs. Although I have steered clear of politics in recent years, the Grove Administration's flagrant assault on the First Amendment strikes at the very heart of our free society, and I find that I can no longer in good conscience remain silent.*

Fortunately, there is an individual whose values, skills and unique bipartisan experience make him an ideal candidate for the Presidency during these troubled times. His name, Jeremiah Lerner, is familiar to all US Senators and most Congressmen, but he is largely unknown to the voting public. I therefore plan to work very hard during the upcoming election season to bring his record, and his experience, and his ideas to the public's attention—beginning right now.

Here the audio continued as voice-over and the video changed to a slow-motion sequence of still images and video footage of Jeremy, each one dissolving into the next.

Jeremy Lerner was born and raised in rural Alabama, earned an undergraduate degrees in mathematics, and attended Harvard Law School, which is where I first met him over thirty years ago. He served as my communications director when I was a Congressman for four years in the 1980's. When I left politics in 1990, Jeremy remained in Washington and became Chief Counsel to the Senate Foreign Relations Committee, a position he retained for twenty-four years. During this time he earned a universal reputation—among all senators of all parties—for integrity, intelligence, and the rare ability to bridge partisan differences."

Now the video reverted to Victor.

In 2015 Jeremy left his job in the Senate, after a quarter-century of service to his country, to return to work for me as General Counsel and CEO of The Oval Office's production company. For the past several years I have worked closely with him in every facet of our business, and I can report that Jeremy is not only smart, hard-working, honest and competent, he is also a brilliant planner and manager.

As the campaign progresses, you will learn more about Jeremy's positions on specific issues, and about his ideas for the future direction of our Nation. Regardless of whether you ultimately agree with his positions and ideas or not, I can say with absolute conviction that Jeremy Lerner will bring integrity, hard work, respect for the Constitution, and managerial competence back to the White House, and I urge you to give him every consideration.

There was a brief trailer, and Victor returned to the screen. He and everyone else in the room had their eyes fixed on Jeremy, who in turn was looking up at Victor with a look of incredulous betrayal.

"You didn't want to discuss this with me first?" Jeremy asked, trying unsuccessfully to mask the trembling in his voice.

"Get over it," Victor replied. "Don't waste these Senators' time. Like me, you can say no. Nobody's twisting your arm. Just try out the idea for a few minutes."

"Why couldn't you have raised this with me first?" he pleaded.

"Because it wouldn't have been *efficient.* It would have preoccupied you unnecessarily, and would not have yielded the candid and spontaneous feedback that is now available to you in this room. If you choose to hear it. You can say no right now, and we can all leave. But I have, as you've noticed, gone to some trouble to put this all together because I believe in it, and I believe in you, and I think you at least owe me the courtesy of hearing what these gentlemen have to say about *my* idea."

Jeremy wondered if he wasn't going into anaphylactic shock, something that had happened to him a decade earlier after eating some re-frozen ice cream. His throat felt swollen, he couldn't speak, and his mind seemed on its way out of his body.

"I for one think it's a brilliant idea," Liman jumped in. "I don't know whether it was part of your thinking or not, but Jeremy would definitely hold the blue state base and probably carry at least two southern states—I would think that Alabama and Florida would be guaranteed. It's a layout that at least has the potential to win."

"The break into the South was my thinking exactly," Victor replied. "Everyone I've spoken with has confirmed what we all know: if we capture even one state in the South, we're on our way to winning."

"I noticed you didn't include anything in the video about Jeremy's languages, that he speaks all of his languages. Did you try to work that in?" Liman asked.

"Not for the initial endorsement," said Victor. "I didn't even think of it."

"Oh, my dear friend, am I going to make you look brilliant. Whatever his languages are—how many are there, Jeremy?"

"Five," Jeremy answered numbly.

"What are they . . .? Never mind, it doesn't matter—Spanish is one of them, right?"

"Right."

"So he can speak to these five immigrant communities in their native tongues. He can tape ads, he can do interviews, the impact could tip the scales in at least five red states. You are absolutely a genius." He looked up at Victor. "This could rewrite the map."

"Irving," Victor said, "may I ask you, if you don't mind, to take a look at some polling and audience rating data that I arranged to collect when Jeremy appeared on two Sunday news programs last November. From what I can tell, the data show that he does extremely well with women in a whole range of categories, with African Americans, and of course among Jews. His recall recognition factor among all women eighteen-to-thirty-four was an 8.2."

"Does he not do well with men?" Liman asked. "Or more to

the point, are there areas where he polled weak?"

"Not really," Victor replied. "His RRF among all men was 6.5, which is perfectly acceptable, do you agree?"

"Absolutely," Liman replied. "Anything above 6 is viable."

"Otherwise we don't really have data that will take us any deeper," Victor said, "but there is nothing to indicate there is a fatal flaw somewhere. Senators, President Clinton, Chairman Sanders, what are your thoughts?"

Maryland Senator Donald Gorman went first. "I agree with Irving," he said, "from an electoral point of view. And I can tell you that I would certainly support Jeremy if he became a candidate. Like you," he looked at Victor, "I have known him for years, and I think he's a great match for the job." He then looked at Jeremy, who was still in a trance. "My only concern is what there might be that's unknown. He's never held an elected office, and has never gone through the vetting that comes with a national campaign. If we were to launch this ship and then it turned out there was even a minor problem, the whole thing could sink immediately. It might be a brilliant play, but we need to be very careful."

"I agree with you, Don," Senator Graham broke in. "The vetting would have to be very thorough, but I'm not as concerned as I might be with some other people."

"Not having been vetted is a risk," Stewart added, "but it is offset by the lack of political baggage. He has no voting record that can be picked apart, no history of public statements or positions on controversial issues. This can be very positive—it makes it a lot harder to attack him or stick labels on him."

Victor turned his attention to Clinton. "President Clinton, you have not expressed your views. Will you share with us what you are thinking?"

"I will, of course, be happy to share with you. I like your idea, Victor; I've known Jeremy for many years and I think there is tremendous merit to his candidacy. However you have to want to be President, and I've still not detected any sense of Jeremy's openness to this idea. Have you recovered, Mr. Lerner? Can you inform us at all as to your thinking?"

Jeremy couldn't decide whether Clinton was mocking him because he wasn't looking very presidential, or was in fact trying to demonstrate to the Senators that he *wasn't* presidential. He considered briefly demanding his forty thousand dollars right then and there, but decided that might not look presidential either. "My thinking is that I'm astonished and flattered. Breathless, really. Surely I'm not obligated to make a decision after only five minutes with the idea."

"If this is really the first time you're hearing of this, I don't think a final decision *is* possible right now," Clinton said. "The short-term question you need to answer is, can the process move forward while you're thinking it out?"

"The process consisting of vetting, I assume . . . and what else?"

Carla Sanders laughed. "Believe me, brother, the vetting is enough for now. By the time you're done with that you may change your mind altogether."

"I concur with you, Mr. President," Liman added. "Jeremy, you need to spend some time with this on your own, talk to your family, etc."

"If you'd find it helpful I'd be happy to talk to you as well." Clinton now sounded very genuine. "I owe you a check, anyhow."

"I may take you up on it," Jeremy said. "You're here in the Hyatt?"

"No, I'm across the street. You have my office number, they'll put you through. But in the meantime, you do have to decide now if you're open to the possibility, otherwise there's no point."

"I'll consider it. I'm open to the next step. Victor, if I went for this, you're okay with me leaving you stranded there in Bulgaria?"

"As far as I'm concerned," Victor replied immediately, "getting you elected President is my fastest route home."

*   *   *   *   *

The meeting with Victor and the Senators ended a little after 10am. As usual Jeremy had a full schedule, which he cancelled outright. When his attending EA asked what he should say if people asked what had happened, Jeremy told him to make something up and waved him away. He looked at his watch. This was prime time for Evelyn; she was off on various 28th Amendment missions, and he knew they weren't due to connect again until dinner. That would not work. He called her private number, and she picked up.

"Hi! What's up, I'm between things."

"I have to see you. Before tonight, I mean. I have to talk to you for a few minutes."

"When?" she asked.

"As soon as you can. It's important; you'll understand when we meet."

"Are you okay?"

"I'm fine. I am. Can you head up to the room now?"

"No, not this minute. Let me do my next thing, and then I'll rearrange the one after that. So let's say forty-five minutes . . . no, an hour. I'll meet you up at the room in an hour. Is that okay?"

"Thanks. That's fine. I'll see you up there."

"Can we talk about it on the phone?"

"No. You'll understand. I'll see you. *Ciao.*"

*   *   *   *   *

When Jeremy arrived at the suite, he found Evelyn sitting up in an armchair with her shoeless feet resting on a low table. She signaled that she was on the phone, so Jeremy took off his jacket, slipped out of his loafers and retrieved two bottles of water from the kitchenette.

She folded up her phone as he returned, and drilled him with a "trying to read your mind" stare. "What's the story?"

"I wanted to talk about last night."

"Okay, what about it?"

"I mean about the marriage thing."

"Okay."

"With clarity of hindsight it seems like a juvenile stunt. I think I saw it in a movie once, with Jeff Bridges. *Winter Kills*, it was called."

"Mr. Efficiency, I have to get back to work. Do you have something you want to say, or ask?"

Jeremy paused to compose himself. "It's just that it was very spontaneous, and of course your answer had to be spontaneous, and somehow that seems to undercut its validity."

Evelyn opened her water bottled and drank. "Look at it this way," she said. "You were letting go. If it was really that spontaneous, that somehow to me seems *more* genuine. If you are having second thoughts, why don't you just say so?"

"I'm not having second thoughts, but you may want to reconsider after I tell you what happened to me this morning."

"I don't want to re-consider, but what happened?"

"Victor has launched a campaign to get me to run for President. I could end up being nominated as a native son of Alabama."

". . . ."

"That was my reaction precisely," Jeremy said. "Listen to this, it turns out Victor has been planning this for *months*. He even had a video endorsement of me all prepared—a five minute infomercial that I knew nothing about!"

"You had no idea? Not even a hint of it?"

"No, nothing. Nada. Zippo. The whole meeting was a set-up, the whole thing! He had me pick the Senators who would attend—he asked me to invite Senators whose judgment *I* would respect! I hadn't a clue that he could be so sneaky, and so well organized about it."

"Well, we know where he got *that* from."

"Right. The old 'teacher overtaken by pupil' routine."

"So where does it stand? The nomination, I mean. What does it depend on?"

"Well, I haven't given them an answer yet. I agreed to consider it, which includes talking to you. I'm going to speak with my sons. Clinton invited me to talk with him . . . and acknowledged that he owes me a check, so now I guess I *have* to go talk to him. There is also the vetting. I'll spend most of the rest of today being asked tons of questions by DNC lawyers. If it all goes well, and we agree on it, I will be put into nomination on the first ballot tomorrow night. It would be announced a few hours beforehand, I imagine."

"Who would your running-mate be?"

"We haven't gotten that far yet. I haven't given it a moment's thought."

"Is there any way to know how you would poll against Grove?"

"Victor even had me polled! Can you believe that? Remember when I did those Sunday morning news shows in November, when the Trask Committee was announced?"

Evelyn nodded. "You were in fine form, I thought."

"Well, too fine, apparently. Anyhow, it was a set-up. Victor had asked me to do two programs, in addition to the one that he was doing, just so he could have me polled! He used our top-secret pollster, the polling operation I put together for him, to poll *me*."

Evelyn re-opened her bottle of water, took another drink, and re-screwed the cap on, watching Jeremy the entire time.

"What are you thinking?" Jeremy asked.

Evelyn continued her silent stare, but Jeremy then realized she wasn't really looking at him, but just cogitating in his direction. He opened his own bottle of water and took a drink.

"Jeremy," Evelyn said, "I really know next to nothing about presidential politics, but the little I know leads me to understand what Victor's reasoning is. You're Jewish, you could easily win Florida; you're from the South, you could probably win your home state; you don't have a lot of political baggage; you're *extremely* handsome and personable."

"Don't flatter me now, this is serious."

"I *am* serious, and what's more important, Victor Glade is serious. Think about this. Having his backing is a huge advantage, and you're a viable candidate in your own right."

"I have zero electoral experience. No track record whatsoever."

"That's part of what makes you such a smart pick. You have no Congressional voting record, no pre-defined position on anything, you're a total outsider—these are plusses, not minuses."

"I take it from your reaction that you're not opposed to this. Remember we're planning to get married, right? None of this was in the equation last night—you're sure you want to take all this on?"

"Are you kidding? This is like fairy tale stuff—I'm excited beyond belief. You could do great things for this country, and I might add selfishly, for the 28th Amendment. I think we cut a fine figure together as a political couple."

"Evelyn," Jeremy's tone suggested a change of direction, "do you find it the least bit odd that your fiancé of twelve hours is suddenly about to run for President?"

"What do you mean *odd*? The whole thing is totally fantastical!"

"My point precisely. To me this has the feel of one of my coincidence events."

"What do you mean? Where is the coincidence?"

"I can't say I know yet. But it's here, I feel it. I've encountered this often enough to recognize it. Which reminds me, that's another reason why you might want to reconsider getting married."

"What, because of your coincidence condition, or whatever you call it?"

Jeremy nodded. "Amitai called it a *probability vortex*."

Evelyn was effusive. "Hey, my attitude is, I'll never get another opportunity like this with anyone else. So if there's a chance—any chance at all—that I could get sucked into a probability vortex with you, please, *please* don't leave me behind."

*   *   *   *   *

At 5am the following morning Jeremy slowly opened the door to the bedroom in their hotel suite, where Evelyn was fast asleep. He had last spoken to her three hours earlier, after finishing with the vetting lawyers, and at that point she had just turned off the light. Since then he had been in conference with the DNC's executive committee, reviewing potential Vice Presidential nominees.

As the day had progressed he became more and more comfortable with the idea of running. Victor had called him again, urging him to take up the mantle, as he put it, and reassured Jeremy of his support. "I am counting on you to win. This Bulgaria thing is losing its charm fast."

He also spoke privately with Liman, who was very persuasive. Both of his sons had responded enthusiastically, his fiancée was on board, and his confidence soared after his meeting with President Clinton. Not only was he becoming accustomed to the idea of running, he was becoming convinced that he could actually win.

He stared at Evelyn as he shed his clothes, and then decided to shower and shave first. When he was done he slid into bed wearing boxers and snuggled up against her back. She stirred slightly.

He whispered into her ear, "I'm ready now, are you?"

"Huh? What? Hi!" She turned around to face him and they embraced. She kissed his chest. "I love your hairy chest, but I'm in no shape to make love. I'm dead tired."

"That's okay. I'm exhausted too, but I needed to wake you up and thought I would see what your limits are."

"Very cute. Why do you need to wake me?" She seemed satisfied as long as she could keep her eyes closed.

"Are you awake?" he asked.

"Yes, yes, I'm awake." She ran her hand again over his chest to prove it.

"Okay. You said you were game to get sucked into a probability vortex with me, and the opportunity has arrived. The coincidence has now fully manifested itself, and its power and beauty and *symmetry* are revealed for all to see."

"Wonderful. What is it then?" she nuzzled some more and smiled, keeping her eyes closed, feeling very cozy and content.

"You're going to be nominated as Vice President. The Party wants you to be my running mate."

*   *   *   *   *

Two minutes after he concluded his acceptance speech, Jeremy held up both arms trying to quell the cacophony, signaling to the crowd that he wanted to continue. This had no effect whatsoever, so he waved Carla Sanders over and shouted to her for help. The message went out on the dozen or so scoreboard-size Teleprompters that hung from the ceiling of the arena, and in another minute he tried with the crowd again and it finally began to subside.

Jeremy looked down at Evelyn and then grasped her around the shoulder. "This is your last chance to say no!" He still had to raise his voice for her to hear him.

"If I'm gonna blow you in the Oval Office, we had better be married!" she shouted back.

Jeremy staggered backwards and almost careened off the podium. A Secret Service agent reached up to help balance him. "It's a good thing the microphone isn't on," he chastised her seriously.

The crowd had now quieted down, and the floor manager signaled to Jeremy that the mike was live.

"Thank you, thank you, delegates, for your cooperation. I have only a few more words to add." Pause. "You may have noticed that the traditional order of content for acceptance speeches is being reversed today." Jeremy had now regained the crowd's attention. "Usually the candidate talks first about his—or her—" he smiled at Evelyn— "personal journey, the unique set of circumstances that led to the privilege of this moment. Then comes the part about the candidate's vision and ideas.

"I have shared with you already some of my plans and goals for the next four years. I saved the 'personal journey' part for last, because in my case it actually calls for a celebration, and I didn't want that to distract from our message and our mission, which are of paramount importance, and which have now—hopefully—been clearly defined for you, and for the citizens of this great Nation, and indeed for all citizens of the world.

"I have been described to you by my long-time friend and employer Victor Glade as an 'organizational genius.' Senator Arnall's generous introduction referred to me as a master of mediation and compromise. But anyone who has worked with me, or knows me at all, will tell you that above all I am obsessed with efficiency. It is second nature to me: every minute of every day I am looking for ways to do things better, faster, smarter.

"When, with your help and support, I am elected President, you can be sure that I will from day one find ways to make our government run more efficiently. The very first thing I plan to do, which will save the taxpayers a cool eighty million dollars or more over four years, is to abolish the office of the First Lady.

"'Hah!' you may say. 'Some genius he is! He's not married, so of course he doesn't need an Office of the First Lady.' But that's actually not the case. While I'm not married now, I am *engaged* to be married, and I *will* be married by the time I get to the White House. So how am I going to be married, in the White House, without having an office for the First Lady?

"The answer is both efficient, and simple," he announced, pulling Evelyn close to him and lifting her up on her toes. "I plan to marry the Vice President!" He then kissed her on the lips in a long, sweet embrace.

And the crowd went wild.

<table>
<tr>
<td>**20**</td>
<td>September, 2020
Lerner / Vaughn Campaign</td>
</tr>
</table>

Like many of his card-playing friends, Jeremy thought of bridge as an addiction—at the very least a chronic compulsion. It was the one thing he could do to relax completely, to be free of all external pressures. So when his Campaign Manager, Julie Sokolov, took him aside after a staff meeting one Saturday morning and privately urged him to quit playing bridge altogether—*cold turkey*—for the duration of the Campaign, he was horrified.

"Please tell me you're joking," Jeremy pleaded. "How could it possibly matter what I do in my free time? Presidents play golf, Presidents jog, Presidents go to the movies—why the hell can't I just unwind the way I unwind?"

"This is not about your choice of activities," she said. Julie was of tallish, olive-skinned Mediterranean stock, with dark eyes, strong opinions, and a deceptively soft voice. At forty-two she was relatively young for her trade, but still a battle-tested veteran who was not prone to making frivolous requests. "The problem is the singleton king of spades thing, and the attention it attracts."

It was true that since Jeremy and Amitai had abandoned the remote dealing experiment in February, the singleton king had returned with a vengeance—appearing on an average about every thirty deals.

"This is an old story," Jeremy replied. "It's been out there in the public for fifteen years. Why is this suddenly a problem?"

"It's a problem," Julie replied, "because it could draw attention to your wider coincidence condition, which is something the opposition would latch onto in a second and *really* make hay out of."

"How on Earth will anyone find out about my coincidence condition?" Jeremy asked.

Julie paused, staring him down with a "you're serious?" look. "Jeremy, you've run a private blog about this for years. It's been seen by unknown dozens of friends and acquaintances—never with any expectation of confidentiality. If I understand it correctly, at one point you had an Israeli scientist working full-time trying to analyze your coincidence condition, and according to Charles his tablet was lost during the attack in Washington, so all of his research about you is floating around out there somewhere. You've had newspaper articles written about the king of spades thing, you've made *speeches*, for Pete's sake, where you've referred to your attraction to coincidence."

"And you think my playing a few bridge hands will lead people to this?"

"Hey, if you could play without the singleton king of spades following you around like a shadow, we wouldn't be having this conversation. But as it is, almost every time you play you draw attention to a phenomenon that is really just the tip of a giant iceberg. That's a bad analogy; it's more like a Pandora's Box. It's really both . . . it's a Pandora's Iceberg. It could sink our whole merry ship here."

Jeremy was sullen. "Your attempts at humor don't make me feel any better about it. Bridge is what I do to relax, you know. It's how I let go."

"Jeremy, we have done *so well* up to this point," Julie said. "If we just maintain the status quo we're winners, so all I'm trying to do is keep an eye on things that could derail us. Your coincidence condition, your probability vortex—whatever you call it—is way, way up there on the list. We should be doing everything possible to minimize this risk, and the king of spades business leads right to it."

Jeremy recognized that she was right, and a compromise was reached. He agreed to play no more bridge in public or even in person, and she agreed he could play on-line, at night, under a confidential, top-secret alias. It was to be put on his schedule as "reading time," and there was to be absolutely no record kept of his games or his singleton kings or anything else. Officially he was taking a hiatus from bridge for the duration of the campaign, and hoped to be able to return to it in the future.

There was, Jeremy agreed with Julie, far too much at stake. With seven weeks to go before the election, most polls showed the Lerner/Vaughn ticket had retained the nine percentage point bump that came after the August convention, and in many areas they had now even improved on that. Nationwide polls for raw vote showed them with a 55/41 advantage over Grove. Even the Electoral College map, by lesser margins, looked promising.

This favorable position Jeremy attributed in some considerable measure to Victor Glade's ongoing support. As soon as Jeremy won the nomination, Victor called from Bulgaria to congratulate him and to offer his help, which—since Victor had put him up to the whole thing anyhow—Jeremy wasn't shy about accepting. He immediately hired several key people from his former *Oval Office* staff to join him on the Campaign, which allowed them to come up to speed quickly with personnel who already knew each other. He also hired three *Oval Office* script consultants to fill key policy advisory posts in the Campaign.

From his studios in Bulgaria, Victor produced a series of video ads endorsing Jeremy, using a dismantled *Oval Office* set as a backdrop. Victor also provided the campaign with access to *The Oval Office*'s substantial archive of issues research and analysis, which enabled them to release from very early on a continuous stream of policy papers and legislative proposals on subjects ranging from animal rights to Zimbabwe.

Comparisons between the Lerner/Vaughn platform and the policies of *The Oval Office*'s Bosco Administration became a constant refrain in the press. The most transparent and certainly most controversial embrace of an *Oval Office* policy was Jeremy's proposed Marijuana Reform and Tax Act, which under a slightly different name had already become law in the fictional world of *The Oval Office* way back in 2016 (presumably engineered so that Victor could feel better about his regular late-night indulgence). And, as predicted on *The Oval Office*, it had little net effect on Jeremy's standing when he announced it. They were able to counter the predicted moral outrage on the right by emphasizing the fifty-three billion dollars in new tax revenue *in the very first year* that would be coming directly out of the pockets of drug dealers.

His proposal to phase-out, by attrition, teacher tenure in public schools was met with rabid denunciations by teachers' unions, but after the dust had settled there was no net erosion of support—any loss that accrued on the left was balanced, apparently, by support from the right. Also borrowed from a recent episode of *The Oval Office*: a proposed budget of $22.5 billion to start a drastic controlled reduction in the number of nuclear armaments extant in the world. This amount was chosen to stand in direct contrast to Grove's most recent defense budget, which requested $22.5 billion to develop small "designer" nuclear warheads whose charges could be shaped and customized for specific targets. Jeremy's support among the military, already respectable for a Democrat, actually increased when he announced his nuclear weapons policy.

Grove at one point tried to make the obvious connection between Jeremy's campaign and *The Oval Office* into an issue, by questioning who his opponent really was—Jeremy Lerner or Victor Glade. He suggested that if Lerner was elected, Glade would actually be in charge, and the government would be "in the hands of an indicted Hollywood mogul." This played well in Grove's own camp and in the press for a short while, but didn't resonate with undecided voters or the general public. Jeremy acknowledged repeatedly that Victor and *The Oval Office* were important influences on his campaign. He described Victor as a key advisor and contributor, and vowed that his very first act as President would be to rescind the outstanding indictment against Victor and bring him—and *The Oval Office*—back home to Los Angeles.

The fortunes of the 28th Amendment rose along with those of the Democrats. In keeping with the spirit of the broader coincidence, Jeremy and Evelyn had decided soon after the convention to marry the 28th Amendment to their presidential campaign. They referred to the Amendment in every stump speech, in every media appearance, and at every town meeting. They envisioned politics as a marketplace of ideas instead of a marketplace of purchased influence, and claimed the Amendment would "restore American democracy to our Founding Fathers' vision." Evelyn retained her position as head of the 28th Amendment PAC, and accepted checks for both organizations at all fundraising events. If the polls held up in seven particular Senate and House races, the upcoming Congress would almost certainly pass the Amendment and send it to the States for ratification.

In public, Jeremy encouraged and celebrated the optimism that prevailed in his camp, but privately, among his inner circle, the take was completely different. Everyone agreed that it could not possibly be over: Grove and especially his crazed puppeteer, Morley James, would not go down this easily.

<table>
<tr><td rowspan="3" style="font-size:large">**21**</td><td>October 1, 2020</td></tr>
<tr><td>Lerner / Vaughn Campaign</td></tr>
<tr><td>Reform, Alabama</td></tr>
</table>

One of the few campaign stops on his schedule that Jeremy looked forward to was a trip on October 1st to his hometown of Reform, which he had not visited in over forty years. Evelyn, who ordinarily had a completely separate campaign itinerary, also had planned to join him for this one stop. She had never been to Alabama or anywhere in the Deep South other than Atlanta, and was baffled at how Jeremy could have emerged, walking upright, from America's closest thing to a primordial swamp. (Much to Jeremy's dismay Evelyn, like many non-Southerners, harbored lurid notions of the South, the way Europeans think of Transylvania.)

However, in terms of campaign manpower, it certainly wasn't *efficient* to have them both booked into a town of a thousand people in a state that had eight electoral votes and was already in their win column, so Evelyn was the first person everyone thought of when a valuable opportunity arose in Tampa to speak at a huge realtors' convention. She diverted to Florida, while Jeremy's campaign plane flew into Northport, outside of Tuscaloosa. From there it was a half-hour motorcade to a Poultry Feed Co-Operative on Main Street in Reform, where Jeremy delivered a stump speech about his proposed Sustainable Agriculture Initiative and received a raucous, whistling welcome from a crowd of about five thousand, which was greater than the population of the entire county.

He then had lunch with the mayor of Reform, Erwin Wade Jr., whose father, Erwin Sr., had been a friend and fishing buddy of Jeremy's father. The restaurant, Jeremy remembered, was a local institution whose claim to fame was that Elvis Presley, passing through on a bus in 1958, had signed the wall next to the cash register. Jeremy asked about it, and there it still was, faded but timeless behind a protective sheet of glass. Also invited to the luncheon were his high school classmates, only a handful of whom Jeremy remembered. His best friend from high school, Tim Moore, had been killed in the second Iraq war in 2005, and Jeremy spent a few private moments with his younger siblings reminiscing about their brother. For hours afterward, Tim continued to pop into his mind. What a waste, he kept repeating to himself, *what a fucking waste!*

After lunch they were scheduled to return to their plane, but at the last moment an advance team reported that Jeremy would be welcome to visit his old home off of County Route 25. The current occupant was a seventy-two-year-old retired teacher who was a staunch Republican and Grove supporter, but also a gentleman who insisted that Jeremy would be made most welcome. He had visiting with him from out of town an older brother, in failing health, for whom the visit might provide some welcome diversion.

So with Mayor Wade and a few of his classmates in tow, Jeremy boarded a pared-down six-car motorcade that included a single press pool van, and made the ten mile trek northward to his original spawning grounds, like a salmon battling upstream.

When they arrived, Jeremy's first impression was that the landscaping had been altered. What he had remembered as a steep hill behind their house now seemed like a slope, and the driveway leading to the County Road was a short stroll from the house; he remembered it as a hike that you had to leave time for if you didn't want to miss the school bus. The house itself, from the outside at least, looked far bigger than he remembered it.

Jeremy was introduced to Albert Gordon, a cheerful, seemingly under-nourished retired history teacher, who had owned the house for the past twelve years, and his wheelchair-bound older brother George, who was frail but obviously brimming with excitement. Albert led him on a tour of the house, the layout of which seemed completely different than what he remembered, and then invited him to join them on their screen porch for "some home-made lemonade or some store-bought iced tea."

There had never been a screen porch when Jeremy lived there, and he began to wonder if they might somehow have come up with the wrong house. He started to say something to the advance manager when he realized that the view from the porch, where he was now being invited to sit, was the view from his bedroom window as a child—and then he got it: the whole house had been reconfigured, added onto significantly in the back, and the area that had been his bedroom was now a screened-in patio.

"I would love to join you out here for a few minutes," Jeremy said. "This is the view I remember as a child. This was my view of the outside world," the distance perspective of which now seemed more in line with what he recollected.

It was warm and muggy, but at 2pm the sun was high enough overhead that no direct sunlight was streaming in. After drinks had been served, Jeremy ignored his press aide's advice and brought up the election and politics. "I understand from our advance team that you're a life-long Republican, Mr. Gordon."

Jeremy's thinking was: this was a Southern gentleman who would never dream of making a hostile comment to a guest in his own home, and he might even be capable of engaging in the kind of "civil discourse" that Jeremy had been insisting publicly was still possible.

"That's right sir, I have been, and despite your personal visit, I'm afraid I will continue to be. But you're still welcome in my home, sir."

"You have been very welcoming, Mr. Gordon—I certainly didn't mean to imply otherwise. It's very generous of you to open your home up to this big to-do, especially since you know our political views are different, and as you know, I'm out here campaigning. The reason I wanted to ask you about politics was to see if there are any issues that we *do* agree on. I'm not asking you to vote for me, I'm just curious to know if we have any things in common."

"I can't say I know everything about your platform. I suspect we probably do agree on *some* things, but not the things that are important to me," replied Albert.

Jeremy turned to the older brother, who was alert and listening to every word. "Your politics lean toward your brother's?" he asked, wanting to include him in the conversation.

"For the most part," George replied in a quiet but steady voice. "But there is one thing I read about that I think is a good idea—one of your ideas, that is, if I've got it right."

"What's that?" Jeremy asked.

"Your idea of giving the army and the armed forces a second mission, to help people that have come upon natural disasters." He was referring to the defense doctrine Jeremy's campaign had packaged under the tag line "Every Mission Accomplished." The idea was that America could best ensure its homeland security by proactively making friends around the globe, rather than making enemies by staging unilateral interventions in countries that don't meet its standards-du-jour for democracy and human rights. The US would dispatch its armed forces quickly, immediately, to countries that had suffered from natural disasters like earthquakes and floods, where the mission would be limited and defined: search and rescue, provide emergency medical and temporary logistical support, and leave. Each mission would be a guaranteed success.

"Albert," George asked his brother, trying to speak more loudly but not succeeding, "do you not think that's a good idea?"

"I'm not sure," Albert replied. "Maybe it is, maybe not. It seems to me we've got plenty to keep our armed forces occupied with nowadays, without giving them more to do."

"Well I was an army pilot for many years, Mr. Lerner," George said, struggling to add some emotion to his voice, "and I know from experience, when you rescue someone who's in dire trouble, either because of war or flood or whatever it is that threatens them—when you save someone like that, they become your friend for life. They never forget, and they always tell other people what you did for them."

"You flew helicopters?" Jeremy asked.

"Mostly in Nam. Did three tours there, first with Chinooks, then with Hueys. I left the service in '78 though, and quit flying. I got married when I got out, and it made my wife too jittery, rest her soul. So I became an aircraft mechanic."

"Did you ever do any flying stateside?"

"Oh, hell yeah. When I was stationed at Ft. Benning, we'd get called all the time to do civilian rescues, in floods and things like that. When Hurricane Betsy hit New Orleans, that was back in '63 before the war, I spent a week of twenty-hour days out there. Never been so tired in my whole damn life. Almost *lost* my life out there too, I had a real close call. Whew, I don't even wanna *think* about that again."

"Do you by any chance remember flying troops to Oxford, Mississippi in 1962?"

"I sure do, I must've made that trip a dozen times back and forth. I was co-piloting on those flights, those was twin rotor-craft that I was still new to."

Here it was. Jeremy had felt it coming as soon as he learned that George had been an army pilot; now he was sure. He was entering a coincidence event—a *probability vortex* What was today? Today was October 1st—naturally! The day Kennedy announced he was sending troops to Oxford was *October 1, 1962*. Jeremy knew that date because he had researched it for his coincidence blog, the very first entry of which was his tale of troop helicopters landing across the road from his home. He and George Gordon were old friends! They had met at this exact location *fifty-eight years ago to the day.*

"This may sound like a strange question," Jeremy asked, just to confirm, but he already knew the answer. "When you were making these flights to Oxford, did you ever land the helicopters to let the soldiers out for a break? You know, to take a leak and walk around?"

"Whoa! On civilian property? We wasn't supposed to, absolutely not! But it's funny you say that, because the first day out to Oxford we had to do that. The BC, the Battalion Chief, ordered us down."

"You remember that specific event?"

"I sure do, that was not something you was ever supposed to do. How could I forget?"

"Why did you get ordered down?" Jeremy asked.

"We—the pilot and me—we was just followin' orders, but I remember what happened. It was a typical Army thing, where they had loaded us up to the gills—full combat gear, ready to go with jeeps, the whole works, double-time, and then they held us on the tarmac for two hours for some reason or other. It was hot as blazes, the troops were cooking in their gear, and they started drinking from their canteens. So finally we take off, and half an hour later the BC's telling us we have to find a place to stop. He was not gonna land a bunch of troops who had to pee in the middle of a race riot. So we found an empty field and landed. But we couldn't have been down for more than . . ." George stopped himself and gave Jeremy a blank look, which Jeremy soon understood to be quizzical. "Why are you asking about this? Did you see us land?"

"Mr. Gordon, you see those fence posts on the far side of the highway, and the field beyond?" Jeremy pointed.

"Yep. I see." His brother adjusted the wheelchair to give him a better view.

"Well you landed in the pasture across the road there exactly 58 years ago *to the day*. As I recall there were seven or eight helicopters. You were flying twin-rotor helicopters, right?"

"That sounds about right."

"It was on a Monday morning?"

"Sounds about right."

"Well, I watched that whole thing unfold from the very room we are sitting in right now, except that this used to be my bedroom, and that," he pointed to an east-facing screen, "was where my window was."

"Whoa!" Albert whistled, and George looked like he was trying to catch his breath. Jeremy also sat for a moment to take it all in.

"How is it that you come to remember all this stuff about that particular morning?" Albert asked.

"Oh!" Jeremy laughed, "For me it was the strangest thing in the world. Remember, I was nine years old. These huge helicopters land across the road from my house. The racket they made was something I couldn't ever describe, and I had never seen a live soldier before in my life. It was the most unbelievable thing, and then they all started to pee in the field. Nobody believed me when I told them! I am finally vindicated!" Jeremy wanted to slap George on the shoulder, or high-five him, but fortunately restrained himself.

Charles stepped into the porch area to signal Jeremy. Even though he was under Secret Service protection, Jeremy still left all security matters to Charles, and Charles dealt with the Secret Service Agent-in-Charge. Jeremy excused himself from the porch for a moment and joined Charles in the hallway.

"I thought you would want to know about this," Charles said quietly. "I just received a secure call from Szulkin, saying it was urgent that I check for an e-mail message from Tzvi. I did, and here it is." He handed Jeremy a small portable tablet.

> *The amount of the loan was $5,000. Event imminent.*
> *Advise take precautions. Cannot provide further info.*
> *Alpha03*

Jeremy's heart jump-started. "This just came in? Just now?"

"About five minutes ago. I got it to you right away."

"Fuck! What is going on here?!"

"Sir, please tell me what you mean, so that I can work with you on this."

"I'm in the middle of one of my coincidence events. The brother in the wheelchair—he and I met here fifty-eight years ago today. He landed an army helicopter in the field across the road, and I watched him from the house here. I was nine years old."

"I don't know what to make out of that, sir, but might I suggest in the meantime that we leave the area immediately?"

"Yes, absolutely, get it rolling. I'll spend another couple of minutes with the Gordons—it will take you that long to get everything else in place." Before he had finished, Charles was talking hurriedly into his lapel.

Jeremy returned to the porch where the Gordon brothers were still discussing the multiple dimensions of the coincidence. "Life is so funny," Jeremy said. "Whenever I ask people if they have ever encountered this kind of incredible coincidence, almost everyone has at least one story." George mentioned a chance meeting with an ex-Army buddy on a cruise ship in the Caribbean, and Jeremy was pleased to see the older man enjoy the recollection.

Charles returned to his side and interrupted cheerfully. "Thank you so much for your fine hospitality." He smiled, bowed slightly, and then quickly hustled Jeremy out the door.

Charles walked him quickly down the driveway. "It looks like the 'imminent event' might already have happened," he said. "A nuclear explosion has been reported just outside New York Harbor."

Jeremy stopped walking. "You're sure about this?"

Charles coaxed him to keep moving. "It's been confirmed. It apparently was small, relatively speaking, and it was several miles to the south of New York City, on a ship headed for Perth Amboy, New Jersey. It happened about ten minutes ago."

As they reached his car, the Secret Service Agent-in-Charge came loping up to them. "You have heard the news, I presume."

"About the explosion?" Charles asked.

"Right. There's been a nuclear detonation in New York Harbor."

"My understanding is that it was short of the harbor, south of the City," Jeremy said.

"Close enough for us to classify it as a domestic nuclear incident. The President is in the air, and our orders are to get you to a nuclear safe site as soon as possible."

"Where is the closest site?" Jeremy asked.

"Ft. Benning, Georgia, outside of Columbus. It's about a half-hour by helicopter from here."

"Let me guess," Jeremy said. "A helicopter is already on its way, and it's going to land in that field over there." He pointed across the road.

"That's exactly right," the Agent replied, removing his aviator glasses to display how impressed he was. "It's due to touch down in about twenty minutes—they have our coordinates. We're to stay put here for now."

"Thank you, Agent . . . ?" Jeremy said.

"Carter, sir. Hal Carter."

"Thank you, Agent Carter. My oldest son is in New York City. I'll try to contact him while we wait."

"I doubt you'll get through. The pulse from the explosion took out a lot of communications, and the networks are overloaded. If you'd like I can have agents in New York City check on him—but I'm sure he's okay. Apparently no one in the City has been directly affected."

"Thanks. I'll try myself first and then let you know. Charles, would you please join me in the car for a minute or two?" An agent standing by the car opened the door for them and they both got in. Charles sat opposite him on the back-facing seat.

"Charles, just sit with me for a minute please while I think this out. Something is happening here and I need to be very careful." Charles nodded and Jeremy went into a trance of concentration, as though he was about to play a bridge hand. His eyes were slightly open but he wasn't seeing anything specific.

Stay loose and concentrate. What information do I have, and is there any line of play that might help me learn what I don't know? What was the "imminent event" that Tzvi was referring to? It couldn't be the nuclear detonation outside of New York. His message had been specific— "Advise take precautions." Why would he tell me to take precautions for an event that was a thousand miles away? Tzvi had to know that I am not in the New York area—he has easy access to that kind of information. But if the nuclear explosion in New York was not it, what was the imminent event? It was something that would threaten me personally, here where I am now. Where am I? I'm campaigning in my hometown in Reform, Alabama, and I was in the middle of a probability event that was tied to this location and time—to helicopters landing in that field. That was it! The incoming helicopter had to be the imminent event. That had to be it!

He thought it through for another few moments . . . what if he was wrong? Was there a safe play? Jeremy opened his eyes. "Charles, what happens if I say no to the helicopter? What if we tell Carter that I don't want to go to a nuclear safe facility?"

"In theory he shouldn't overrule you. But if your life is in immediate danger he's authorized to take any and all action necessary to protect you—with or without your consent."

"My life is not in immediate danger."

"No, but if the Agent-in-Charge decided it was, he could act unilaterally."

Jeremy thought for a moment. "Let's assume that Agent Carter—who seems reasonable enough—doesn't go overboard about this. I tell him I don't want to take the helicopter, and I don't want to hole up in a nuclear safe facility. What happens?"

"He'll report that you refused recommended protection, and keep doing his job."

"Make it so," Jeremy said to Charles. "Find Carter and decline the helicopter. And ask him to recall it so that it doesn't land here. If he can't do that, somebody's got to go back to the Gordon brothers and explain to them why a helicopter may be landing yet again in their front lawn—once every fifty-eight years—whether they want it to or not."

"You're sure about this?" Charles asked.

"I'm positive. I'll explain it to you, but first let Carter know right away. Then when you come back, bring Mayor Wade with you— the tall gentleman with the boots and the tie. Ask him if he would join us back here in the car for a minute. It will answer a lot of your questions."

A minute later Charles returned with the Mayor and they clambered in, sitting on the banquette opposite Jeremy. "Erwin," Jeremy said, "thank you for joining us, I won't keep you but a minute."

"If thar's any way I can render assistance, I want to hear it. Is everything okay?"

"Everything's fine," Jeremy said. "Please bear with me for one moment," and he turned to Charles. "What was Carter's reaction? Any problem there?"

"No, he just asked if we were sure. He's calling off the chopper, and waiting for a signal from us. Seems fine with it."

"Well, that's a relief. Whew." Jeremy took a deep breath. "Good. Okay. Next step. Mayor Wade, we are going to be heading out in a few minutes, but before we do I wanted to ask you for a favor."

"I'm eager to help if I possibly can."

"Would it be possible for your own police—local or county, don't say anything to the Feds—to quietly stake out the area around this house as soon as possible? Let's say within a one mile radius of here, for up to three hours after we've left?"

"What are we looking for?"

"Men with high-powered rifles or RPG's who might be waiting to bring down a helicopter taking off from *that* field." Jeremy pointed across the highway.

"That sounds to me like the kind of thing our police would take an interest in. You don't want the Secret Service to know about this?"

"No I don't, and I'll tell you why. I'm far from sure that there's anyone out there. I'm working on a hunch, and I don't want to go crying wolf to the Secret Service, if you know what I mean."

Wade nodded thoughtfully.

"Also, if by chance I'm right, could you, or your Sheriff, or someone else locally, take credit for anything you come up with? It's important that the lead not be attributed to me or my campaign. It was part of a routine patrol, or whatever."

"No problem. Mr. Lerner, I must say you have brought more excitement to this town in one day than it's had altogether since the Civil War. It will be an honor to assist you however we can."

"Mayor, I can't thank you enough." Jeremy pumped the Mayor's hand in thanks. "Please be as discreet as possible—you can do this outside of open frequencies? Do you have any unmarked vehicles?" Jeremy pulled the latch on his door and an agent finished opening it from the outside.

"Mr. Lerner, your mission is safe with me." Wade stepped out of the car. "I was the County Sheriff up until two years ago. I know exactly how we're going to go about it."

"Thanks." Jeremy saluted him.

When the Mayor had left and the door was closed again, Charles looked wide-eyed at Jeremy. "I'm not sure I'm following. You think there might be an ambush set up for the helicopter that was ordered?"

"I don't believe the explosion in New York is the imminent threat that Tzvi is warning us about. His message advised me to take precautions, so it has to be referring to something that's threatening me here, where I am now. He knows where I am, he has to know that. And where am I now? I'm in the middle of a coincidence event that's tied to helicopters landing on this property."

"Got it. I see. I think." Charles continued to try and process it.

"Look at it two ways," Jeremy explained. "Either the event in Tzvi's message refers to the attack in New York, in which case it's too late and is a thousand miles away anyhow, or it's referring to some other event that is *still* imminent, and still a threat. I'm betting that the helicopter that was dispatched for me is the key to the threat. That fits neatly within the coincidence pattern that I'm used to. Take my word for it."

"Okay. I understand. And you've dispatched the local police to see if anyone is staking out this area, maybe with the intention of firing on it after it picks you up."

"*Voilà! Exactement.* "

"There's only one problem," Charles said.

" . . . ?"

"Your theory assumes that gunmen were positioned here in advance. That could happen only if the person who sent them here knew in advance that a helicopter would be arriving for them to shoot down. *Ergo, that* person would have to have known in advance about the nuclear detonation in New York, because that is what is triggering the helicopter."

"You are correct on all assumptions. What's the problem?"

"If you assume that Grove—or his people—are behind an assassination plot here, you're also assuming they knew about the nuclear bomb in New York Harbor—or that they're responsible for that too?!"

"Charles, you read the same security briefings that I do. There are at least three *Oval Office* TAG scenarios that envision stealing or stopping the election by staging terrorist attacks and using those as an excuse to declare a National Security Emergency." TAG scenarios were reports issues by the Threat Analysis Group of *The Oval Office's* security department, which continued to make its information available to Jeremy's campaign.

"Yes, but I can't believe they would actually go this far. A nuclear bomb?"

"Charles, *our own people* have been saying there is a greater than fifty percent probability that they would try something like this within two weeks of the election if they were on a losing track."

"Okay, okay, assume that's the case. We've got to get back to here and now. Your idea is that someone knew that a helicopter would be coming here to ferry you out, and they've had gunmen positioned in this area, in advance, to try and bring it down."

"If they knew when the nuclear explosion was going to go off," Jeremy said, "they would know exactly when the helicopter would be requested."

"And if you happened to be assassinated at the same time that a nuclear terrorist attack was taking place elsewhere, the nation's attentions would be divided, to say the least."

"*Kon-nyeshsz-na.*"

Charles sat quietly, trying to comprehend it all. Jeremy let him think. "Okay," he finally said, "I get it. I see it. I'm not saying I believe this is what's happening, but I'm with you on the premise. So what's next? We're sitting ducks here in the middle of nowhere . . . we've gotta get out of here pronto."

"Okay, but we want to give Wade as much time as we can to put some men into place before we leave, so speak to Carter and buy us a couple of more minutes."

"Are you kidding? We want to be out of here immediately— like *right now!*"

"Why? What difference will a few minutes make?"

"Sir, you're thinking about an ambush of a helicopter that picks you up and leaves; I'm thinking of an ambush *by* a helicopter when it arrives. What if the chopper that was supposedly coming to pick you up instead attacked us?"

"Jesus, sorry, I didn't think of that. Okay, get us going. Make sure Wade can reach us directly if he needs to."

Charles punched open the door and immediately they both heard it: the unmistakable whop-whop of a helicopter in the distance. They looked at each other quickly, and then Charles leapt out. Jeremy got out and stood behind the open car door.

"Agent Carter!" Charles called out, and then added a piercing whistle. Carter walked up.

"There's a chopper coming in." Charles pointed at a distant speck in the eastern sky. "I thought the one we were expecting was recalled."

"As far as I know it was," Carter answered. "The Duty Officer acknowledged and said he would order it back. But this is a few minutes earlier than the one I was expecting anyhow."

Charles and Jeremy exchanged looks of disbelief.

"Hal," Charles said quickly but calmly, "you're saying you have no positive ID on this aircraft?"

"No, I don't. Why?"

"I urge you to consider it a possible threat. Please act now, I'll explain later."

Carter gazed at the slowly enlarging speck for a second, and then at Charles, straight in the eye. Then he stepped back and surveyed the array of cars and personnel—the Agents standing outside their cars waiting for departure instructions, the press van with its three doors still open, the Mayor walking back from the Gordon's house. The whop-whop was distant but noticeably louder.

"Okay, Charles, you seal yourself up in there with PC1, buckle up and everything. I'm not planning to move you right now, but be ready to go." As Charles got in, Jeremy heard Carter begin his commands. "All units, Local Red, I repeat, Local Red, no drill! Units three and four, deploy ADW stet, target is incoming chopper due East, fire on my command only. Units one and five . . ."

The door closed and the compartment hissed. Jeremy and Charles both scooted to the opposite side of the car, buckled themselves in facing each other, and got a dim but direct view of the proceedings through the dark glass. Two cars had maneuvered their way out of the line-up on the shoulder of the highway and sped toward town. Charles explained to Jeremy that it was probably a decoy to try and draw the chopper away. Trunks popped open and agents scrambled to remove shoulder-launched SAM's and activate them. Now the noise of the chopper could be heard through the limousine's soundproofing. The intercom clicked. "You're all tied in back there, gents? The car's already in gear—be ready to go."

"We're set," Charles replied, "thanks."

Three large bazooka-like weapons were now trained on the helicopter as it began its slow descent into the field across the road.

It was certainly making no threatening moves, and looked to have no armaments at all. Charles fumbled for his audio. "Carter, Witt here, do you see? This is State Police, this is not a chopper from Ft. Benning."

"So what does that mean?"

"Just sit tight. Maybe this isn't the threat I was thinking of. Let's see what happens."

Carter kept the weapons trained on it even after it had landed, and when the pilot's door opened, a hand emerged from the top waving a white handkerchief. The heavy weapons were lowered. Charles tried opening the door but it was still locked down. He pounded, and several moments later it decompressed and opened. Jeremy followed him out and immediately shaded his eyes with his hand to counteract the sudden increase in light. Through his simmering vision, he could see that the pilot of the helicopter had hopped out and was struggling with something on his belt. An agent lifted his rifle again to cover the suspicious moves, but finally all became clear: the pilot had now gotten the top of his pants open, his zipper down, and was pissing into the backwash.

To Charles this seemed quite reasonable. "Hey, if I was landing a chopper and suddenly saw three SAM's locked onto me, I would have peed instantly. This guy must have a sphincter of brass."

*   *   *   *   *

Forty-five minutes later they were back on the plane. Jeremy settled in a forward conference room and was alone, completely, for the first time in days. He closed his eyes and breathed deeply for half a minute, and then called Evelyn. She had arrived in Tampa and was talking to him from a car on her way back from the Realtors' Convention. He practically melted when the first thing she asked about was his son in New York.

"That is *so* thoughtful. Thank you so much for asking. I've not reached him yet through regular channels, but I'm sure he's okay. He'll call me when he can."

Charles knocked on the door and stuck his head in. "Nancy Oliver is on the phone from Washington. She's prepared to brief you about New York." Nancy was the campaign's National Security Advisor. She ordinarily accompanied Jeremy on the plane, but had been in Washington for a Congressional hearing. A former Air Force captain who joined the NSA, rose to become a Deputy Director, and left the Agency eleven months into the Grove Administration, she had been working as a script consultant for *The Oval Office* when Jeremy invited her to join the campaign.

"Evelyn," Jeremy said, "I'm putting you on an open mike. Charles, please put Nancy through to here, and why don't you join us."

In moments Nancy's image appeared on one of the ceiling-mounted video screens. "Hi Nancy, is the audio okay?"

"Fine, we can hear you fine." Charles tapped on the door and came in.

"Nancy, I'm here with Charles Witt, and Evelyn Vaughn is with us on another line. What's the story in New York?"

"I got a call about ten minutes ago from Colonel Warren," Nancy began, summoning her nearly basso presentation voice that Jeremy always found so comforting, "who brought me up to date on what the White House knows." Warren was the Administration's national security liaison to the Lerner campaign, whose job it was to keep the potential President apprised, in a general way, of pending national security matters. He was an Air Force intelligence officer who had toadied up to the Administration sufficiently to be offered a posting in the White House, and no one in the Lerner campaign trusted him. But Nancy herself was ex-Air Force and was able to maintain cordial relations.

"I have also gotten information from other sources, and I should say in advance that a lot of what I'm going to say has not been independently confirmed. But let me give you what I'm working with right now.

"By nuclear bomb standards, this was not big: they're estimating 18 kilotons, which is a little smaller than the blast at Hiroshima. It was either a small device, or a larger one that misfired in some way. It detonated at sea-level—I'll tell you about the ship it was on in a second—at a point about twenty-two miles due east of Perth Amboy, which was its destination. The radiation has been identified as Russian

NEAL RECHTMAN

in origin, a product of the Ozersk military reactor, and probably quite old. If current wind patterns hold, it's possible the radiation cloud could remain at a high altitude over most of Long Island, and not settle to ground level until it's out to sea. By volume it is not a large cloud, but there is no question that it is lethal. All North Atlantic air and sea traffic has been diverted."

"So there is going to be some radiation poisoning, I take it." Jeremy said. "Some people are going to get sick or be killed by this?"

"I can't imagine there won't be, but right now I have no casualty estimates for you. We might learn something about that in the next hour," Nancy replied. "For now, though, we can start with the eighty-nine-man crew of the *Desert Ruby II*." She described the ship to them as a huge supertanker that had taken on its cargo fourteen days earlier at Doha, in the Persian Gulf, made one off-shore port call in Cape Town to transfer off a sick crew member—maybe that's where the bomb came on—and was scheduled to arrive at the Chevron refinery in Perth Amboy at around 11am. It was broadcasting its approved transponder signal and was therefore marked at the exact point and time of the detonation.

"If the same detonation had occurred after the ship docked," she reported, "it could have killed upwards of twenty thousand people immediately, and perhaps another 100,000 or more through radiation and longer term effects."

"What about the situation in New York City?" Evelyn asked. "Some of the news sites are reporting traffic gridlock, and no one can get through by telephone. We can't reach anyone in New York."

"People can't reach their families," Nancy said, "so there is a massive scramble in many directions. There are ten million people living on Long Island, and you can be sure all ten million of them are headed west. The Verrazano Narrows Bridge is closed, so the back-up has got to be monumental."

"Why is the Bridge closed?"

"It was left swaying by the blast wave. They're checking it out."

"Got it."

"Is the emergency broadcast system working?" Charles asked.

"It is," Nancy said, "but it is not clear how widely it is being heard, or listened to. The electro-magnetic pulse may have fried every radio receiver in its path, we just don't know. In theory, a detonation at sea level will produce an asymmetrical pulse, which should make it weaker."

"Nancy, I take it we don't have anyone on the ground in New York who we're in touch with," Charles said.

"That's correct."

"Let's make that our first priority."

"I will notify you when the first call gets through."

"Nancy," Jeremy asked, "where's the President?"

"He was campaigning in Michigan, and is now on Air Force One circling over Ohio at 42,000 feet.

"Please also let me know when he plans to address the nation. I've got a very bad feeling about this."

*　　*　　*　　*　　*

As the day progressed, the sequence of events that unfolded began to line up remarkably with one of the threat scenarios described by *The Oval Office*'s TAG team. The nuclear detonation was followed by multiple terrorist attacks around the country: a rocket propelled grenade was shot into the Mall of America in Minneapolis; a pair of coordinated truck bombs crippled, but did not collapse, the 154-year-old Roebling Bridge in Cincinnati; a series of disc bombs were detonated through the BART system in San Francisco. By late afternoon a total of six attacks, in addition to the one in New York Harbor, had been reported, taking over thirty lives at last count.

Because all commercial airline traffic had been halted when the security level was raised to Red, Jeremy's plane was grounded at the Tuscaloosa Regional Airport. CAT's were still flying, however, so by sundown Evelyn had rejoined the campaign. She arrived at the plane just in time to share a take-out Chinese food buffet that had been set up in the forward conference room, where Jeremy and his staff were following the rapidly unfolding events.

"Sir," Leslie called out, pointing with her chopsticks to the console of displays hung from the ceiling, "the White House is declaring a National Security Emergency." She brought up the volume and they all listened: it was a statement being read from the White House Press Office. Grove would be addressing the nation at 7pm Eastern Time, in about fifteen minutes.

Everyone looked at everyone else, and immediately recognized that anticipating these events might have helped to eliminate the shock, but did nothing to make it less real. Under powers already granted by Congress after the July 4th attacks, the President could at any time declare a National Security Emergency— Patriot Act III's euphemism for martial law. The legal pretext for such a declaration was to permit the deployment of regular US Army troops into urban areas during a crisis, however it also gave the President a host of new powers of decree, vaguely defined, that could lead anywhere. The only statutory check was the Supreme Court, which was required to ratify by a simple majority, within five days of its issuance, the NSE Declaration and each subsequent decree issued under its authority.

The conversation turned to the line-up at the Supreme Court, which virtually always sided with the Administration on any matter related to national security. Evelyn, who had continued to follow the Court closely after she left law school, was not entirely pessimistic. She pointed out that the Administration's typical majority was only 5-4, and that this was a far from typical situation. The Justices had their own place and history, and she did not think they would be eager to have the Constitution swept away on their watch.

Evelyn's analysis was interrupted by Julie's assistant Eric, calling through the intercom. "President Grove is calling, sir. He's on line three." Eyebrows rose all around. Julie signaled for everyone to vacate the conference room, but Jeremy countermanded her with a wave. "Thank you, Eric. I'll pick it up in a moment." He put the call on the conference phone.

"Mr. President."

"Mr. Lerner, I assume you are aware that I have declared a National Security Emergency," Grove began.

"I have been following the news," Jeremy replied. "I am here with my senior staff."

"I'm calling to let you knew that I also plan under NSE authority to order a three-month postponement of the elections. I would like to invite you, and I urge you, to endorse this action as a gesture of bipartisan unity during a time of national crisis." He then rambled on in a similar vein—no time for politics as usual . . . public welfare first . . . etc.—with Jeremy tuning in and out, stunned as he was by the proposition.

"Mr. President," Jeremy replied, when the President finally finished, "with *chutzpah* like that, maybe you should be the one running as the Jewish candidate. Any attempt to tamper with the elections, regardless of the state of national security, will be met by widespread opposition, not only from my campaign but from all quarters." In theory he knew this to be true, because every TAG scenario included the results of hypothetical polling that had been done to assess what public and media reaction would be to the portrayed events. But the results of a hypothetical poll were bound to be different from those of a live poll conducted after a full day of real terrorist attacks around the country, and as soon as the call with Grove was concluded, Jeremy reminded Julie that all of their polling would need to be rerun.

Minutes later President Grove began his televised address and everyone settled back to listen. He first offered a somber recap of the day's events, and did so with such a genuine sense of outrage that Jeremy became convinced that Grove knew nothing about the origin of the attacks. Morley James had probably engineered the day's events entirely on his own, and from his point of view the key to such an operation would be limiting the number of people who knew about it—a factor whose significance Jeremy had learned all too well from Tzvi. In that context, President Burton Grove would be the *last* person James would want to know about it; the President's every minute was accounted for and every conversation was documented. Jeremy had always thought that Grove looked a little like Alfred E. Neumann, *Mad Magazine*'s idiot mascot, so the notion that he might know nothing about the events swirling around him was not too difficult to conjure.

Grove gave the combined tally from the day's seven separate attacks: 131 confirmed dead and over 500 hospitalized with injuries. Attacks had taken place in Minneapolis, San Francisco, Cincinnati, Miami Beach, Orlando and Galveston. There had been no arrests, and Grove urged the public to remain vigilant at all times. He lambasted

Russia for its lax security with nuclear materials, and reminded everyone that over a thousand pounds of bomb-grade nuclear material had unaccountably disappeared out of Russian inventories over the past decade.

Grove then shifted from outrage and *alarum* to sympathy, expressing his deepest sorrow for those personally affected, and from sympathy to intractable Montana determination. "Although there is no nation against which we can make a formal declaration of war, make no mistake about it: we are at war. We are fighting the most heartless enemy this nation, and indeed this world, has ever faced. This is not a war that we can afford to walk away from, or ignore, or leave to others to fight, because if we lose it we lose the very foundation of our civilization: we lose the rule of law. There can be no peace or liberty or justice in a society where random violence is the norm and terrorists target innocent civilians as they go about their daily routines.

"If the terrorists play by their rules, and we play by ours, we are doomed to lose this war. Terrorists do not get permission from anyone before they blow up a bridge and kill thirty-seven people, they just blow it up. Yet when we identify a terrorist, or even *try* to identify a terrorist, we have to get permission from a judge to act against that individual person—by which time it us usually too late. If we are to make progress in our fight against this enemy, we need to be able to move far more quickly than we do now."

He then officially declared a National Security Emergency, invited the Supreme Court to ratify his declaration, and announced three immediate actions he was taking under NSE authority: a ninety-day suspension of writs of habeas corpus in Federal courts; a ninety-day suspension of all warrant requirements for searching, detaining or investigating suspected terrorists and their property; and a ninety-day postponement of the general election, until Tuesday, February 2, 2021.

Grove slid into a softer, but chastising, voice. "Before my address to you tonight, I spoke with Mr. Lerner, the Democratic nominee, and notified him of my decision to postpone the elections. I invited him to endorse my decision, and advised him of the public's expectation that the nation's leaders would set aside 'politics as usual' during a time of national crisis. Mr. Lerner declined my invitation, and he is of course free to pursue whatever course of action he feels is appropriate for a presidential candidate in light of today's events.

"In my case, however, in addition to being a presidential candidate, I am also *the* President, and in consideration of today's events I cannot in good conscience devote another minute of my time to 'politics as usual,' even if it is my re-election campaign. For the next ninety days the focus of every single member of the armed forces and every single Federal employee will be to find out who these terrorists are and to stop them. As Commander in Chief and Chief Executive, it is my responsibility to set the example and lead this effort, and I believe the circumstances call for me to devote all of my attention and energy to this task, at this pivotal time in our Nation's history.

"If Mr. Lerner wishes to contest my legal postponement of the elections and divert resources and attention away from our anti-terrorism efforts, he is free to do so. If the Supreme Court fails to ratify the postponement and elections are held next month, I will of course abide by the Court's ruling and the vote of the Electoral College. As long as I am President, however, from this moment forward, I will do nothing but pursue these terrorists until they have been caught or killed and I will not rest until their attacks on our citizens have stopped.

"May God ease the pain of those who have suffered today, and may God bless America. Thank you."

The screen changed to a talking head whose voice Leslie immediately muted out with a remote. The sudden silence gained an ominous quality as it expanded, as though everyone was waiting for a signal that it was okay to breathe. All eyes turned first to Jeremy, and then to Evelyn, who was seated next to him.

"Well it's one thing to be prepared for an event," Jeremy finally said, "and another to actually have it happen." There was in fact nothing Grove had said that they had not in some way anticipated, but Morley James' packaging, as always, was a work of art.

"This works for them on so many levels," Evelyn said. "A postponed election also means the 28th Amendment won't move forward. If there are no changes to the current Congress, it'll never even get to the floor in the House. This could really turn out to be a disaster."

"We're going to have rebuttal time," Leslie spoke up. "We have to plan what our response is going to be."

"Tell me about it," Jeremy said. "And I'm not liking our options here. If I challenge the postponement, Grove has preemptively characterized that as 'politics as usual' and detrimental to the war effort—it makes me out to be a virtual traitor. If I go along with the postponement, that gives Grove three months to engineer various headline-grabbing victories in the war on terrorism—easy enough to do if you're staging the attacks yourself."

"Do we really know that?" Charles asked. "Are we sure that is what's happening?"

"I don't think we have any proof," Jeremy said. "If we did we'd be using it. But if anyone has doubts, I urge you to go back and read *The Oval Office*'s TAG Scenario B-27, Bravo-27, which I just reread a couple of hours ago. The TAG's have been predicting—with uncanny accuracy—how all this might unfold. Now that it's actually happening, why should we suddenly stop believing them? Their information is better than anyone's."

"It's not a matter of not believing them," Evelyn said. "The problem is that we're not seeing these events the way everyone else is. Everyone else feels like war has been declared on the US by an unseen and, for all intents and purposes, unstoppable enemy, and they're terrified. We think we know who the enemy is, so our reaction is not the same."

There was a knock on the door, and Marilyn Brown, Leslie's assistant, stuck her head in. "Sorry to interrupt," she said, and nodded at Jeremy. "Even if we don't know yet how we're going to respond, we need to make a statement of some kind very soon. The press has gone wild. I have seen a lot, and these people are over the top."

"We'll have a statement in five minutes," Leslie said. "Tell them fifteen minutes to be safe."

"Got it," Marilyn acknowledged, and withdrew.

"I agree with Evelyn," Julie resumed. "Our perspective is off. We need to start to look at this as everyone else is looking at it."

"Okay, I see you point, I've got the picture," Jeremy said, sounding annoyed. "Leslie, work up a statement that doesn't commit us one way or another. I recognize the seriousness of the situation and the need to make progress against terrorism; I'm horrified at what has happened; my sympathies, *et cetera*. That kind of thing. Then at the end say I'm evaluating the situation, and will announce tomorrow what my response is to Grove's decrees."

"We should give them a time," Leslie suggested.

"How about noon?" Jeremy proposed.

"I advise earlier," Julie said. "Grove has thrown down his glove in front of you, and the whole country is waiting for you to react. The longer you wait, the more indecisive you seem, the more time Grove's *spinmeisters* have to set you up. You don't even want to *know* how this is being played on Fox."

"Like I care," Jeremy said.

"You should care,"

"You're right. Okay, set it for 9am. We'll have a decision by then anyhow, it's just a matter of getting *our* packaging right. Morley James has been planning this maneuver for months, and we've got twelve hours."

He then addressed Julie, his Campaign Manager, who was sitting to his right. "I agree we need—I need—to reframe how we're looking at this. But I can't sit in this aluminum tube anymore, I've gotta stretch my legs. Let's break for a half hour or so." He then turned back to Evelyn on his left. "You'll join me for a walk?"

"A stroll on the tarmac at the Tuscaloosa airport? How romantic!"

Jeremy cast her a facetious smile, and then turned back to Julie. "So we'll meet back here in, say, forty-five minutes, at eight o'clock. Let's have you, Leslie, Evelyn of course, Charles, Gordon Kramer, and see if you can get Victor and Irving Liman to join us by Web or phone. Charles!" Jeremy shouted, to catch him before he ducked through the doorway. "Evelyn and I want to go for a walk. Please see what you can arrange."

*   *   *   *   *

Within five minutes a small security detail had been put

together, the press was un-invited, and they were able to exit the plane with a relatively small entourage. The fresh air that Jeremy had so eagerly anticipated at the head of the aluminum staircase was not there; the prevailing scent was kerosene. "Take us to the nearest grass!" Jeremy called to the Agent-in-Charge, "—of the *landscaping* variety."

As they walked, Jeremy realized that Evelyn looked not only somber, but also exceedingly pale, open-casket pale. He looked up and around at the airport lighting, which had a blue halogen cast.

"Are you okay?" Jeremy asked. "I mean physically. We're all wracked mentally."

"I think so," she said, "but I'm having trouble accepting that we have a President who is killing his own citizens in order to stay in power!"

"As I said, I don't think Grove knows what's happening. That's the reason he's able to come off sounding so convincing about it. This has Morley James's handwriting all over it."

Evelyn was not relieved in the least. "The fact that we have a White House Chief of Staff who would kill his own citizens is devastating."

"I'm no less horrified than you, my dear, but I'm not surprised. *The Oval Office's* security people have had this guy pegged for years. Morley James is a dangerous, dangerous man."

They reached the front of the terminal and, behold! Right across the road was a park, an actual, named city park, the Robert Cardinal Park, with benches and grass and trees! Agents did a walk-through, prompting a young couple to exit voluntarily at a less than casual pace.

"Sir," Charles called out from where the couple had emerged, "if you wanted some grass of the *non-landscaping* variety, they have that here as well." Jeremy and Evelyn headed toward him, and halfway there were greeted by a visible cloud of marijuana smoke that had been left by the departing couple. "Well, it beats the smell of kerosene," Jeremy said, and began dusting off a bench for them to sit down on.

"We have also known that the last two Supreme Court nominees were political hacks," Evelyn said, "but we barely seemed to make a dent in their confirmation."

"I'm beginning to see Grove's point about playing by your

own rules instead of the opponent's rules. The reason Democrats never get anywhere is because they are playing by rules defined by civil law and rational thought, whereas the Republican guiding principle is more like 'it's okay to cheat as long as you don't get caught.'"

"So you're saying liberals need to adopt those kinds of methods?" Evelyn asked.

"I'm not at that point yet. But I can't help but wonder how far it will have to go before we are forced to change our methods. We're on the verge of losing everything here."

*   *   *   *   *

Thirty minutes later, in the campaign plane's forward conference room, Irving Liman addressed the meeting from his side of a split-screen monitor he was sharing with Victor Glade. He suggested looking at the decision they had to make in terms of campaign tactics. "A presidential campaign is always either in attack mode, or in a passive mode," he argued. "Usually attacking is for underdogs, and passive is for favorites, candidates who enjoy a safe lead, say, of five points or better. As of yesterday, you were a decided favorite, and for the last month you've maintained a passive strategy, focusing on your own ideas and leaving the attacks in the background. You want to appear as though you've already beaten your opponent, and are totally occupied with preparing to do the job. Do we all agree with that?" There was a general nodding.

"So, look at our options and what they represent in terms of tactics. Option A, challenging the Administration's decree and arguing against postponement, is clearly the attack route. Option B, endorsing the postponement and hoping for the best in three months, is passive. Everyone still with me?"

Mumbled acknowledgements arose.

"So what I'm trying to get to is, should the campaign now be shifting its tactics from passive to attack? If we confront the Administration and the Supreme Court, which is what our fighting instinct says to do, that switches us from passive to attack. I am *so* reluctant to give up our superior, passive position, which is so hard to secure, and which I'm not convinced we'd lose if we remained passive. It's really too soon to tell how these events are going to affect the public."

"You would accept Grove's invitation?" Evelyn was incredulous. "You'd go along with the postponement? You really think there will be an election in three months? Does anyone here believe that?"

"Of course not," Julie said. "If he can decree one postponement, he can decree another one. They're not going to run in an election unless they know they're going to win it."

"Evelyn," Liman continued, "you may well be right. I wouldn't want anyone to refer back to this meeting in the future and report that I believed Grove when he said there would be elections in three months. I can't read the future like that. All I can tell you is that this is not the time, in my opinion, for us to be engaging in political attacks. Terrorists have just devastated the country. Hundreds of people are dead, and our life in America as we know it seems on the verge of unraveling. When people are afraid for their lives and their families' lives, are they going to respond to political attacks? I'm thinking not. If you disagree, please speak up."

"That's why Grove's speech was so effective," Julie said. "He has assured every man, woman and child in this country that he is personally working to defend them; the fact that he is a virtual idiot who can barely read to find the men's room is, of course, irrelevant."

"The hundreds of people who are dead have been *killed by their own government!*" Evelyn blurted out. "And we're going to take a passive approach?! *I think I'm going to be sick.*"

"Evelyn," Liman replied. "I empathize, I truly do. Jeremy will tell you how strongly I feel about the state of our country. But I don't think in either the short- or long-term you will advance your goal of occupying the White House by attacking Burton Grove right now. You instinctively want to go on the attack, *but you don't have any ammunition.*"

"Evelyn," said Jeremy, "put on your prosecutor's hat. You might absolutely *know* that someone is guilty of a serious crime, but if you don't have the evidence, you don't indict. If you do indict, you do nothing to bring the person to justice, and in the end you look foolish."

Julie broke in. "What do we actually need to prove? What if we just planted it as a story—got a talking head to speculate about the possibility of the Administration's complicity in the attacks."

"Another way to accomplish the same thing would be write it into *The Oval Office*," Victor said. "We could have some rogue elements in the Bosco Administration manufacture a terrorist incident for some misguided end, but like your idea, Julie, it wouldn't happen fast enough to have any impact on this decision, which we have to make now: do we gamble everything on the Supreme Court and have our answer in five days, or cooperate with the Administration and see what happens in three months?"

"Sir," Charles said, addressing Jeremy, "this grand conspiracy that we're all taking for granted and no one else knows about: obviously we have no proof, or we'd be using it, but do we have any evidence at all—of any sort—that the Grove Administration is connected to today's attacks?"

Everyone looked at Jeremy, who was looking sheepish. "No, I don't think so . . . not unless Mayor Wade has nabbed us a couple of would-be assassins lurking in the tall grass of Western Alabama."

There was a knock on the door and Julie's assistant Eric stepped in. "Sir," he said, facing Jeremy, who was standing up behind his chair, "sorry about the interruption. Erwin Wade is holding on campaign line one. He is the Mayor from Reform who you met this afternoon. I explained that you are not available at this very moment, but he insists that I should let you know he's calling. Do you want me to handle it?"

"No!" Jeremy almost choked. "Please, put him through right away. Everyone here will tell you, I've been expecting his call."

*　　*　　*　　*　　*

The two men picked up for questioning by Pickens County Sheriff's deputies forty-five minutes after Jeremy's entourage left were carrying high-powered Slam rifles of the same type used in the July 4th attack on the helicopter in Dupont Circle. Each of the men had a valid license for the weapon, each had been in his own pick-up truck, and initially they claimed that they didn't know each other. They also both said they were going hunting, but neither of them had any specific ideas about where they were planning to hunt or what they were hunting for in Alabama with .50 caliber armor-piercing rifles. Neither of them had a hunting license. Then it was uncovered that the trucks were leased to two different Birmingham construction companies that operated out of the same address. Finally, the sheriff's office learned that their cell phones each had a hidden intercom function that was powered by the same encryption software. As of now they had established that the men knew each other, and they were continuing to hold and question them.

An exuberant Mayor Wade reported all this over the open speakerphone in the conference room. He began to relate the men's names and driver's license numbers when Charles interrupted.

"Sir, Mayor Wade, pardon me. This is Charles Witt—we met earlier today. I was with you in the back of Jeremy's car. If you don't mind I'm going to record this call so that we've got all of this information documented."

"Oh, by all means, please." He proceeded to read out the men's names and ID information. Charles also took notes on a legal pad as Wade spoke. When he was done, Charles asked for and received the Mayor's e-mail address.

"Has the press picked this up yet?" Jeremy asked.

"Not yet. I wanted to check in with you first. You think these men were really out there to try and shoot down a helicopter?" Wade asked.

"Mayor Wade, the men were there to shoot down a helicopter *with me in it.*"

"Understood. So how do you want me to proceed at this point—with the press and otherwise?"

"I'd like you to just continue doing the *most* excellent and professional job that you've been doing so far. Please continue with your investigation. You are keeping copies of your interrogations of these men?" Jeremy asked.

"Absolutely," Wade replied. "It's all being videotaped."

"Great. Make sure you have back-up copies as well, off-site. I'm serious about that. At some point DHS is going to come and take over this case." Charles nodded his enthusiastic agreement.

"How would DHS find out about them?" Wade asked.

"Well that leads us back to the question of the press. If reporters take an interest in these arrests, feel free to give them whatever information you deem appropriate. Maybe you can get them to help you with your investigation, I don't know. But once the press picks this story up, DHS will come to you. There's nothing you can do to stop them from taking it over, but try to uncover as much as you can before they do. These men were apprehended as the result of your department's own initiative . . . ?"

"Absolutely, it's all described in the reports."

"Mayor Wade, I cannot thank you enough for your diligence in this matter. My security chief, Charles Witt, with whom you were just speaking, will stay in close touch with you for the next few days."

"I will keep you posted. I saw the President's speech a while ago. I'm sure your hands are full. We wish you the best here from Reform."

The line clicked off, and all eyes fell in silence on Jeremy, who left the quiet in place for a few moments.

"Sir," Charles asked, "I'm trying to get a better handle on the coincidence thing, because it really seems like it could impact your safety in some way. Is this coincidence—Mayor Wade calling right now—part of the same event you were in earlier today, with the helicopters? Are you still in some kind of vortex, if that's what you call it?"

"Not now, Charles," Jeremy said. "I understand your concern. We'll talk about it later. The immediate issue is, what do these arrests mean for the decision we're trying to make. Heads up, everyone! Follow along with this and correct me if there is some flaw in logic that you see.

"Is it safe to assume, first of all, that seven terrorist attacks occurring on the same day is not a *coincidence*. Most if not all of them had to have been coordinated at some level. Can we stipulate that?"

Heads nodded.

"Now, thanks to the Pickens County Sheriff's Department, we know there was yet another attack planned for today, an eighth attack, and that was an assassination plot against me. We also know that the people who planned it had to have known about the nuclear attack in New York, because the whole assassination scheme was predicated on a helicopter coming to take me to a nuclear-safe location. *And* we know that these people had to have knowledge of internal Secret Service protocols. In fact, the only reason the assassination wasn't attempted was because *I declined to board a helicopter that had been ordered for me by the Secret Service.*

"So now the question is, is this enough evidence to give traction to our theory that the Administration is behind the attacks? 'Do we have enough evidence to indict?' I guess is the right way to frame it."

There was silence again, everyone was on overload.

"Irving, Victor, what are your thoughts?" Jeremy looked up at the monitor.

"You are far, far ahead of me on this," Irving responded. "I see nothing wrong with your logic, and I think the assassination story will have huge traction. Is it a smoking gun? I think it's too soon to tell."

"Victor?" Jeremy prodded.

"Not only are you far ahead of me, but I am still stuck on what Charles was saying about the security situation. I know you don't want to deal with this now, but look at what you just said, yourself, a few moments ago: *You are not safe in the hands of the Secret Service—their security has been breached.* You should refuse their protection. I can send a security team to cover for you until you can make other arrangements."

"You're in Bulgaria, for Pete's sake!" Jeremy said.

"We can have two dozen agents there in less than 24 hours. I'll lend you Amanda Marx, she'll help you set it all up."

"If you refused Secret Service protection because of this thing," Irving added, "that would add a lot of drama to your story. If they've actually been compromised that is really outrageous — that's not something I can recall ever happening before."

"I really don't want to get bogged down on this. Charles, if you think we should refuse Secret Service protection, I'm fine with it, just do it."

Charles nodded an acknowledgment, opened up his small tablet and began typing.

"Irving," Jeremy continued, "leave aside for now the question of whether or not the assassination plot is a smoking gun. What does it say about our tactical mode—the passive/attack thing you were talking about earlier?"

"If someone is actually trying to *kill* you," Liman said, "I don't think the public would expect you to react passively to that. Actually I think the opposite is true. Your question is a good one. The assassination thing puts us in a very different position than before. Julie, what do you think?"

"I agree, switching now to offense feels right. Even if we don't have a smoking gun, we've at least got ammunition, as you say. The Secret Service thing will be a huge scandal. My only concern is that we're basing everything on these two men who've been arrested. If they were to suddenly disappear, for example, or their story turned out not to be what we think it is now, we would have absolutely nothing. We'd be looking very foolish."

"Evelyn," Jeremy asked, "what do you think?"

"I certainly see some risk, but in this case I see a much bigger risk in not contesting these decrees. We're five days away from a dictatorship here."

<table>
<tr><td>**22**</td><td>October 2, 2020
Lerner / Vaughn Campaign
Tuscaloosa Regional Airport</td></tr>
</table>

The following morning Jeremy left the plane, still parked in Tuscaloosa, and made the ten-minute motorcade trip to a nearby airport hotel, where a small ballroom had been secured for his press conference. He started out very subdued, offering his condolences and prayers to those who were directly affected by the attacks of the previous day. The click of cameras and the jostling of reporters could easily be heard behind his voice.

He then shifted gears. "President Grove has invited me endorse his plan to postpone the upcoming election, and suggested that if I don't, I will somehow be giving aid and comfort to the enemy. The election, he claims, will distract him from his non-stop, single-minded pursuit of the terrorists who are wreaking havoc on our society.

"First of all, I can't help but point out how hollow this promise of hard work sounds, coming from a President who has spent more time on vacation than any other President in history. But more importantly, I am declining the President's 'invitation,' and will be challenging all of his emergency declarations before the Supreme Court, because my view of the terrorist threat is almost exactly the opposite of his: my contention is that it is the Grove Administration's foreign policy that is responsible for the wave of terrorism we face today, and the longer he is in office, the worse it is going to get.

"President Grove's various unilateral interventions in the Middle East have resulted in tens of thousands of civilian deaths, not to mention our own military casualties. When people in Saudi Arabia and Iraq and Afghanistan are killed or injured as the result of Grove's policies, the families of these people—who feel every bit as strongly about their loved ones as we feel about ours—become our bitter enemies. In his four short years in office, President Grove has succeeded in earning the ill will and outright hatred of millions of people around the world.

"It will take this country decades to recover from this Administration's foreign policy, and if Grove succeeds in postponing the upcoming Presidential election, we may never recover at all. From the President who brought you warrantless surveillance of American citizens, legalized torture, and Patriot Act III, we now see the ultimate debasement of the US Constitution: the hijacking of an election.

"If the Grove Administration's emergency declarations are allowed to stand, it will mark the end of this country's 244-year-long experiment in democracy. Our President today arrogates to himself powers that were last wielded here by King George in 1775.

"It is now up to the Supreme Court to decide if we move forward as a democratic nation and an evolving civilization, or we regress and implode to the same point we were at two and a half centuries ago. I can only hope and pray that wisdom and mature judgment in the Court will prevail over partisan loyalties at this pivotal point in our Nation's history."

Jeremy looked up from his prepared text and paused, and every reporter in the room suddenly leapt up and began shouting questions. But he raised his hands again after a few moments, and waited for an opening. "I have one more statement to make," he said, speaking deeply into the microphone, "on a different topic. Then I will be happy to entertain your questions."

A semblance of quiet began to return, but he remained silent until he had everyone's attention. "Effective immediately, my campaign will pay for its own security, and we will be refusing the protection of the US Secret Service. We are taking this action because we learned yesterday evening of an apparent assassination plot against me that appears to have been based on inside knowledge of classified Secret Service procedures—" The room exploded with howled and shouted questions, none of which were intelligible to anyone.

When he could be heard, Jeremy tried wresting control by using his own loudest voice. "The plot was uncovered by local authorities in my hometown of Reform, Alabama, where I was campaigning, and two arrests have been made. The few details that we have, at this point, we are making available to you in hard copy as I speak, and there will obviously be more about this later; but for now I won't be taking questions about this. I welcome, however," —he was now shouting to be heard— "your questions about our plan to fight ratification of Grove's emergency declarations, and our goal of restoring constitutional government to the United States of America."

23	October 3, 2020 Lerner / Vaughn Campaign Washington, DC

Jeremy's campaign arrived in Washington late Friday evening and set up shop at a Holiday Inn on C Street SW, just a few blocks from the Supreme Court.

Mayor Wade called Saturday morning to let them know that DHS and Secret Service agents had arrived in Reform to take custody of the two assassination suspects. They had also presented a Homeland Security Court Permanent Restraining Order prohibiting all local authorities involved in the case from making statements to the press, but by then it was too late. One of several reporters whom Leslie had given the lead to the previous evening had been able to link both suspects to a man named Malcolm Adwar, a former State Department Arabist who now worked for the American Patriots Foundation as a Middle East policy analyst.

The same connection was made independently by CNN later in the day and a media frenzy ensued, not only because the American Patriots Foundation was a high-profile conservative think-tank that was often referred to as the "White House Personnel Office" by Administration insiders, but also because Malcolm Adwar was *missing*. His company ID showed him leaving work the previous day, October 1 — the day of the attacks—at 2:17pm; he never arrived home, and had

NEAL RECHTMAN

not been heard from since. His wife had filed a missing person's report with the Montgomery County Police at 11pm that night.

As soon as Adwar's picture became public, Charles forwarded it by e-mail to Amanda Marx at *The Oval Office* in Bulgaria, with the covering message, "Is this who I think it is?" Two hours later the reply came back: "It is. We have compared it with our surveillance footage and confirmed the match with image telemetry."

Adwar was the anonymous man that *Oval Office* security personnel had videotaped on several occasions meeting in public places with the two Corel technicians who were suspected of having planted the bugs. So along with dozens of investigative reporters, DC detectives, FBI, DHS and Secret Service agents, *The Oval Office* put together its own posse to try and track Adwar down. Amanda had even considered recommending to Victor that they retain a bounty hunter, but the only one she would consider hiring was already working the case.

If only because so many people were looking for him, Jeremy was sure that Malcolm Adwar would never be found. Morley James would never leave a liability like that outstanding.

Despite the irrelevance of public opinion to Supreme Court deliberations, Jeremy pushed to get some type of polling re-started—anything that would reveal the public's frame of mind. The earliest data began to come in Saturday afternoon, but both Leslie and Gordon cautioned him about drawing any conclusions or even inferences. "I know, I know," Jeremy said, "but I can't stand the feeling of no pulse. Now at least I know the beast is alive."

"The beast is alive," Evelyn said, "but its fate is in the hands of the Supreme Court, not the electorate." She had wanted to say *Forget the fucking polls, they're meaningless!*, but recognized that everyone was already sufficiently on edge. Evelyn and Carla Sanders of the DNC had worked the phones almost non-stop through the night to line up their legal team for the Supreme Court arguments, which had been scheduled for Monday at 10:30am. By noon Saturday they had concluded a round of meetings with potential counsel, and had chosen William Barwick of Jones Day's appellate practice to lead. They also retained Marc Enright of the University of Michigan, who had been so successful representing the Democrats in the Michigan Senatorial recount in 2018, and Harriet

Sullivan of Georgetown Law Center, whom Evelyn knew personally and pushed to bring in.

At two in the afternoon the staff gathered yet again around a Chinese food buffet that had been spread out on a credenza in the living room of Jeremy and Evelyn's hotel suite. "Someone correct me if you think I'm wrong," Evelyn said, "but I rate the Chinese food in Tuscaloosa several notches higher than this stuff. These vegetables are all overcooked." A general agreement emerged amid the finger licking and lip-smacking.

"Jeremy," Evelyn asked, as she bathed an egg roll in mustard and duck sauce, "gourmet Chinese food is part of the 'New South,' is it?"

"I can tell you it wasn't part of the Old South," Jeremy said. "When I was growing up in the 1950s, the only Chinese restaurant in the entire state was a place in Birmingham called Joy Young's. It was a three-hour drive from Reform. We went there once a year and met my uncles and their families, so it was always a big party of fifteen or twenty people. There were three dining rooms on three different floors. Everything was in gold and red: the carpets, walls, the ceiling, the tablecloths. There were mirrors everywhere. The waiters would slide down the banisters carrying their trays, and they never wrote down your order—they memorized everything. There could be twenty people at the table, but the waiter never even took out a pad, and always got it right."

"If I ever meet a Martian," Evelyn said, munching away, "I'm hard pressed to think that I'll find his childhood story any more exotic than yours."

There was a quick knock on the front door as it was opened from the outside by a bodyguard. Charles came in and Jeremy waved him over. "Please join us for some Chinese food that is second rate compared to yesterday's Chinese food."

"Thanks very much, sir. I'll pass. Could I get you privately for a few moments?" The urgency in his eyes was transparent to everyone.

Jeremy wiped his hands on a napkin and stood up. "Join me over here," he said, and walked over to a window overlooking the Mall. It was 3pm and the sun was already well down its descending arc over the southwest horizon. The roof of the White House was visible in the distance.

"Sir, Szulkin has called to let us know that Tzvi has sent a message. Says it's urgent. Your last instruction was to not even respond. Does that still hold? I thought you should know that this has come in."

"My instruction stands," Jeremy said. "Don't retrieve his message, don't even go to the Web site where you would log in to get it."

"You're sure?" Charles asked. "What if it's another message like the last one that is warning you of imminent danger? His last message may have saved your life."

"He may have saved my life, but his communication also coincided with a nuclear blast that could have killed 20,000 people. I've made up my mind; it's not worth the risk."

"Do you want me to notify you if additional messages come in from him in the future?"

Jeremy thought about that. As he did, Evelyn approached them, smiling, but Jeremy did not acknowledge her so she stopped a few feet short.

"Yes, I do want to know if and when messages come in. Don't respond in any way, but let me know immediately, as you did today, either in person or over a secure channel. Thanks for checking back on this." He nodded and Charles left.

Evelyn walked up to him and they both stood looking out the window. He put his arm around her shoulder and pointed to the White House. "So near and yet so far," he said.

"Jeremy, is anything wrong?" Evelyn asked.

"You mean aside from the fact that the country is being run by an berserk, homicidal theocrat?"

"I mean in terms of your personal safety. Charles walks in and flashes a look like that, *everyone* is going to wonder what's up. It's not like someone hasn't been trying to kill you."

"Well, rest assured, no one has tried to kill me again, at least not yet."

"I take it you are not scrimping on security."

" . . . ?"

"Okay, okay. I have another question for you," Evelyn said. "I've been meaning to ask you since last night. How did you know there were going to be men staking you out with Slam rifles? That couldn't have been just a lucky guess."

Jeremy unwrapped his arm from her shoulder and nudged her to look at him. She looked up and he met her gaze, but didn't say anything.

"What is it?" she asked.

"It's awkward," he said.

"What's awkward?"

"The answer to your question, how I knew there were going to be gunmen there. Let's go for a walk."

*   *   *   *   *

His security detail had already staked out an area of the Mall where it was easy for them to protect Jeremy when he went out for one of his minimum twice-daily fresh air excursions. After they crossed the street and escaped the small contingent of reporters, supporters, and protesters that had camped out in front of the hotel, Jeremy began telling Evelyn the unlikely story of his cousin Tzvi, their history of deadly coincidences, his recently revealed connection to Israeli intelligence and to Amitai, and his most recent mysterious warning that led Jeremy to uncover the assassination plot.

"It was Tzvi," Jeremy related, "who first told me that you were an assassination target. Remember, the day we first met, I left our meeting for an outside lunch, and then came back and told you someone was trying to kill you? My lunch that day was with Tzvi, where I learned for the first time of his involvement with Mossad."

"You're kidding!" she almost squealed. It was the most girlish sound Jeremy had ever heard her make.

"No I am *not* kidding. The night before, remember the air taxi that picked you up in Detroit and dropped you off in Burbank? That was all arranged by Tzvi. That CAT flight was a secret Israeli intelligence operation."

"That makes no sense. Why would Israeli agents care about whether or not I'm an assassination target?"

"It's complicated, to say the least. Tzvi claims that the threat against you was in some way associated with a terrorist they were tracking."

"This really is almost too fantastic to believe. The pilot was a very nice man with an Irish name, Loughran, or something like that. You mean to tell me this man works for Israeli intelligence?"

"According to Tzvi, the pilot did not even know it was an operation. The CAT he works for, AirShares, is owned by an Israeli company that is controlled by the Mossad. It was the cabin attendant, the woman, who was 'handling' you, as they say in the trade."

An instantaneous memory flash stopped Evelyn in her tracks: the flight attendant had been a young woman with a slight accent that Evelyn had pegged almost immediately. *What kind of airline would hire an Israeli to do customer service?* she remembered thinking, because the woman seemed remarkably cold and distant for a stewardess.

They were coming up to Madison Drive, facing the National Gallery of Art. "We should head back," Jeremy said. He came up to her and took hold of her hand. They turned and began walking back towards Independence Avenue. One of the three close-in bodyguards started talking into his collar.

"Will I ever meet this Tzvi?" Evelyn asked. "He's really a blood relative of yours?"

"He is, but I doubt you will meet him—not through me, anyhow. It just isn't worth the risk. My last communication with him on Thursday coincided with a nuclear detonation that could have killed thousands of people!"

"Correct me if I'm wrong, but was it not his message on Thursday that also saved your life?"

"Actually, I get most of the credit for avoiding the assassination attempt. The message I got from Tzvi was very vague, only that an 'event' was imminent, and that I should take precautions. I was the one who reasoned out what the actual threat was. It was related to a coincidence vortex I was in at the time."

"What vortex was *that?*" Evelyn knew, from her own experience, how incredible these could be.

He related as briefly as he could the story of George Gordon, the helicopter pilot who had landed across the street from his home when he was nine years old, and who now crossed paths with Jeremy at the

THE 28TH AMENDMENT   239

exact same location, fifty-eight years later *to the day*. "The coincidence was keyed on helicopters, so I guessed that it had to be related to that."

"Still, if Tzvi hadn't contacted you, you never would have seen it coming."

"That may be true, but an atomic bomb also went off at the same time that his message came through to me."

"Jeremy, think about that for a second. It's just crazy to think that there's some connection. How could an e-mail from your cousin trigger an event somewhere else?"

"Maybe it's not cause-and-effect, maybe it's just coincidence, but as I told you, my coincidence pattern with Tzvi has a violent twist to it. After Thursday, the stakes are *way* too high for me to be playing this game. In fact, when Charles dropped by a little while ago, it was to tell me that another message had come in from Tzvi. We're not even going to pick it up."

"You're not going to look at it?"

"No. It's not worth the risk. For all I know it may already be too late. I'm worried that his e-mail alone, without any response, might align with some terrible event."

Evelyn fell silent as they walked. The sun was almost down and they picked up their pace. The sound of multiple sirens rose in the distance. As they approached Independence Avenue, Evelyn spoke up again. "Jeremy," she asked, "if your cousin Tzvi was able to warn you about the attempted assassination, the real question to be asking is how *he* knew about it."

"The man's a spy. However spies get their information, that's how he got his." They had reached Independence Avenue, where the modest Saturday afternoon traffic had yielded to numerous DC police cars racing westbound. Charles came up to them. "Sir," he said, looking at Jeremy, and then he glanced at Evelyn, "M'am, we have to bring you back into the hotel right away, as soon as we can get across the road here safely. There are reports that shots have been fired at two Supreme Court justices."

Jeremy looked down at Evelyn, who was wide-eyed and speechless. "This is becoming a fucking nightmare," Jeremy said. "*I really have to get Tzvi to stop contacting me.*"

Moments later, in the distance, there was a muffled but obviously powerful explosion.

*   *   *   *   *

Back in the hotel, they went directly to the campaign war room on the second floor and were immediately briefed by Charles. Two Supreme Court justices had been targeted. Justice Arnold Byron was leaving an armored sedan in front of his townhouse when he was struck by at least two bullets, fired from a rooftop almost a quarter-mile away, and was in critical condition at the Georgetown Medical Center. At almost exactly the same time, an auditorium at George Washington University, where Justice Constance Baylis Wilson was speaking, was raked with gunfire from a passing truck. Numerous people were injured by flying glass, but the Justice was unharmed. Ten minutes later, the abandoned truck exploded at the corner of 18th and K, killing and injuring an unknown number of people. That was the explosion that Jeremy and Evelyn had heard while waiting to cross Independence Avenue.

Jeremy's first thought was that this was yet another incident staged by Morley James to demonstrate to the Justices just how dangerous these terrorists could be. What did not make sense, however, was that Justice Byron, whose life was hanging in the balance, was a reliable supporter of the Administration, while Wilson, who was uninjured, was far more independent-minded. If the attacks on the Justices were engineered by the Grove camp, one would have expected them to try and take out Wilson, and leave Byron unharmed. Charles pointed out that they could have done it that way purposely, to deflect any speculation that they were behind it, or it could have been an accidental outcome. "Maybe the idea was to miss both of them, just shake things up a little. But when you try to engineer events this way," Charles said, "a lot of things can go wrong, and they don't always turn out as planned."

"In the meantime," Evelyn asked, "have they made any arrests?"

"Not that I know of," Charles said. "Remember, this only happened thirty minutes ago."

"Could other Justices still be in danger?" asked Jeremy.

"That's unlikely," Charles said. "They are all going to be locked down tight wherever they are until the dust has settled."

Jeremy looked at Evelyn. "What does this mean for Monday's session?" he asked. Doesn't the Court have to ratify Grove's decrees within five days, or they are automatically rescinded?"

"That is my understanding of it," Evelyn said. "I've read Patriot Act III, and that's how it's supposed to work, but the first thing I'm going to do now is go back and read it again."

"What if the Court is incomplete, or can't come into session within the required five days?"

"This is going to be a showdown of lawyers," Evelyn said. "The law is written the way it's written, and there may be precedents that can be brought to bear. But if these Justices want a particular outcome, they'll find a way to get it. This Court has already done some outrageous things in the name of national security."

24	October 5, 2020 Lerner / Vaughn Campaign Washington, DC

To Jeremy, "outrage" seemed far too mild a term to describe the judicial farce that played out on Monday. In contravention of all Court precedent, a semi-conscious Arnold Byron "participated" in the deliberations through a live video link to his hospital room. In order to emphasize his presence, Chief Justice Goodwin on several occasions threw in acknowledgments like, "As I'm sure my colleague Justice Byron would agree, . . ." and "Justice Byron has made similar arguments in the past," but Byron himself never uttered a word or did anything to signify he was aware of what was taking place.

For security reasons the gallery had been closed to the press. There were two live video feeds to a remote press pool, so the visual realities that were abundantly clear from inside the courtroom were never seen by the public or press. A full transcript of the proceedings was released concurrently with the decision, making it seem like an ordinary session of the Court with nine justices present. Evelyn, who sat with Barwick and their other counsel throughout the oral arguments, was horrified that only two of the dissenting Justices made reference to the circumstances of Justice Byron's vote, which they had to do in a separately issued opinion.

"The Supreme Court as an independent institution is dead,"

Evelyn said as she read the details of the decision on her tablet. She and Jeremy were sitting in the campaign's hotel war room along with their legal team—Barwick, Enright, Sullivan—and various staff coming and going. A row of wireless monitors had been set up on the top shelf of a coat rack and offered up a parade of muted talking heads.

"Is there any other legal route that can be pursued?" Jeremy directed his question to Barwick.

"You mean in terms of going back to the Supreme Court?" Barwick asked.

"Anything at all," Jeremy said.

"Well, as you know there's no appeal from here," Barwick replied. "If we had compelling new evidence we could revisit . . . but absent that . . ."

"I'm not even sure new evidence would make a difference. This Court is an entirely partisan operation."

"I was just going to ask." Jeremy directed himself to Charles, who had encamped at the end of the table and was reading messages on his tablet. "Charles! Has any progress been made on the evidence front, anything at all?"

Charles closed his tablet and looked up. "Sir, nothing significant to report. No further word on the two riflemen in Alabama, and nothing on Malcolm Adwar. He would appear to be the key to everything."

"I assume you are coordinating with *Oval Office* security on this?"

"I'm in touch with them on a regular basis. They have their own interest in Adwar, as you know."

Now Jeremy garnered everyone's attention by scanning the room. Conversations trailed off and the silence expanded.

"Today has not been a good day," he finally said, addressing everyone. "Not for this campaign, and not for this country, and not for the world at large. It would be absurd not to acknowledge at least that.

"On the other hand, I am not convinced that today's lost battle represents the end of the war. There will hopefully be another day tomorrow, and another one after that, and in theory after ninety such days there will be an election to win, although, frankly, if we haven't exposed what's happening by then, I suspect it will be too late for everyone.

"All this being said," he continued, "I personally have no intention of simply walking away, and I'm sure that Evelyn concurs with me in that view." Evelyn had begun nodding her assent even before he finished the sentence. "There is too much at stake, and there is too much to be done. For those of you who wish to stay with the campaign, I'm prepared to guarantee salaries until the next scheduled Election Day, which is February 2nd, if I'm not mistaken. If you don't wish to stay with us, we thank you for your efforts and wish you the best in your next endeavor. Please let Julie know your intentions by breakfast tomorrow."

*   *   *   *   *

Later that evening, Evelyn and Jeremy had dinner alone together for the first time in months; they tried and could not remember when they had last had a private dinner. They ordered a bottle of good wine and every available appetizer on the hotel's room service menu, and had it set up in their suite with candles and linen and silverware.

"Let's talk about our wedding!" Evelyn suggested as they sat down, and she raised her wine glass to begin the meal. "We haven't even picked a date yet."

Jeremy executed the toast with a clink and took a sip. "You still want to marry me even though I'm not going to be President?" He tried his best to look earnest.

"Didn't you ask me to marry you *before* you were asked to run?"

"I did indeed, and I'm glad to know that you remember it that way."

"Well I do, and of course I still want to marry you—the sooner, the better. When do you have in mind?"

"How about over the holidays—you know, sometime between Christmas and New Year. Politics are at a standstill then, and we'll have a better shot for a few days' privacy."

"That's fine with me," she said. "And where?" Evelyn

began pulling various appetizers from a tray onto her plate.

"Somewhere warm, that's all I care about. I want it to be outdoors, and I don't want to be bundled up in coats. How about the back yard of Victor's home in La Cañada Flintridge? I don't think you've ever been to his house, have you?"

"No, I haven't, and I'm very curious to see it."

"A river runs through it. Literally. Anyhow, I will ask Caroline to arrange it." Jeremy put down his glass and began filling his plate.

"You're sure it's available?"

"He's encouraged me to use it. The Feds quit it months ago, and he keeps paying his staff there. Victor owns and maintains three homes in the US, and the poor guy is living with his family in an industrial park in Bulgaria, for god's sake. He won't even be able to come to the wedding!"

"Maybe we should offer to have the wedding there," Evelyn suggested "so that he could attend. He is after all the . . . "

" . . . *Shad'chan*—right you are. That really is a very considerate gesture. It would also help shrink the attendance. There are not a lot of people who are going to fly to Bulgaria between Christmas and New Year's to attend a wedding."

"Actually, I take it all back. Think about it . . . you—*we*—are not going to want to be out of the country at all over the next three months, I would think."

"Ah, right you are. Absolutely. And I'm glad of it, too, because I'm one of those people who wouldn't want to go to Bulgaria in the middle of the December for *anybody's* wedding—not even my own."

They paused and began to eat, and reviewed the various dishes they had sampled.

"Shall I assume that your desire to honor the *shad'chan* signifies your willingness to have a Jewish ceremony?"

"I have no religious tradition in my family whatsoever. I'm more than happy to latch onto yours. This is going to be a small and intimate affair, yes?" Evelyn sounded hopeful.

"The smaller the better. I'm thinking in the dozens."

"How big is Victor's house?"

"*That's* not something you need to be concerned about. A small event for him was 100 people."

"Hmmm." Evelyn considered that. "Are you going to organize our 'event,' as you call it?"

"I'll arrange for the rabbi and take care of the ceremony if you'll do everything else."

"Done. Perfect."

"You're going to do it yourself?" he asked.

"No, of course not. I'll hire someone to do it. *A professional.*"

"Now we're talking." Jeremy was happy that they were making progress; this was something he wanted to spend as little time on as possible.

"You should be thinking about who you want to invite. It may not be as easy as you think to keep it that small."

"I'm merciless when it comes to things like this. I'll have no problem whatsoever. My immediate family and a few friends. That's it."

"Lamest fast words," Evelyn said.

"What does that mean?" Jeremy asked.

"Lamest fast words? That's 'famous last words,' Spoonerized."

Jeremy thought about that, grinned, and resumed eating.

"Speaking of family, I want to get back to your infamous cousin Tzvi. How well do you know him? Would you say you are close?"

"Well, we've known each other since 1973, so that's forty-seven years, almost half a century. Are we close? Not in the sense of buddies who spend a lot of time together, and the few times we have been together have almost all had this added element of catastrophe."

"You really believe that contact with your cousin triggers violent events?"

"No, I'm not saying it triggers, I'm saying it coincides with. You saw what happened the other night. Through *three* intermediaries, I heard that Tzvi had left a message for me in a throwaway public mailbox. Ten minutes later, we learn that two Supreme Court justices have been shot."

"And you're still not planning to pick up his last message?"

"Are you kidding? Absolutely not!"

"Jeremy, whatever coincidence there was between Tzvi's message and the Supreme Court shootings, it's now *over*. It's history, it happened

Saturday night. In the meantime his message is sitting there—and the last message you got from him saved your life. Are *you* kidding? Pick up the goddamn e-mail! It's probably a message warning you that *I'm gonna fucking kill you if you don't pick up his message!*"

Jeremy sat with an artichoke leaf poised artfully over the table, on a frozen trajectory to his mouth. Several seconds later he put it down.

"Evelyn, consider the bigger picture. Since I have known Tzvi, our few meetings and communications have coincided with five assassinations and attempted assassinations, three terrorist attacks—one of which was a nuclear bomb—one *coup d'état*, and one full-scale war. You really think it's a good idea for me to be in touch with this man?"

"I have a question for you." Evelyn had cooled off slightly.

"What?"

"You say that all Tzvi had to do was send you a message—you didn't even pick it up—and that triggered one of these events?"

"Yes. No. Not triggered, but coincided with, yes."

"So what if he sends you another message? How are you going to stop him from sending you more messages?"

"I've thought about this. I was hoping he would see it himself, but he obviously hasn't so far. At some point I might have to communicate back to him that it's got to stop."

"Right. Exactly. If you really want to put an end to this, you've got to let him know that."

"Okay. Maybe that will turn out to be the case. What of it?"

"Think about this," Evelyn argued, "the man sent you a message marked urgent that you've not responded to or even opened up. If it's that urgent, at some point he's going to think his message didn't get through, and he's going to try again. By not responding, you're practically begging for him to contact you again."

Jeremy sat thinking.

"If your objective is to stop future communications," Evelyn continued, "the longer you wait to tell him that, the more likely it is that he'll contact you again. The coincidence from last Saturday has already happened. You want to precipitate another one?"

"So what are you suggesting?" Jeremy asked.

"Call him right now! Call him this very minute, on the telephone! Find out what his last message was about, and tell him to stop all future communication. You'll be done with it once and for all."

Jeremy hated being out-maneuvered like this. He gave her a sideways look—was she really a better lawyer than he was?

"I'll call Charles," Jeremy said, and he pulled his earpiece out of his pocket.

"What's with Charles? Call Tzvi!"

Jeremy compressed his cheeks into a patronizing smile. "Don't press your luck, sweetheart. I'm going to contact him, but I'll do it my way."

Evelyn retrieved her wine and leaned back in her chair; to the victor go the spoils.

"Charles," Jeremy said when the connection came through, "meet me in the war room in ten minutes with your secure tablet. Clear everyone else out; just you, me and Evelyn. We'll be using it for about fifteen minutes."

When he clicked off, Evelyn looked at him oddly. "Why kick everybody out of the war room? He could just as easily come up here."

"There are no windows in the war room," Jeremy said, pushing his chair back from the table and standing up.

"All right . . . ." She paused, expecting some further explanation, which was not immediately forthcoming. "What is the significance of that?"

"With no windows," he said, extending his hand to help her stand up, "there can be no flying glass."

*   *   *   *   *

Ten minutes later they were hunched behind Charles, peering over his back at his tablet screen. He navigated to the public mail site, entered the login and password, and Tzvi's message popped up.

*I have urgent information relevant to your campaign that I can only discuss in person. If you are willing, I can call on you at your hotel as a visiting relative. I'm in DC until Monday evening 10/5; call my mobile secure only 011+972+48+8726935 * 2282*

"What did I tell you?" Evelyn boiled with excitement. "The last message from Tzvi saved your life. This one is going to save your Presidency!"

"Why would you assume that?" Jeremy asked.

"Because it fits your coincidence pattern with Tzvi," Evelyn replied. "I've seen this enough times now to recognize it."

"If you recognize the pattern so well, you also must recognize that people could get hurt. That doesn't concern you at all?"

"It does, but the stakes are too great," Evelyn said. "You've gotta take that chance."

                    *   *   *   *   *

"Tzvi, I'd like you to meet my fiancée, Evelyn Vaughn." Jeremy made the introduction as he welcomed his cousin into their suite. "Just the other day, I had been telling Evelyn that it was unlikely she would ever meet you, and here I am eating my words. She has a tendency to make me do that."

"I think I understand, but even if I don't, I am still charmed to meet you," Tzvi said, offering a brief nod of his head but not a handshake. "I have read a lot about you, and my wife Ditza is a big fan."

"That's very kind," Evelyn replied. "It has been a roller coaster ride for us both, to say the least."

"Maybe the ride is not over," Tzvi speculated, addressing both of them. "But unfortunately it is for me, because I am literally on my way back to Israel. My plane leaves very soon. I was headed for the highway when you called. Is there any chance you could accompany me to the airport?"

"Probably not in the time frame you have in mind. My public schedule for today was finished hours ago; it would take half an hour at least to move me out of here in an automobile, and it would have to be my car."

"*Ai-zeh balagan!*" Tzvi cringed.

"Translate . . . ?" Evelyn tugged at Jeremy's sleeve.

"A *balagan* is a fuss, a big production, a *rigmarole.*"

"Maybe you could just walk me to my car," Tzvi suggested. "I have a car waiting downstairs."

"That works for me. It will keep our time together to a minimum. I'll get my jacket and I'll be right with you." Jeremy alerted Charles, who was right outside their door, and got his coat out of the closet. He grunted as he put it on; like most of his outerwear, it was bulletproof and weighed several pounds. Tzvi bid his goodbyes to Evelyn; Jeremy kissed her on the cheek, stepped into the hallway, and demanded that she return to the war room. "I'm serious," he said, "don't make me more anxious. Charles, make sure Evelyn stays in the war room until I get back, got it?"

Charles nodded, and Jeremy and Tzvi exited into the hallway, flanked by half-a-dozen guards.

"Perhaps we could speak in Hebrew," Tzvi said in Hebrew as they walked down the hall. "Less chance of being overheard."

"No problem," Jeremy said, also in Hebrew. "In close quarters like this, it's probably a good idea."

They were held at a corner until an elevator could be summoned and checked. "So, Tzvi," Jeremy said, "I have a million questions, but first of all, how did you know to warn me about the plot in Alabama? How could you have known that was about to happen?"

"Jeremy, my dear cousin, we have too little time. Let me tell you about Adwar—this will answer *all* of your questions."

"Malcolm Adwar? What is your connection to Adwar?" Jeremy asked.

"Let's refer to him as Aleph. Aleph is one of our agents. He's back in Israel with us."

"Adwar—*Aleph*? Is an Israeli agent?!" Jeremy's breath went away.

"Shhh! Quiet!" His voice lowered a notch. "One of our most successful placements ever, I might add."

"We all assumed he was connected to in some way to the White

House or to Morley James."

"Well that's more proof of his success: Morley James thought the same thing. But he was our man from the very beginning, and we pulled him no more than an hour before they were going to take him out."

The elevator came and they got in with two bodyguards. They let the ride go by quietly. Three other guards were already waiting in the lobby when they got out.

"I'm beginning to see the picture," Jeremy said. "Even when he was working for the State Department, he was working for you?"

Tzvi nodded. "He's been under deep cover for over a decade. When he was offered the job at the American Patriots Foundation, we were reluctant to give up such a fantastic spot in State. There was a lot of debate about that, but it turned out to be an excellent decision."

"Okay, so Aleph was tied to the White House in some way through his job at APF. Does he know about the terrorist attacks—can he connect the White House to the attacks at all?"

"Now is not the time for the details. It's enough to say that he can absolutely tie people in the White House to everything: to the nuclear bomb, which, by the way, was not on the tanker—the tanker was torpedoed; to the riflemen in Alabama; and to the July 4th attack as well, which was also an assassination attempt. Aleph's information might not reach all the way to Morley James—it depends on how some of the middle players react once they are revealed. But these middle players are all White House employees, all working for James or his assistant Carla Rush."

"When you say he can connect, you mean he can prove? He has evidence?"

"One hundred percent," Tzvi said.

"Jesus." By now Jeremy's heart rate had shot up. His mind whirled with high speed calculations of options and consequences, a sensation that was magnified as they raced past a revolving door spinning in the opposite direction.

They emerged into the cool evening air and were greeted by only modest cheering and chants from a sparse crowd. Jeremy breathed deeply. "What needs to happen in order to get this story out?" Jeremy asked.

"There are a number of conditions, and it's not clear to me that they can all be met. First of all, Aleph has committed crimes, so he will testify officially only if he receives full immunity. Second, he knows that the Grove Administration would do anything to see him silenced, so he is not willing to surrender himself physically to any government agency. And, most important of all, we have maintained for years an elaborate alibi that disassociates him entirely from my organization and from Israel, and he will only come out if that alibi remains intact." Tzvi pointed to the end of the block where a dark sedan was idling at the curb. "That's my car, down there," he said to one of the bodyguards, and the phalanx wheeled and marched in that direction.

"So," Tzvi resumed, "it's complicated, which is why I couldn't do this with you by e-mail. I want to find a way to help you, but I don't know if it's possible; what's happening in your country is really unimaginable. It's bad not only for you, but for everyone. What has happened to your Supreme Court?"

"Please, don't get me started," Jeremy said. "It's been a bad day." They arrived at the car and stopped walking.

"What is the best way to do this?" Tzvi asked. "You guide *me* this time. This is your territory. How can we get Aleph's story out there? We can't do it through the press."

Jeremy paused, looking at his cousin with the fondest of smiles, and then suddenly reached out and surrounded him with a bear hug, not letting up for some seconds. "Tzvi, I urge you to do all you can to get your person to come forward, but it can't involve me. We must not be in touch anymore. I'm terrified that some violent event is going to unfold while we're talking here right now. I am tortured, *tortured* every night by thoughts of Amitai. This can't happen again."

"You need not remind *me!*" Tzvi hissed. "Remember, I was the one who introduced Amitai to you. If it makes you feel any better, blame it on me. But do you see what you are missing?"

"What do you mean? Please just say it—*we must finish up here.*"

"Your country is on the edge of an abyss . . ."

"What is *te-hohm?*" They were speaking in Hebrew, and Jeremy didn't recognize the word.

"*A hole! A giant hole with no bottom!* Your country is about to go into one! *You* are the leader of the opposition. There are long-term, historical implications to your actions. You cannot afford to be haunted by one man's death. What's at stake is much greater."

"You think I'm ignoring the stakes?" Jeremy switched to English. "The last time you contacted me, two Supreme Court justices were shot at! The time before that, *a fucking nuclear bomb exploded!*"

Tzvi locked onto Jeremy's glare, held it for a few seconds, and then let go. "Okay. I agree. We will stop our communication. But I am not sure I can deliver Aleph on my own. We're not going to do anything that will risk our agent, or his connection to Israel."

Jeremy held up his hand. "Tzvi, there is no need to explain or defend. The most important thing for us to do now is to end this meeting. I can't help you with Aleph, but I will refer you to someone who perhaps can."

"*Nu? . . .*"

"My friend Victor."

"Ahhh, Victor Glade the actor? President Bosco?"

"Victor and I have been close friends for more than thirty years. Until very recently, as you know, I worked for him. Because of that he already knows who you are—I had to tell him back in November when all of this started to happen."

"That was part of the risk profile, we figured you might tell him."

"Well then, there you have it. Your 'risk profile' won't increase at all, because Victor already knows who you are. Contact him and say that I have referred you to him as a Code Twenty-four, which verifies my introduction. You can speak to him in complete confidence; there is absolute trust between us. He would be in an excellent position to advise you. He's in Bulgaria, you know"—Tzvi nodded—"which may make it easier to communicate with him. He will have a big incentive to help you: he and his family desperately want to get back to the US."

Tzvi repeated to himself, "twenty-four," first in Hebrew and then in English, and then reached out to embrace Jeremy once more. "Maybe one day this will all be figured out and we can speak again," he said.

"In the meantime, cousin, please, *please* do not contact me, don't even *try* to contact me. We have to go it alone from now on."

Tzvi saluted, they shook hands, and Jeremy's bodyguard phalanx shifted momentarily to allow Tzvi to leave. When he was gone, they refilled the gap immediately. Jeremy then walked briskly back to the hotel and took the mezzanine stairs two at a time to get to the war room, where a raucous poker game was under way. People started to stand up, but he motioned for everyone to stay. Evelyn came up to him, and they ducked away into a corner of the room.

"What did he have to say?" she asked. "What, what, what, what . . . spill it now!"

Jeremy told her everything. When he was finished, Evelyn said, "You can thank me later."

"I'll thank you right now. Thank you." Jeremy was not feeling celebratory. "Let's just hope the consequences don't outweigh the benefits."

"I thought you said there was no cause-and-effect, that it was just a coincidence."

"What does that matter? If people get hurt, do you think they care about our analysis of the cause? Have you checked the news?"

"I've been looking at Reuters and CNN—nothing so far."

"Let's just hope it stays that way. I feel like I've been hanging onto the edge of a cliff for ten minutes."

25	October 12, 2020 Plovdiv, Bulgaria

The first live feed of the 211th episode of *The Oval Office* started with its usual stream of lead actor credits scrolling to the snappy cadence of a snare drum, and then settled on a sepia silhouette of Victor as President Bosco, poised deep in thought, with a fade-in caption, "Created and Produced by Victor Glade."

The very first scene, however, was a long shot of Victor standing on a disassembled set, leaning against a tall director's chair, on the same stage he had used in his video endorsement of Jeremy at the convention and in his subsequent commercials. The camera began a slow zoom-in.

"You may recognize me as President Alvin Bosco, the character I portray on the NBC series *The Oval Office*. My real name is Victor Glade. In real life, I'm a father, husband, actor, writer, and entrepreneur. I am *not* a politician, and I have no political ambitions—" Victor began strolling the stage slowly, but maintained his eye contact with the audience— "unless you consider my family's desire to return to our home in Southern California a *political ambition*.

"As many of you know, several months ago the Administration of President Burton Grove, in the aftermath of a devastating terrorist attack, tried to arrest me and close down *The Oval Office*. Very fortunately, we had a plan in place to move our personnel to a back-up facility, so we were able to continue production here in Bulgaria, and I'm able to speak to you freely this evening.

"I am still a loyal and grateful American citizen, however, and I care deeply about the future of my country. For that reason, I have agreed, for the first time in the history of *The Oval Office*, to suspend the telling of our story in order to report some hard news.

"The remainder of our show this week will consist of an interview with Malcolm Adwar, a former employee of the US State Department and the American Patriots Foundation, who has a horrifying story to tell. Mr. Adwar will describe how many of the terrorist attacks that have taken place in the US over the past several years have been ordered or condoned by high ranking officials in the US government. The recent attacks of October 1st, for example, including the nuclear detonation outside New York City, were all engineered by operatives of the current Administration. Mr. Adwar also has evidence connecting the Grove Administration to no fewer than three attempted assassinations, and to a secret effort to sabotage the careers of lawmakers and candidates who have endorsed the 28th Amendment.

"At this point, I would be doing an injustice to Mr. Adwar if I told any more of his story; it is his to tell. I will add only that I have personally seen the evidence he is presenting to back up these claims, and I assure you it is both credible and concrete.

"Mr. Adwar is complicit in some of the crimes that he will describe, and will not give sworn testimony in these matters until complete and unconditional immunity has been guaranteed. If representatives of the US Justice Department, or perhaps the Supreme Court or Congress, would like to question him in person, or see the evidence that is in his possession, they are welcome to visit him here in our studios in Plovdiv, Bulgaria, where he has agreed to remain for the short term. He will also make himself available to the press, via Web conference, through facilities we already have in place here."

Victor had by now meandered back to his director's chair and restored the pose that he began with.

"The recent capitulation of the US Supreme Court to the demands of the Grove Administration is a testament to the power of fear as a political weapon. What we are about to learn, however, is that the fear being used by the Grove Administration is fear that *the Administration itself has manufactured.*

"The Constitution assigns responsibility for checking and balancing Presidential power to the Courts and Congress. Hopefully, with the following revelations, these institutions will now recognize that they must reassert their authority and put an end to this Administration's unprecedented abuse of Executive Power."

- The End -

APPENDIX 1

PROPOSED 28th AMENDMENT TO
THE U.S. CONSTITUTION

Section 1. General election campaigns for seats in the United States Congress, and for the office of President, shall be conducted in accordance with the limitations and requirements set forth herein.

(1) The Legislatures of the respective states shall acquire and allocate public funds for the purpose of financing Congressional general election campaigns conducted within their states. The Congress of the United States shall acquire and allocate public funds for the purpose of financing both Congressional and Presidential general election campaigns. No poll tax or other direct voting tax shall be levied to finance said general election campaigns.

(2) A fixed sum is to be budgeted for each covered general election, in an amount agreeable to a simple majority of the authorizing legislators. In setting budgets for Congressional general elections, the state legislatures shall assume a contribution from the Federal treasury of one dollar for each dollar of authorized state funds.

(3) Each of the state legislatures, and the Congress, shall establish appropriate regulatory oversight to ensure that general election campaign funds are acquired and disbursed in accordance with the law. The cost of such oversight and enforcement shall be incorporated into the budget for each general election and, in the case of Congressional campaigns, subject to the matching contribution from the Federal treasury specified in the preceding sub-section 2.

(4) Candidates appearing on the ballot of a covered general election who received ten percent or more of the total votes cast in an immediately preceding primary (or primary run-off) election will qualify to receive

public funds for the general election campaign.

(5) Public funds budgeted for disbursement to qualifying candidates shall be allocated in direct proportion to the percentage of primary votes each candidate received, relative to the total number of primary votes received by all qualifying candidates.

(6) For each covered general election, the amount of money disbursed to the candidate receiving the largest share of public funds shall represent the maximum amount of money to be spent by any candidate running in that election.

(7) All candidates appearing on the ballot of a covered general election, other than the candidate who received the largest share of public funds, shall be authorized to solicit private contributions to supplement their allocation of public funds (if any), up to a combined amount not to exceed the maximum amount defined in the preceding sub-section 6.

(8) Covered general election campaigns shall last no more than eighty days. Funds allocated to or raised by candidates pursuant to this Amendment shall be the only funds used by the candidate in the conduct of their general election campaigns.

(9) No individual, committee or organization, other than a candidate's personally authorized General Election Campaign Committee, shall raise or disburse funds on behalf or in support of individual, named candidates during a covered General Election.

Section 2: This article shall be inoperative unless it shall have been ratified as an Amendment to the Constitution by the legislatures of three-fourths of the several States within twenty-five years from the date of its submission to the States by the Congress. Upon ratification, the Amendment shall apply to all Federal general elections held after the third anniversary of the ratification date.

APPENDIX 2

HOW BRIDGE IS PLAYED

Four card players, playing as two 2-person teams, sit at a square card table and are each dealt 13 cards (a 'hand') out of a standard 52-card deck (North-South is one team, and East-West is the other). The players then place bets in a round-robin auction (clockwise around the table, beginning with the Dealer) with respect to how many 'tricks' they think they can win using their team's combined (26) cards. This process, known as bidding, ends when the highest bid is passed (not contested) by any other player.

N-S Vulnerable
Dealer--East

North--Seeger
♠ 5 2
♥ A Q 6
♦ A 7 6 2
♣ J 8 6 5

West--Gates
(Dummy)
♠ K
♥ K 5 4 2
♦ K 9 4 3
♣ 9 7 3 2

East--Clinton
(Declarer)
♠ Q J 10 8 6
♥ 10 9
♦ 8 5
♣ A K Q 4

♠ A 9 7 4 3
♥ J 8 7 3
♦ Q J 10
♣ 10
South--Jeremy
(Makes opening lead)

North--Seeger	East--Clinton	South--Lerner	West--Gates
	1 ♠	Pass	1 No-Trump
Pass	2 ♣	Pass	Pass
Pass			

In the above deal from Chapter 6, Clinton is the Declarer (the winning bidder). His bid of "two clubs" was passed by all other players, which means he needs to take a total of eight tricks--a basic "book" of six, plus *two* more--with clubs as the declared trump suit (explained below).

When the bidding is concluded, the play for tricks then begins with the player sitting to the left of the Declarer leading (placing on the table, face up) a card from his hand (his choice). After this initial lead is made, the partner of the Declarer puts his cards down on the table for all to see, while the other players keep their hands hidden. This hand exposed on the table is now called the 'Dummy', and the clockwise play for the first trick continues with the Declarer selecting from the Dummy a card of the same suit that was led, and then each of the two remaining players (North and East in the above diagram) contributes a card, again each playing a card in the same suit (♠ , ♥, ♦, ♣) that was led. The player who played the highest card in the led suit wins that four-card trick, and it then becomes his/her turn to lead another card (any suit) to start the play for the next trick. If after all 13 tricks have been played the Declarer has won fewer tricks than his 'bid', his team loses points. If the winning bidder does win as many tricks as his bid (or more), his team wins points. A series of hands (usually 24~28 in competitive play) comprises a game (also sometimes called a "rubber").

Among the myriad fine points to bridge, one of the most crucial is what card to play when you don't have a card in the suit that was led. In the bidding sequence that takes place immediately before the play for tricks, the winning bidder (Declarer) "declares" what rule is going to be in effect for that hand when you don't have a card in the led suit.

If the winning bidder has declared a 'trump' suit (either ♠ , ♥, ♦, or ♣), that means when you don't have a card in the led suit, you can instead play any card of the designated trump suit, and that will win the trick--unless another player who *also* doesn't have any cards in the led suit plays a *higher* card of the declared trump suit.

The winning bidder can also, however, declare that the hand is to be played under a "No-Trump" rule--meaning that no suit will be designated as the trump suit, and if you don't have a card in the led suit, you must surrender a card from another suit and you lose the trick.

That's basically the game of bridge. There are different bidding systems (called conventions) and different methods of scoring, but the play--the taking of tricks--is always the same.

The format of play referred to most frequently in *The 28th Amendment* is called duplicate bridge, where teams of players compete against each other playing the same set of pre-dealt hands. In bridge clubs and at tournaments this is accomplished by pre-dealing a deck of cards into four bridge hands, and then tucking each of the four 13-card hands face-down into separate slots in a portable aluminum rack called a "board." These boards are then passed from table to table in a sequence that gets them played by all of the competing teams, and each team's score on a particular board is compared with all of the other teams' results for that same board.

Ambitious readers may wish to follow the "trick by trick'" narration below (think of play by play radio coverage of a basketball game; duplicate bridge is played at a similar tempo that must be maintained or your team gets penalized). I have repeated the diagram of the deal next to the chart so that you can easily reference it while reading the play-by-play: try to visualize what cards remain after every trick, or, alternately, cross out on the diagram the cards played at each trick so you can keep track of the remaining cards for subsequent tricks.

Trick	Description of Play	Won by N/S	Won by E/W
1	Jeremy leads his singleton trump, the ten of clubs. Clinton calls for the two of clubs from the Dummy, Seeger plays the five, and Clinton wins in his hand with the club ace.		X
2	Clinton leads the spade six from his hand; Jeremy puts up the ace, killing the singleton king of spades in the Dummy, and Seeger follows suit with the five.	X	
3	Jeremy leads the queen of diamonds; Clinton covers with the Dummy's king, Seeger plays his ace, and Clinton contributes the five from his hand.	X	
4	Seeger leads the two of diamonds; Clinton plays the eight from his hand, Jeremy wins his ten, and the three is played from the Dummy.	X	
5	Jeremy leads the three of hearts; Clinton plays low (the two) from the Dummy, Seeger wins his queen, and Clinton plays the nine from his hand.	X	
6	Seeger leads his two of spades. Clinton plays his spade queen, Jeremy follows with the three, and Clinton – having no more spades in Dummy -- throws his heart four.		X
7	Clinton plays the king of clubs. Jeremy throws his seven of hearts (having no more clubs); Clinton plays the three from the Dummy, and Seeger follows with the club six.		X
8	Clinton plays the queen of clubs from his hand. Jeremy throws his heart eight; Clinton follows with the seven from the Dummy, and Seeger with his club eight.		X
9	Clinton leads his jack of spades. Jeremy follows with his three, Clinton plays the diamond four from the Dummy (out of spades), and Seeger wins by trumping with his jack of clubs.	X	
10	Seeger plays his heart ace. Clinton follows with the ten from his hand, Jeremy plays the jack (his last heart), and the heart five is played from the Dummy.	X	
11	Seeger plays his diamond seven. Clinton trumps with the four of clubs in his hand, Jeremy plays his jack, and Clinton plays the last diamond in the Dummy, the nine.		X
12	Clinton leads his ten of spades. Jeremy plays his seven; Clinton throws away his now-good king of hearts in the Dummy, and Seeger follows with his six of hearts.		X
13	Clinton continues with the spade eight, Jeremy covers with his nine, but Clinton has a trump, the nine of clubs, remaining in the Dummy to win the trick. Seeger's last card was a diamond.		X
	Total Tricks Taken	6	7
	Clinton's bid required him to take eight tricks, and he only managed to take seven, so his team was scored for "down one".		-1

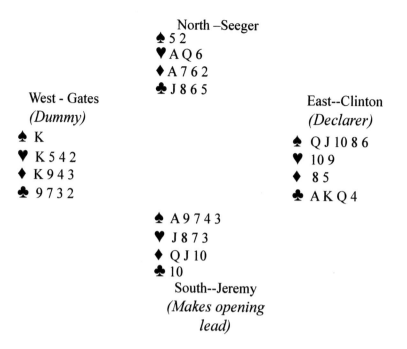

North –Seeger
♠ 5 2
♥ A Q 6
♦ A 7 6 2
♣ J 8 6 5

West - Gates
(Dummy)
♠ K
♥ K 5 4 2
♦ K 9 4 3
♣ 9 7 3 2

East--Clinton
(Declarer)
♠ Q J 10 8 6
♥ 10 9
♦ 8 5
♣ A K Q 4

♠ A 9 7 4 3
♥ J 8 7 3
♦ Q J 10
♣ 10
South--Jeremy
(Makes opening lead)

The bidding went as follows:

North-- Seeger	East-- Clinton	South-- Lerner	West-- Gates
	1 ♠	Pass	1 No-Trump
Pass	2 ♣	Pass	Pass
Pass			

East's two-club bid is passed out, which means that Clinton is the "Declarer" (winning bidder). His objective is to take at least eight tricks (a basic "book" of six tricks, plus *two* more) with clubs (♣) as the designated trump suit.

Jeremy, sitting to the left of the Declarer, chooses the ten of clubs as his opening lead (experts may question this lead, perhaps with good cause). Gates then lays his hand down on the table as the Dummy for all to see, and the play of the hand proceeds as described in the chart on the left.